BLACK GOD

BLACK GOD

A Story of the Congo

BY

D. MANNERS-SUTTON

LONGMANS, GREEN AND CO.

LONDON · NEW YORK · TORONTO

1934

LONGMANS, GREEN AND CO.
114 FIFTH AVENUE, NEW YORK
221 EAST 20TH STREET, CHICAGO
88 TREMONT STREET, BOSTON

LONGMANS, GREEN AND CO. Ltd.
39 PATERNOSTER ROW, LONDON, E C 4
6 OLD COURT HOUSE STREET, CALCUTTA
53 NICOL ROAD, BOMBAY
36A MOUNT ROAD, MADRAS

LONGMANS, GREEN AND CO.
480 UNIVERSITY AVENUE, TORONTO

MANNERS-SUTTON

BLACK GOD

FIRST EDITION

PRINTED IN THE UNITED STATES OF AMERICA

CONTENTS

BOOK I

BLACK GOD

M'KATO sat on the right bank of the Little River just at the point where travellers found the river shallow enough to cross by foot. He sat there quietly, all day and every day, watching the people who crossed by the ford, and never made any disturbance whatsoever. He was regarded by the people who lived on the banks of the Little River, as a harmless old man with queer notions, but so long as he continued to make no disturbance, they were quite prepared to allow him to sit there as long as he pleased.

When he was asked why he sat there, he always gave the same reply: that the river was the narrowest that he had yet come to, and as he had to use his foot to throw an assegai, he could not throw very far.

The answer seemed irrelevant, and the white men who asked the question and were given this response merely shrugged their shoulders and said: "Queer old fish," as they went on their way. The black men who asked the same question and received the same answer, also shrugged their shoulders and went on their way, but they did not say: "Queer old fish," as the white men did, because they saw nothing unreasonable in M'Kato's reply.

3

When the Marist Mission was built on the hill that rose
up from the right bank of the Little River, and Father
Domenique came across the ford for the first time, looking very fat and hot perched up on his white mule, with
his topee somewhat awry on his head, he stayed to ask
the same question of M'Kato, and M'Kato gave the same
answer, a little wearily, as travellers were becoming more
frequent, and he had so often to repeat it.

Father Domenique was so surprised that he took off
one of his old leather sandals, and gave his mule such
a welt with it that the animal travelled up the hill which
led to the Mission at a speed that astonished itself even,
and brought the brothers out of the Mission in great haste
to see what ailed the dear Father who was arriving for
the first time so precipitately among them.

But nothing ailed Father Domenique, except, perhaps,
that he had at last been given an answer that he could
not say a prayer about.

He pondered over M'Kato's reply for some considerable time afterwards, but he was never able to find any
feasible explanation for it, not even after he had been ten
years at the Mission and had seen the settlement of
Chembi come into being, and with it the ferry across the
Little River, not even after he had been twenty years at
the Mission and seen the ferry and the queer misshapen
ferryman, Lardi, swept away by flood waters, nor yet
again, when thirty years had elapsed and M'Kato was no
longer sitting upon the river-bank, and an iron bridge

was being constructed over the very spot where Chicot Brown had thrown his father into the swirling rapids of the Demon's Boiling Pot, for love of Flore, the courtesan. He only continued to wonder in his gentle old way and to pray for the black soul of M'Kato, who he knew later on would have a bad time in Purgatory. He remembered M'Kato specially in his prayers, not linking him up with the other black brethren for whom he prayed regularly at morning Mass on Sunday, but mentioning his name and asking the Virgin Mary for special lenience every time that he went down upon his knees in front of the rather tawdry altar in the Mission chapel.

He felt, somehow, that M'Kato needed this special intercession ; he had once given M'Kato a rosary, and ever afterwards had been rather uncomfortable as to the use that M'Kato had made of it.

When M'Kato left the Little River for good (the morning of Humphrey Brown's demise), he did not take Father Domenique's rosary with him, but left it hanging as it had hung for years upon the twig of a gnarled and knotted furze bush. Father Domenique found it there and took it home with him, but he never liked it afterwards ; the beads always seemed hot and alive to his touch, so that he could not say his prayers by it with any sort of tranquillity. In the end, he returned it to its original owner, a friend of his youth, one Fra Angelico in the Carthusian Monastery just outside Florence, but Fra Angelico never wrote to thank him for it. Perhaps he had no reason to, for shortly afterwards he was found dead in his bed, with the rosary that Father Domenique had returned to him clutched tightly in one hand. They buried him with it, as it seemed impossible to detach his fingers from the last bead near the cross.

WHEN Father Domenique arrived at the Mission, hot and dusty and out of breath on his speeding mule, he found a low, rambling, whitewashed building, with a small space of cleared land at one side of it, which was used by the black children attending the Mission School for their unintelligible and dusty games.

The first alteration that Father Domenique made in the life of the Mission, before he had been there many days, was to relegate these dusty games to a small square beside the school-house, and to set the brothers to work turning the patch of cleared land into a garden. In time, poinsettias, magnolias and cannas bloomed there in a riot of colour, and even red roses from Father Domenique's own country of Basque.

At night the perfume of the Mission garden was exotic, but the brothers of the Mission never enjoyed it, as they went to bed so early, almost as soon as the sun went down. When the sun hung blood-red and torrid over the narrow river, like a splash of vermilion paint thrown against the sky, the brothers said their prayers in the cool shade of the little whitewashed chapel, and made their way afterwards through long, dim corridors to their cells. They knew nothing of the fire that burnt in the

7

big round sun hanging so low over the purple river;
they knew nothing of the fire that burnt in the blood of
the black men and women who wandered by the waters
of that river, nothing at all of the excitement of the
tropic night that was closing in upon the river and land
and people—a night of bottomless silence, passionate
perfumes, and the darkness of desire—except, perhaps,
Brother François, who sometimes opened the window of
his cell stealthily, and putting his head through the aper-
ture, sniffed the air greedily as if he could never get
enough of it.

By right, the roses that Father Domenique planted in
his garden should have been white ones (pure and spotless to lay at the feet of the plaster statue of the Madonna
that graced the Mission chapel), but he was rather childish in some matters, and he liked the red flowers best.
They were never the undoing of any priest but one, and
that was Brother Joseph.

Father Domenique, the gentle-hearted lover of flowers,
liked to entertain a guest occasionally at the evening
meal of the Mission. An Arab trader, a big-game hunter,
a doctor studying tropical diseases, any traveller, as a
matter of fact, fording the Little River, and taking the
trouble to mount the steep hill to the Mission, was
sure of a welcome and an invitation to supper from its
director.

But in the wet season travellers were few; no one appeared to relish crossing the river when its waters ran
full and turbulent over its bed, so Father Domenique had

then to fall back upon one of the brothers for company at supper.

But he did not like that, for he was rather shy in the presence of the brothers ; they all seemed so much older than he — not in years, but in knowledge — that he felt in their presence like a small child constantly being set right by its elders.

He always deferred, as long as possible, asking any of the brothers to sup with him and linger over the good wine that was sent out to the Mission by an uncle in the Basque Country, who, having lived longer than is considered necessary, had developed a taste in wine denied to the ordinary mortal of three score years and ten. Father Domenique would look wistfully out of the window of his study during the wet season, and say : "Surely someone will attempt the river today," and when no one did, he would send reluctantly for one of the brothers.

There were three brothers at the Mission. Brother François, with his coarse jokes which he had learned outside the whitewashed walls of the Mission, and would have done well to forget within them ; Brother Antoine, who always drank too much of Father Domenique's wine and had once toasted Mary Magdalene in the seventh glass ; and Brother Paul, at the other end of the pole, narrow, carping, critical of anything that might pertain to the graces of life. Father Domenique did not like any one of these three at his table, and always put off asking them so long as there seemed the glimmer of

ning, so that he could go to rest with the comforting thought that today there had been so many more blooms in his garden than yesterday. Brother Joseph had not attended matins ; he was not in his cell, Brother Paul reported, after going there to look for him. He was not anywhere in the Mission, it was found later on. Brother Joseph had left the Mission for good, and taken with him twenty-four of Father Domenique's choicest rose blooms.

The gentle, kindly old priest did not begrudge the young and fiery one his roses, if only he had cut them with a knife instead of plucking them so ruthlessly with his hands ; the bushes never quite recovered from the harsh treatment to which they had been subjected ; some of them withered and died of it.

For a long time Brother Joseph was not heard of at the Mission ; it was thought that he had died in the jungle.

THE day that Brother Joseph left the Mission M'Kato counted the first bead on the rosary that Father Domenique had given him. He was rather doubtful about the wisdom of doing so at first, but Brother Joseph had forded the river with such hurried, frightened foot-steps, had turned back so often, and yet gone on again, that M'Kato knew it must be some stronger force than just his own will that was propelling Brother Joseph's legs through the shallow water. So he counted his bead and waited again, as he had been waiting for many a year on the banks of the Little River.

M'Kato had sat waiting on the banks of the Little River long before the Marist Mission had been built on the top of the hill that sloped up so swiftly from the right bank of the river. When he had first come to the river there had been no building of any sort in the vicinity, just a narrow, little river of no particular fame, turbulent in the wet season, calm and tranquil (except for an occasional stretch of rapids in its course) in the dry season — a river without even the formality of a name, so insignificant and unimportant it was in a land intersected by many rivers.

M'Kato, standing by it for the first time, measured it

with his eye. "This," he said aloud, "is the narrowest river that I have yet come to, and so I will sit by it as Kundi, the witchman, bade me."

So he sat upon its right bank and watched the events that happened by it, day in and day out. Dry season, wet season made no difference to M'Kato ; there he sat, cross-legged and immutable, like some black god intent upon creation.

That he was engaged upon any such practice would never have occurred of course, to any casual observer, such as the men and women who came to the Little River and forded it, or crossed by the ferry after it came into being. Warriors, missionaries, hunters, traders, black women with baskets on their heads, white women holding aloft large umbrellas, negroes from Sierra Leone, Arabs from the Nile, Englishmen with small moustaches, Italians, Greeks, and rapscallion Portuguese from the Angolian coastal towns, passed and repassed, a moving line of people intent upon their own affairs with little thought to give to the still figure squatting on the riverbank.

It would never have occurred to M'Kato, either, that he was attaining godhead, for he was a simple soul, with no aspirations towards Deity. He was merely sitting upon the banks of the Little River according to the instructions of Kundi, the witchman, and although the time might be long and his bones ache for movement, for the panting breath and the pain of running, he intended to sit there until he had achieved his life's task.

With this idea in mind he kept his thoughts focused only upon the end, as the old witch doctor had bade him. "Let not your thoughts stray from their course, O Zulu," Kundi had told him, "the end alone concerns you, not that which is happening about you." So the amazing changes that came upon the Little River during the years of M'Kato's vigil there left him entirely unmoved; although he was aware of them, he paid them little heed.

First came the Mission, and with it Father Domenique on his white mule. And when the Mission had been built for a year and a day, Brother Joseph hurried through the ford one moonlight night. After that events marched more slowly. M'Kato had been sitting by the river for some twelve years when the settlement of Chembi came into being. Chembi was at first a trading-store roofed with iron, where ivory was weighed and bargained for, with a wooden residence for the trader-in-ivory next door. Then it became a series of such stores and such residences, and after a year or two it could boast of a square with a little garden in the centre, which was always bare of flowers, an hotel (something of a white elephant as no one appeared to board at it), and one or two short streets, edged by low, wooden bunga-lows, all with mosquito-proofed verandahs and gardens in a state of supreme desolation.

Chembi was spoken of as one of the coming trading-stations in the Congo. It was situated near the old ivory route to the west coast, and ivory still came down that way to the sea; but instead of reaching the coast, it was bespoken by the traders of Chembi, and measured and weighed in the hot little iron-roofed stores, and paid for in good hard cash, or in calicoes and brass wire and nails, according to the status of the seller.

Ivory bearers came through the long grass in single file towards Chembi, the huge tusks swung between them in a kind of network of ropes, and the smaller ones balanced adroitly on their heads. They usually came at dusk, and their coming was heralded in Chembi by the peculiar noise of the swishing grass, long before they ever arrived there. The grass grew high, as high as the waists of the bearers, and as they divided it with their naked black legs in walking, it fell apart with a sharp cutting noise. *S-s-s-wish, a s-s-s-wish,* it went, *s-s-s-wish, a-wish,* and as there were often many hundreds of bearers, the noise was considerable. When it reached Chembi, the clerks in the trading-stores would brace their shoulders, take their pens from behind their ears, and say : "Well, well, here comes some bone," as if it were the last thing that they were expecting, although they kept their ledgers solely for the purpose of recording transactions in bone, and drew their salaries because of these transactions. In the early days of the settlement by the Little River this coming of ivory was the only diversion that the Government employees had (and everyone was a Government employee then) ; later, things were a little better, when the Compagnie Navigation du Congo Belge ran a boat up the Little River to Chembi once a fortnight. It was then that Chembi became of some importance, and was marked upon newly-drawn maps of Central Africa. Residents then sought for a name for the Little River, but could find none. The black men did not know of one. It was too insignificant a river for them to bother about the naming of it. Finally Trader Voss of the I.N.T. Stores said : "Let us ask that old black man who sits there on the bank all day long ; he should know better than anyone, as he never does anything else but gaze at the river."

So they asked M'Kato, and M'Kato, without moving his position in any way, or even looking at the white men who questioned him, said : "It is the smallest river in the land. I call it the Little River."

And so the matter of a name was settled, for afterwards the white residents of Chembi always spoke of it as the Little River, and the surrounding black men adopted the name also.

WITH the advent of Chembi came Lardi, the ferry-man. Previous to the building of the white settlement on the left bank of the river, travellers had been content to ford the Little River in the dry season, and make a detour of it when the rains were on. But when the settlement came to contain fifty or sixty inhabitants, a ferry became a necessity, for the white men and women, trading-store clerks and their wives, Sisters of Mercy, bankers, missionaries, etc., did not care about taking off their shoes and stockings — or socks as the case might be — to wade the river, or again make a hammock journey of many kilometres in the wet season, in order to avoid the turbulent and unruly little river.

The white residents talked about a ferry in a dilatory way, but before anything could be decided about the matter, they woke up one morning to find old Lardi sitting on a raft moored to the Chembi bank, waiting for passengers at a sou a time.

Where old Lardi had come from, what he had been engaged upon before becoming the self-appointed ferryman of the Little River, no one knew, or troubled to find out. That he was an Arabeezi could be judged from his evil countenance, and his greed for money made it apparent that he had had long association with Arab traders and slavers ; probably at one time or another he had been one of their band.

As well as being evil of countenance, he had a peculiarly misshapen body which gave him the appearance of a dwarf, and with this, he combined the soul of a satyr and the spirit of a devil. He was the demon jester of the Little River, and no one knew what he would be up to next.

He would perhaps ferry a passenger half-way across the river, and then inform him that he had to wade the rest, while he himself stood upon his head on the raft, chuckling ingloriously to see immaculate duck trousers becoming water-splashed and muddy. He might ferry another to the very brink of the chutes and announce his intention of sending him to perdition, and not all the promises of brass wire or sous would move him from his declared intention, until tiring of the jest himself, he would land the passenger up river, several kilometres probably, from the destination he wished to achieve.

But the white men never laid hands upon Lardi, though they would have given much to do so many a time. There was something so evil about him, that they felt Satan would have risen to his instant aid and wrenched him from their grasp. He was the only one of the black people by the Little River that the Reverend Llewellyn Jones, the director of the Baptist Mission, did not try to convert. Father Domenique also let well alone ; once he had crossed by the ferry, but Lardi had tickled the hoofs of his white mule to such an extent that the animal had pranced off the raft into the river waters, and Father Domenique had been almost thrown from his back. Ever afterwards, the good priest had forded the river as of old, and had tried not to see the ferryman making mouthing faces at him from the precincts of his raft.

But it seemed to be M'Kato that old Lardi wished to annoy most ; he considered the silent black man, sitting on the bank just above where he moored his raft, a good subject for his jesting. Whenever he had a moment to spare from his ferrying, he would jump up the bank, hopping on feet and hands like a weird brown toad, and caper before M'Kato, calling him lewd names, tormenting him with poking fingers, trying in every way to disturb and withdraw M'Kato from the seclusion of his thoughts. But Lardi was no more to M'Kato than the flies that buzzed about him and sometimes settled upon his ears or nose, just something to be brushed aside and ignored, so at length Lardi had to give up his tormenting from sheer lack of opposition. But he never ceased to instruct his wives to stumble over the figure of M'Kato every time they came down to the river with baskets of fruit and vegetables upon their heads.

Lardi, on his earnings as a ferryman, kept a seraglio bigger than the chief of the surrounding district of Akesi. It was said that when he tired of a wife he tickled her to death. His reputation was as evil as his countenance.

He amassed great wealth as ferryman. For a time he kept his money tied up in a villainously dirty piece of

calico, which was always beside him upon the raft, and
which he opened every now and again to count the coins
surreptitiously. But after a little while, his money bag
becoming so bulky, he had perforce to dispose of it in
some other manner. It was then he began his seraglio,
and put all his money into the buying of wives. He
bought his women with astuteness and shrewd insight
into character, choosing the lean, wiry type of woman-
hood rather than the damsels whose rounded forms would
have been the joy of any other sultan. The lean ones
made better workers, Lardi declared.

His wives worked his garden and his manioc fields.
They sold the produce of garden and fields in Chembi,
and were always carful to bring him the coins that they
were given in exchange for these commodities. He
counted them carefully, and if there was so much as one
short even, the wives were apt to feel his disapproval in
a manner which he considered to be playful, but others
might take to be demoniacal. His youngest wife shewed
evidence of his playfulness in the rent lobes of her ears ;
she had at one time pitted her wits against his, and had,
unfortunately, been the loser.

In all Little River history Lardi, the ferryman, was
without doubt one of its pre-eminent figures. He at-
tained a celebrity never vouchsafed to others, not even to
the Zulu, M'Kato, who sat through the best part of his life
on the river-bank. North, south, east and west, by the
trading routes, stories of the Demon Ferryman of the
Little River were carried afar, and when his end came,

as it did in a jest as fearsome as ever he had played upon any of his victims, he was remarked upon and missed by all.

But not so M'Kato. When he came to leave the Little River, only two remarked his going : Father Domenique with gentle pity for a lost soul that had passed out of the reach of the admonishing hand of the Church, and Trader Voss, the only white man who ever came anywhere near fathoming the reason for M'Kato's years of meditation on the banks of the Little River.

WHEN M'Kato first came to the Little River he was a young man, but even so he was at a great disability, for his arms ended at the wrists abruptly, as if at one time his hands had been cut off sharply with an axe. He was a finely made young man, tall of stature and lithe of limb. His features in profile were clean-cut, cleaving the air like a bird ; he had a broad, low forehead with a tendency to shelve backwards, and his nose was Roman rather than negroid. As a young man his forehead was puckered into a wrinkle of concentration between the eyebrows, which never seemed to smooth itself out. As a middle-aged man this wrinkle had grown so deep that it resembled a knife-wound that had been healed with the edges gaping apart. The years of M'Kato's patient sitting by the Little River had, perhaps, deepened the wrinkle to this extent, for he had little else to do but sit and concentrate through the years ; that, as a matter of fact, was what he was there for.

M'Kato was not of the tribes that dwelt in the vicinity of the Little River ; he had journeyed far to find the river. On his mother's side, he was a Zulu, on his father's a Wakemba. Perhaps the blood of his mother's people accounted for his somewhat Cæsarian type of features, for certain castes of the Zulus account themselves as being descended from the Roman Cæsars who came to Africa, and when they returned to Rome after their victories there, left behind them more children than they need have done.

M'Kato had spent the best part of his boyhood on the banks of the Limpopo River, much farther south and east in the great Continent than the Little River. On the banks of the Limpopo he had lived with his mother and his sister, M'Tessa (who had been born with him at a birth), and had been herd-boy to Tarvisio, the wily old chief who ruled over the villages on the banks of the Limpopo for the greater part of its course. It was from Tarvisio, a fat-bellied old rascal if ever there was one, that M'Kato first learnt of the white man and his ways. Tarvisio had fought in the Zulu war, on the white man's side. It was said by his enemies that he had fought on both sides, but Tarvisio always denied this ; certainly he had sold a few head of cattle to the enemy upon occasion, but that was commercial enterprise, and had nothing to do with war.

Tarvisio liked the white men ; they made good laws, he said. For instance, he explained to M'Kato one day, if you stole your neighbour's cattle, they did not allow your neighbour to come down upon you with battle-axe and spear to retaliate. No, indeed, they set up courts of justice where the matter could be discussed at great length, and many witnesses called for both sides. The witnesses were always so numerous and took such a long time to tell their stories, that the stolen cattle were all killed and eaten before the time came for judgment to be passed, and no one, not even a white judge, could condemn a man for stealing cattle that did not exist.

But M'Kato, whose wits were sharp enough, pointed out that such a law could work both ways. One day it might be Tarvisio's cattle that were stolen.

In that case, Tarvisio replied, he would not put into operation the white man's law, but would rely upon his own. Tarvisio told M'Kato many other tales about the white man, which aroused in M'Kato such a sickening sense of disgust, that if ever a white man came to the Limpopo River, M'Kato would take his herd away from the lush grass that grew upon its banks to the arid plains that extended for some miles behind the village of Tarvisio's residence, and there he would wait with his beasts, until his sister, M'Tessa, came to tell him that the white travellers had departed.

When he and M'Tessa came to leave the Limpopo and travel many miles through Africa, until they finally reached the Kafue in Northern Rhodesia, he was always careful to avoid towns and settlements where white men dwelt. He taught M'Tessa to have this same hatred of the white man, although he never explained to her why she should have it, or repeated to her any of the lascivious tales of the Zulu war days that Tarvisio had poured into his own ears.

"All white men are bad," he said over and over again, and at length M'Tessa came to believe it as an undisputable fact; that was the reason, no doubt, why she screamed so much when she was being carried over the threshold of the house of Humphrey Brown at the Kafue.

THE old chief, Tarvisio, was not a Zulu, although he ruled over a certain portion of Zululand, and his six wives and numerous concubines were all Zulu women. He was of the Wa-kwafi tribe (outcasts from the Masai) who hold land in the east of Africa, a tribe of big men, good warriors upon occasion, but mostly addicted to agricultural pursuits. On the banks of the Limpopo River Tarvisio carried on the usual pursuits of his clan. He had a large herd of cattle and goats, and M'Kato, during his boyhood, was herd-boy to the old chief. He was a good herd-boy and enjoyed the life. When he was not engaged with the herd, he was busy whittling away at reeds that he dragged from the river to make pipes. M'Kato then had his two hands, and as he had all the finger-cunning of his father's people, the Wakembas, who had been famous as craftsmen and smiths for generations, he was very successful with the pipes. They were sweet-toned, and he played upon them while his cattle and goats grazed near by. He had all the love of the Wakembas for a quiet, pastoral existence, and he wanted nothing more from life than to be allowed to whittle his reeds and mind his herds in peace.

His mother did not like his playing upon the pipes so

much ; she was always urging him to put away the reeds and practise throwing his assegai more. M'Kato never understood his mother's fierce and warlike attitude towards life. "A sharp knife and a swift assegai," she would say to M'Kato, "are your two best friends." But M'Kato preferred his pipes. He liked to lie idly in the deep grass on the banks of the Limpopo, and blow into his pipes rather than throw an assegai at the hippopotami that sunned themselves on the fat little islands gracing the middle of the river.

M'Kato was just beginning his initiation into the tribe of Tarvisio when his mother died. She died of a fever that the witch doctor could not cure. For three days he poulticed her with warm mud-packs, till the sweat stood out in great beads upon her forehead, but on the fourth day she died. The witch doctor said that it was because she had no desire to live. He told M'Kato so secretly, behind the palm of his hand, and M'Kato was amazed that it should be so, for his mother had never expressed such a thought to him.

But that night, when the women were wailing round the dead body of his mother, he sat beside the grey-green waters of the Limpopo, and thought of many things.

He thought, among others, of how sullen and afraid his mother had always appeared when she had come from the hut of Tarvisio. His mother, being a widow, had slept alone with the younger women of the tribe ; but sometimes she had been summoned to Tarvisio's hut after dark, and had always gone with a firmer and prouder step than usual, but came from it in the morning, cowed and afraid.

M'Kato, as he had begun to undergo his initiation, understood these things. He thought of his sister M'Tessa, who had just finished her period of seclusion at puberty, and of lascivious old Tarvisio who, now that their mother was dead, would be ready enough to cast eyes upon her. Having been born with M'Tessa at a birth, M'Kato felt a peculiar tenderness towards her; he felt that he would kill Tarvisio if ever he saw the same sullen look upon the face of his sister that he had seen so often upon his mother's.

For the first time in his hitherto calm and pastoral existence, the proud, warlike blood of his mother's clan stirred in his veins. But he could not kill Tarvisio, he knew that; the old chief's hut was always too well guarded, and when Tarvisio walked abroad, behind him walked a henchman carrying battle-axe and spear. He had many enemies, and he was a cautious old man. So M'Kato sat all night upon the banks of the Limpopo River, thinking of what could be done in the matter. Before a false dawn appeared in the eastern sky, causing the wild beasts that had come to drink at the river under protection of the darkness to scuttle home to their lairs too early, he had decided that he would take his sister away from the Limpopo; he would take her far away, out of the reach of Tarvisio's long arm, that he knew stretched for many miles along the banks of the river.

He was sorry to leave the river, on the banks of which

he had been so happy, whittling away at his pipes and minding the old chief's herd. He was sorry, too, to leave the herd, because Tarvisio had promised him, as his payment for minding it, that if ever a calf were to be born with a white face and a black splash upon it, then it was to be M'Kato's. In the ordinary course of events, it did not seem likely that such a thing would happen, as the cattle of Tarvisio were all brown ; but at no great distance down the river on the opposite bank, there was a piebald bull that Tarvisio's son-in-law had just bought from some neighbouring cattlemen, and M'Kato had planned to drive Tarvisio's cattle down that way some time when the old chief was away in battle, sometime when the river was low, and the cattle could be relied upon to cross it of their own free will.

M'Tessa was a girl of agreeable disposition, so she made no demur when M'Kato told her that they were leaving the Limpopo and going to journey very far indeed. They set out one day at sunrise. Tarvisio did not cause them to be followed and brought back, although he was perfectly well aware of their departure, and was sorry not to be able to enjoy the charms of M'Tessa, who was a firm, lithe woman like her mother, and so much younger. But he knew also of the piebald bull down the river, and sooner or later he would have to go into battle with some neighbouring tribe, and M'Kato would be left to do what he pleased with the herd. Tarvisio was not minded to set M'Kato up for life with a herd of brindle calves.

M'KATO and M'Tessa travelled many hundreds of miles before they reached the Kafue. In the first place it was not their intended destination, but M'Kato, in avoiding the settlements of white men, misdirected his steps, and instead of finding the land of his father's people, the pastoral Wakcmbas, came to the swampland in Northern Rhodesia, which is known as the Kafue.

According to M'Kato's reckoning this was some twenty-four moons after he and M'Tessa had set out from the Limpopo River. The Wakembas, he knew, dwelt north of the Limpopo ; they were quiet, pastoral people, who cultivated their land and did not hold much intercourse with their neighbours. With them M'Tessa would be safe ; she would, perhaps, marry into the tribe ; and as for himself, well, he would find another river that he could sit by, whilst he whittled away at some reeds.

But between the Limpopo and the land of the Wakembas the white man dwelt, and M'Kato was afraid of the white man, afraid for the sake of M'Tessa. Worse even than the fate that she would have had at the hands of Tarvisio would be her fate at the hands of the white man. Tarvisio had told many lascivious tales of the Zulu war days to M'Kato, of half-caste babies that were born of proud Zulu belles, and had to be thrown to the crocodiles in the rivers because no Zulu woman would acknowledge a half-caste child as her own.

"The crocodiles in the rivers of Zululand," said Tarvisio, "became so gorged and fat-bellied in the days after the war that they were easy prey to any carelessly-flung spear."

There were other tales too, which the old chief told with relish, and which, at the time, M'Kato had listened to with indifference ; but after the beginning of initiation he had remembered them with a kind of fascinated horror.

When he set out from the Limpopo with his sister his main thought was to keep her away from the eyes of white men. This involved considerable deviation from a direct route north, and so it was that, after trekking for some twenty-four moons, brother and sister found themselves in the vicinity of the Kafue, instead of in the land of the Wakembas. The Kafue was swamp-land, set about with tall reeds and rushes, unhealthy and fever-ridden, but beside it the soil was rich and fertile. That was the reason why Humphrey Brown had his plantation there. On a tall hill back of the Kafue Humphrey Brown's house was perched. It was unhealthy in the lowlands of the Kafue, but up on the tall hill the air was clear and free from fever.

M'Kato and M'Tessa had walked many weary miles ; they had been some time without food, as they had recently passed through country where the tribes were hostile and drove them forth from their villages with sticks and stones. So it seemed to M'Kato when he came within sight of the plantation, and saw the white man's house perched up on the hill, that for once he would have to put aside his dislike for the white man and work for him. But he was careful to hide M'Tessa away before going to the plantation. He took her a mile or so away from the tall hill and built her a rough shelter of brushwood. With her he left the pipes that he had brought with him from the Limpopo, and then, promising to return before nightfall with food, he set out to see the white man that dwelt upon the hill.

At the plantation Humphrey Brown looked M'Kato over with a speculative eye. He appeared strong and capable, and when Humphrey Brown asked him what he could do, though M'Kato could not understand him, he was sharp-witted enough to guess what the white man was asking him, and made a pantomime of driving cattle along. It was then Humphrey Brown's turn to fail in understanding, and at last, M'Kato, looking up at the sky for inspiration as to how to demonstrate effectively his one-time occupation by the Limpopo, beheld a trail of white clouds for all the world like a herd of white goats with a herdsman behind, playing upon pipes just as M'Kato had played. He pointed to the sky, because he knew that Humphrey Brown must see the same things as he did, despite the colour of his skin.

Humphrey Brown laughed till the tears streamed down his round red face. "Ha ! ha ! he ! he ! A canting Chris-

tian is he ? Well, we'll soon knock that out of him.
Hey, you there," he called loudly to his head boy, "set
this nigger to work clearing some of the swamp-land, and
see that he does work."

And so M'Kato was taken away by N'Miko, the head
boy, and set to work with axe and chopper to clear
brushwood from the swamp-lands. When he was given
his ration of mealie meal at dusk he managed to steal
away with it to M'Tessa, who was waiting rather fear-
fully for him in her brush shelter. Dogs, she told
M'Kato, had come and prowled about her shelter, large
dogs, probably belonging to the white man. They had
bared their teeth at her, and it was only with a stout stick
that she had been able to drive them off. That night
M'Kato built another shelter for M'Tessa, still further
away from the plantation.

M'Kato worked at Humphrey Brown's plantation for
three moons. There were many things that he did not
like about the place, but he never spoke of them to
M'Tessa, because it was necessary for him to stay for
three moons, in order to obtain the five shillings which
the white man paid to his black labourers once every
three months.

M'Kato was careful never to mention his sister to the
head boy, N'Miko, as he did not trust him any more
than he trusted his master ; but he managed to steal away
to M'Tessa every evening with half of his ration of
mealie meal, though this was against the rules of the
plantation. At dusk all the labourers were sent to their

quarters on the edge of the swamp-land, and were supposed to stay there until they began work the next day at sunrise.

There was always enough for two in M'Kato's rations; Humphrey Brown was generous enough in that respect, but there are worse things in life than an empty stomach, as M'Kato very soon found out. For instance, the heavy sound of the flogging whip which always seemed to be on the air when dusk descended on the Kafue; the loud barking of dogs, shrill screams followed by a death-like silence. M'Kato could not ask about these things, as no one on the plantation understood his language with the exception of N'Miko, who had once worked in Zululand, and had picked up a word or two of Zulu; but when M'Kato asked him, he would say nothing.

M'Kato disliked N'Miko, the head boy, almost as much as he disliked Humphrey Brown with his red, bloated face, and his heavy hand which descended too often upon M'Kato's head. N'Miko also had a heavy hand, and he carried a sjambok swung from his belt, with which he touched up the plantation workers now and then if they were lazy. He did not use the sjambok on M'Kato, because M'Kato was strong and a willing worker, and, strange to say, N'Miko did not return M'Kato's dislike. There was something fine about M'Kato, and N'Miko, bully though he was, recognized this.

When he saw M'Kato working away, knee-deep almost, in the mire of the swamp-lands, in order to gain the five shillings that would help him on his way to the land of the Wakembas, he felt a little qualm of conscience for the lies he had told. There would be no leaving the plantation for M'Kato at the end of three months, he knew that. It was only when the labourers were weary and aged with work that they were allowed to leave Humphrey Brown's plantation.

On one side of the plantation there were the Kafue swamps which no man could cross ; on the other, the kennels of the loud-barking dogs. Humphrey Brown saw to it that no labourer left him of his own accord ; that was one of the reasons that he was so successful as a plantation owner, and was looked up to by the white residents of Northern Rhodesia as a pioneer to be proud of. Even the bishop said, when he dined at his table : "Marvellous what you have achieved in so short a time, Captain Brown. When I passed through these parts a few years ago, there was nothing but a fever-infected swamp. And now——" The bishop spread his hands in a gesture of admiration and approval.

"What the niggers need is discipline," said Humphrey Brown. "I learned how to manage men in the army. The heavy hand, and they respect you."

"Quite so, quite so," agreed the bishop, mellowed by Captain Brown's excellent wine. " 'Spare the rod and spoil the child' ; and after all what are our black brethren but little children ? We must bring them up carefully."

Humphrey Brown, pouring the bishop out another glass of wine, was not quite certain about the "carefully," but he let the word pass.

When the bishop departed next day, carried in a hammock by two bearers, with a huge white umbrella held over him by a third, and followed by a train of porters over a mile long, Humphrey Brown was glad. Now things could go on as usual at the plantation. Visiting missionaries were a nuisance; he always lost a boy or two when any of them stayed at his house, because he could not very well let the dogs out while they were there. It was well that the bishop came only once a year, and his subordinate perhaps twice or three times. There were not many missionaries then in Northern Rhodesia; it was only the beginning of the great missionary season in Africa.

"Find out," said Captain Brown to his head boy one day, "where that new nigger, M'Kato, goes after dark. I have watched him, and every night he steals away into the bush with his mealie meal."

"Perhaps to a wife, B'wana," suggested the head boy with a snigger.

"Well, he can bring her to the plantation quarters then. Watch him, and find out where he goes."

So N'Miko set spies to watch M'Kato after dusk, and very soon afterwards, he was able to report to Humphrey Brown that M'Kato stole away to the camp of a woman, with whom he shared his food, but as he stole back again and slept in the plantation quarters, it appeared that the woman was not his wife. She was a fine, straight, lithe young woman, added the head boy with a leer, anxious to propitiate his master.

"When M'Kato is working in the swamps, bring her here," instructed Humphrey Brown.

The next day the head boy and two others (it took three strong men to hold M'Tessa) brought her to the house of Humphrey Brown. M'Kato, working far away in the swamps, heard shrill screams, and knew that they came from the throat of M'Tessa. He dropped his axe, and ran as swiftly as he could to the house on the hill. He was just in time to see M'Tessa dragged, screaming, over the threshold of the white man's house.

A LITTLE while after that M'Kato left the Kafue and journeyed north. Humphrey Brown made no protest at his going; M'Kato was no longer any use as a worker because his arms now ended sharply at the wrists — his hands had been cut off.

It was a pity, the other boys on the plantation told him, that he had struck Humphrey Brown. It was a dangerous thing to do, to lift a hand against a white man. Why had he not waited until after dark, and then at some distance with an assegai——? They were afraid to do it themselves, but he, M'Kato, had more courage apparently.

But M'Kato could not understand what they said to him. Before he set out, N'Miko, who still liked M'Kato although he had cut off his hands, took him aside and whispered in his ear : "Go to Kundi."

"Who is Kundi, and where is Kundi ?" asked M'Kato, who could understand N'Miko because he spoke in Zulu.

"A witch doctor there," answered the head boy, pointing north vaguely.

"How shall I know him ?" asked M'Kato.

"He is very old, and he wears a monkey skin upon his left shoulder."

"I will go to Kundi," said M'Kato wearily, but he had not much faith in witch doctors since the one of Tarvisio's tribe had let his mother die so easily. Besides, what witch doctor, however clever at his craft, could give him back his sister, or a new pair of hands ?

M'Kato saw his sister once, before leaving the Kafue. She was dressed in gaudy calico, and hung about with strings of coloured beads. M'Kato did not recognise her until she spoke to him. This pert, provocative-eyed girl, the serene and agreeable M'Tessa ?

When he questioned her, she said that she liked living in the white man's house ; it was more comfortable than a brush shelter, but the funny thing that she slept upon she could not get used to. She shewed M'Kato the trumpery baubles round her neck and arms, but he could not admire them ; he could only stare and stare with growing horror at his sister. Finally, she left him rather angrily, and M'Kato went upon his way in search of Kundi, the witchman. M'Kato thought that probably his sister had not noticed the loss of his hands, as she was so taken up with her baubles.

M'Kato left the Kafue with the sun setting in vermilion splendour over the swamp-lands, its reflection turning the dark, dank waters to a sinister pool of blood. M'Kato, skirting the swamp-lands, bound for the north, thought this appropriate ; he would always remember the Kafue as a place of blood — there had been a pool of it about his feet after his hands were cut off.

It was a pity, he thought now, that the labourers had

bound up his stumps so tightly, for if they had not done so there would have been more blood. All the blood in his body would have made a sizeable pool — nothing of course to equal the tremendous stretch of dead water that was quivering a farewell to the fast vanishing sun — but sufficient perhaps to attract people's attention.

M'Tessa might have seen it and felt some sorrow, or that other white man who had come once to the plantation, and conducted queer rites under the shade of a large tree in the labourers' quarters, and afterwards had inspected the labourers, and bound up a sore or two, and applied healing ointment to nasty scratches. M'Kato wondered if he carried anything in his bag that would make new hands ; he knew that the white men could sometimes make new teeth ; Tarvisio had told him so. At least, that white man would have done something in the matter, M'Kato felt, if the pool of blood had been large enough, and he had been there to see it.

M'Kato carried nothing with him on his journey to Kundi, not even his pipes. They were still in the brush shelter that was now deserted ; and although M'Kato regretted having to leave them, he could not do otherwise on account of his mutilated arms. He walked for some little way on the outer edge of the swamp waters, his feet slopping in and out of the mire, but when he reached the uncleared land behind the plantation, he left the swamps, and made his way through the jungle. It was heavy with a dusk mist, and the perfume of the tree orchids was overpowering ; occasionally a cricket chirped in the rotted leaves at his feet, fire-flies darted about like so many falling stars, and from bough to bough of the trees overhead, monkeys swung, chattering and screaming and throwing down leaves and twigs spitefully upon M'Kato's head. But M'Kato went steadily onwards along the tiny track that wound through the bush, walking at an even pace ; he did not notice the white mist closing in upon him, or the bright spots of light, now here, now there, made by the fire-flies. His eyes were blind to all but one thing, and that was his two foreshortened arms that swung out before him. In the darkness he could see them ; they were ever before him, even though he walked with his arms behind his back.

In his ears the song of the crickets and the noisy chattering of the monkeys became as one thing : the rude, excited voices of the plantation workers as they, half-cowed, half-bellicose, had stood about him at the chopping-block. And in his nostrils was not the exotic perfume of orchids, but the hot scent of blood. Blood, blood, blood ! he could smell it everywhere as he walked, on the ground, in the mist ; it seemed to drip upon him from the trees.

M'Kato walked until the dawn began to shew through the network of tree-boughs like light through shutter slats ; then the small track widened suddenly, the bush decreased in density, and gradually M'Kato found himself coming into increasing brightness. He came at length to a stretch of arid plain that led to a rocky plateau. M'Kato was then both tired and hungry, for he had eaten nothing since leaving the Kafue. Once during the night, he had stayed to drink at a water-hole, lying flat upon his stomach and lapping up the water like an animal, but of food he had eaten nothing; and when the sun began to burn down upon him as he crossed the arid plain, he felt sick and dizzy. He was used to eating at dusk and dawn.

Under the shadow of the plateau there appeared to be a small hut, and when M'Kato saw this, he turned his steps in its direction. But when he came to the hut he found that it was merely a shrine, a crude erection of boughs, in the shady interior of which was an altar bearing two wooden figures. These figures were coarsely carved and gaudily stained with colouring matter, and were of man and woman, symbolical of generation. M'Kato went into the shrine, and when his eyes became accustomed to the shadow, he gazed intently at the two wooden figures on the altar. It seemed that it was necessary for him to gaze at them for a long time; he felt that there was something that he could learn from them, something that would help him to solve the problem of his life in the future.

He noticed with what care the genital organs of the two figures had been carved in comparison with the coarse work of the rest of the bodies, how enlarged they were, and yet wrought with such delicacy and mystery, as if they had been something of vast importance, but a little beyond the comprehension of the carver, and therefore had to be rendered in mystic symbols.

M'Kato said suddenly and aloud : "That is a mighty force !"

He heard a hoarse chuckle behind him, a chuckle that might have come from the throat of a hyena, but came instead from a little shrivelled-up old man, crouched away in the corner of the hut, almost hidden in the dark shadows that enveloped its interior. M'Kato swung round swiftly, his handless arms raised in a defensive attitude.

"Put down your arms, O my brother," said a voice as hoarse as the previous chuckle, "for you have just said a mighty truth, and there is never any need to defend a truth by battle."

M'Kato lowered his arms. "And who are you, O my father, who speak the tongue of the Zulus, and yet are not of their race ?" asked he, peering through the gloom at the little, shrivelled-up old man.

The withered old man crept out of his corner. "Ha ! ha ! he ! he ! ho ! ho !" he chuckled. "In a Zulu kraal did I spend my childhood, and a tongue once learned is not easily forgotten."

M'Kato was silent.

"You are tired, O my brother, you have walked a long way. I have a hut not far from here, up on the rocky ridges yonder. Come and rest in it, O long-travelled one," then said the little old man.

THE two men went out from the shrine into the blinding sunlight that beat down upon the plain, the tall, lithe younger man striding ahead, and the little bowed old man hopping along, with bent knees, in a great effort to keep up with him.

"Perhaps, as you know the direction so well, it is to your hut that we are going," suggested the older man, with one of his hoarse chuckles.

M'Kato immediately slackened his pace to meet the requirements of the elder man.

They climbed to the plateau, and set among the rocks there was a hut of leaves and boughs, as coarsely constructed as the shrine on the plain below. In the interior was a heap of blankets, a pile of bones, and various crudely carved figures like those in the shrine, but not as yet complete in the carving.

"Enter," said the little old man to M'Kato, and spread a blanket for him to rest upon. "I am Kundi, the witch-man ; this is my hut, and you are welcome in it."

M'Kato sat down upon the blanket listlessly. Kundi brought him a gourd full of water and a baked cake of mealie meal. "Eat, drink, and be refreshed, O Zulu," he said.

M'Kato's head drooped forward with shame. He could not take the gourd or the food because he had no hands.

"Think you that I am blind?" asked Kundi sharply. "Sit up, and I will hold the water to your lips, and afterwards the food."

M'Kato obeyed the witchman.

All the long hot day M'Kato slept in the hut of Kundi, the witchman; he woke at sunset much refreshed, and would have gone upon his way, but Kundi bade him remain. "When the moon rises, we have many things to speak about," he said.

The two men waited silently until enormous shadows crept out from their lairs and spread themselves across the plain. Then, over the distant black ridge of the jungle, a large white moon appeared like a dead face in the sky.

"Now is the time for you to tell me all," said Kundi, and taking up two bones from the pile in the corner of his hut, he placed them upon the glowing ashes of the fire which smouldered near the doorway. As they became charred by the fire, they gave forth an acrid, pungent odour.

"N'Miko told me to come to you, O Kundi," M'Kato said at length.

"I know not N'Miko," answered Kundi, "but that matters little, because all men know me. Tell me your story."

M'Kato told it briefly, and with shame; he could hear

again the screams of M'Tessa in his ears, and he could smell blood all about him.

Kundi heard him through patiently, and then taking the two charred bones from off the fire, he spat upon them, and going outside his hut to the stockade where he kept his fowls, seized a white rooster, wrung its neck, and hung it over the fire in the doorway of the hut. Its blood dripped down into the smouldering fire and raised a dark smoke. Kundi, squatting cross-legged and hump-backed, gazed intently into the dark vapour rising from the fire. Presently he spoke : "I see a little river, narrow and yellow, with rapids in its course."

There was silence for some time, and then Kundi took the two charred bones, and flung them back on to the pile in the corner.

"An assegai is swift, but thought is surer," said Kundi ; "a combination of the two is certain."

M'Kato listened respectfully to the witchman. "Go through the land until you come to the narrowest river, and when you have found it, sit upon its banks and wait," Kundi instructed him.

M'Kato, his voice seeming to come from a great distance, said : "Why must it be a narrow river ?"

"Because you will have to throw your assegai with your foot, and you will never be able to throw very far," replied Kundi.

The rooster continued to drip its blood into the ashes of the fire, and the thin black smoke arose and curled away upwards outside the doorway of the hut, but there was now no picture in the smoke, as Kundi, the witch-man, had taken away the magic bones. Presently the smoke died away, and the ashes of the fire fell into ruins and grew cold.

Kundi and M'Kato sat by the cold ashes long into the night, and Kundi told the younger man many things, so when M'Kato left him at sunrise, he felt weighty with knowledge. He felt soothed, too, and almost contented ; if it had not been for his foreshortened arms which would swing out into the line of his vision, he would have gone happily upon his way.

"I have nothing to pay you with," he said to Kundi, before leaving, "not even a blanket."

Kundi, the witchman, gave one of his hoarse chuckles, and hopped a few steps on his bent old legs. "Pay me when you have accomplished your task," he replied. "Come back this way, and tell me all about it. But perhaps I shall be dead by then ; I am old now, very old."

"Will it be so long then ?" asked M'Kato.

"How should I know ?" retorted Kundi hopping a few steps more. "Now go upon your way, O Zulu, and come back some day and pay me what you owe me. I want two bags of mealie meal and a goat, and remember that the goat must be with kid."

AFTER M'Kato left Kundi he crossed a series of
rocky plateaux which led into the Tree Country.
Kundi had spoken of this Tree Country to M'Kato.
The Tree people were disposed to be friendly towards
strangers, he had said, so M'Kato could not do better
than keep in their country for a while, at least, until he
became expert in the use of his teeth and toes. He would
give him a charm, too, that he could shew to the witch
doctors of the tribe, and they would supply him with
food.

For three nights and days, M'Kato crossed the plateaux,
only resting in the hottest hours of the day. The plateaux
were lion-infested, and M'Kato, with no means of protecting himself, had no wish to dawdle there. So he
walked steadily through the night and day, only staying
to eat and rest when the sun was high in the heavens,
and burning down on the rocky plateaux with fierce intensity ; he slept in what shade he could get, behind the
high boulders on the plateau, but that was little enough.

When at length he reached the end of the rocky ridges,
and saw stretched before him a green and gracious country, with tall trees spaced well apart and in between long
meadows of verdant grass, he felt a vague sense of comfort, and a promise of peace to come.

Kundi had supplied M'Kato with food in the form of mealie cakes ; these he carried wrapped up in a piece of cloth, slung over his shoulder. He managed, with the aid of his teeth, to extract a cake now and then from the bundle, but when he came within sight of the Tree Country, and knew that he would soon be in a land of hospitality and abundance, he sat down and made his first good meal since he had left Kundi's hut. When he had eaten his fill, he lay down (for it was near dusk) in the shelter of a high boulder, and prepared himself for slumber. He meant to sleep well through the long night, and enter at dawn into the green and enchanted land. But he could not rest ; a hunger had come upon M'Kato that he knew no food could assuage.

He lay huddled up upon the fast-cooling earth, and gazed upwards at the myriad stars frosting the dark night sky. The wonder of life was upon him, its fear and its fascination. He had seen it in the shrine on the arid plain below Kundi's hut, he had heard of it from old Kundi, and now he knew it for himself ; all the unrest of the Universe was upon him, torturing his limbs and burning his heart. Far away across the plateau came the long-drawn mating-call of a lion. M'Kato, listening, felt that he must rise and lift up his voice to the thousand stars in a like call, but when he did so, his voice was only lost in the darkness ; there was no response.

He rested upon the earth again ; the stillness about him was profound, the lion had ceased his calling, the lioness had come to him. The quietness seemed like a menace that surrounded M'Kato in a circle of threatening figures. His restless energy was hemmed in ; it was too much for his body, but he could not free himself from it, for the circle of stillness pressed hard upon him and thrust back his inquietude. He huddled all night upon the ground, burning with his inextinguishable desire. M'Kato knew that the time had come for him to take a wife.

At dawn he rose and went into the Tree Country. He walked steadily by day through the peaceful green land, and at night, curled up at the foot of one of the friendly trees. His desire troubled him no longer ; he slept well and quietly, worn out by the day's march. That this hunger would return to him, he knew, but he would guard against it ; in the Tree Country he would take a wife.

When M'Kato's supply of mealie cakes gave out, he found the charm that Kundi had given him, made of monkey-skin and the hair from the tail of a sacred giraffe, very useful ; for every witch doctor to whom it was shewn, immediately spread the best food that his village could produce before M'Kato, and pressed a further supply upon him when he went upon his way. The witch doctors always knew of M'Kato's coming before his arrival, and also of the charm that he carried with him, so food was always in readiness for him, laid out with much ceremony before the village shrine.

But apart from the message of command that Kundi's charm carried, the inhabitants of the Tree Country were hospitable, kindly people, and travellers never went unfed through their land. They were experts in sign language, so, although they could not talk to M'Kato with their tongues, they always managed to make him feel that he was welcome among them.

There were seven different clans or tribes in the Tree Country, and each clan took its name and status from one of the species of trees that were spaced so evenly through the land. There were the Big Tree men (the *Babaos*), the Little Tree Men (a species of wild cotton were the little trees), the *Ashorin* Men, the Tall Tree men (the beeches), and the Bent Tree men, a race of incredibly old men who were short and shrivelled and twisted like the trees whose name they bore. Kundi had been a Bent Tree man when he had lived in the Tree Country and practised his magic there. There were also the Mango Tree men, who were looked down upon by the other tribes, as their trees, though useful, were insignificant ; and the Bird Tree men, so called because their trees bore flowers which were like the feathery plumage of a bird ; and also in their tribal rites, they always used the bird fetish, and were able to understand the language of birds as well as trees.

Each clan knew the language of its own trees, and the witch doctors knew the language of many ; that was how they always knew of M'Kato's coming before his arrival. The trees, talking to one another, spoke of the man without hands who was walking amongst them, and of the charm that he carried ; and the witch doctors, listening, prepared food in anticipation of his arrival.

Long friendship and mutual understanding between the trees and the Tree Men have taught the wise old fathers of the race the tree language and the tree magic ; and from generation to generation, it has been handed down from father to son, a deeply hidden, mysterious thing, guarded jealously from the interference of strangers.

The trees know everything. They have lived through many ages ; they have gathered a store of knowledge from times past, and as life is a circle that repeats itself, then in the past there are to be found all the visions of the future. Man cannot see these visions, for he does not live long enough ; one age is his only, but the trees stand through the centuries. This, a witch doctor in the Tree Country, one Luala, told to M'Kato, first in sign language ; and then, as M'Kato stayed some time in the village of Luala, and became familiar with the spoken tongue of the Tree People, he was able to talk more freely with him.

Luala grew to have a great affection for M'Kato, and helped him in many ways ; he gave him a grass hut to dwell in, and in exchange for the charm of Kundi's, his niece, Tela, for a wife.

Tela was a fine, upstanding young woman, strong of arm and body, and well versed in all methods of agriculture. When M'Kato came to the end of his wandering and found the narrowest river, while he settled down on its banks to his great task, she would cultivate a garden, and thus they would be able to eat and live.

This was satisfactory, M'Kato felt, as he would need a great deal of time to himself. Luala was also satisfied, as he had long wanted to possess a charm of Kundi's, knowing the old man's marvellous powers in magic.

The trees said that Kundi had lived too long; he was not as old as they were, but he was very old indeed in the way of men, and therefore knew much magic. He was the most powerful witch doctor in the land, and the trees knew how wide was the land. Kundi was a Bent Tree man, and therefore taciturn. The Bent Trees never spoke much; they waved their bent old boughs, and laughed up and down their shrivelled trunks, but they did not speak much, because they were so very old, the oldest of all the trees. The Bent Tree men were silent also, and Kundi was the most silent of all the clan. Presently, he would not talk at all, and then he would have achieved all knowledge, for wisdom never speaks; the very essence of it is silence and secrecy.

Luala repeated this over and over again to M'Kato, so M'Kato became sparing in the use of speech, and on his forehead, there began a furrow which gradually deepened as the days passed, and M'Kato's speech grew less, and his thoughts greater. M'Kato's appearance, too, took on a different aspect; his face lost the rounded curve of youth and became thin and sharp-edged. By the time that he left the Tree Country he had the appearance of a man going on towards middle-age. This, of course, was not so, but M'Kato's silence and preoccupation, his peering into the future, his finally living in the future instead of the present, brought the years quickly upon him.

All day long he would sit in the shade of one of the trees and gather his thoughts together in concentration according to Kundi's instructions. When first he had come to the Tree Country he had been impatient to be upon his way in search of the narrowest river, but as the moons came, grew big, and faded again, one after another, he grew more content to leave the matter in the hands of the Tree people. Luala had asked the trees to discover the smallest river, and they were busy searching for it. Trees stood everywhere in the land ; they would pass on the news one to another, and when the river was found and compared in width with all other rivers, then its direction would be passed back to Luala. This would simplify M'Kato's journey, and as he was now related to the Tree people by marriage the trees were glad enough to do anything that they could for him, although he had no understanding of their language.

L UALA watched the trees each day for news of the narrowest river. He had spent his life in watching the trees, so there was not a sign which they made that he did not understand. At length came a day when the trees had news for him. "Keep north," they said, "and then west, west of the large lakes, and you will come to the narrowest river in the land. It is a little river with rapids in its course, and its only use is for the wild beasts of the jungle to drink at after dark, but you asked for the narrowest river, and we have found it for you."

Luala passed the news on to M'Kato, and M'Kato immediately prepared for his journey north. Tela was to go with her husband ; she was content to leave her own country and journey into the unknown. Men were scarce in the Tree Country, and she counted herself lucky to have a husband, stranger though he was, and without hands.

The men of the Tree Country were not warriors, but their neighbours on the right were powerful savages with filed teeth, so when they invaded the Tree Country, the Tree Men always lost in the encounter. It was one thing to know that the enemy was bearing down upon them (which they always did through the goodwill of the

Trees), but it was quite another to array themselves against the enemy, being a weaponless people who had no knowledge of the art of war !

Sometimes the savages with filed teeth carried off some of the women, which evened matters up a little ; otherwise the Tree Country would have been overrun with women. As it was, there were four women to every man, and the chiefs sat round their fires at night and spoke of polygamy, which their neighbours on both sides seemed to practise without evil results. It had never been the custom with the Tree people, and the chiefs hesitated to break old laws ; they themselves did not even keep concubines.

But it was permissible in the Tree Country to exchange wives, provided that the exchange was made within the clan. They usually consulted the witch doctor about such matters, and the witch doctor consulted the trees. The trees were strict and had a great sense of morality. For instance, when the old chief of the Bird Men, against all laws and codes of his clan, cast his ancient, toothless wife from him and took unto himself a young and comely maiden, they were so incensed that they killed him next day. At least, he was found dead upon the ground with the great trunk of a tree fallen upon him, and after that none of the other chiefs thought of following his example.

When M'Kato and Tela set out upon their journey, Tela took with her a bag of mealie meal, some dried beans, and rough implements for gardening, which the Tree people used in the cultivation of the soil. She also took unknown to M'Kato, the charm that he had given to Luala in payment for her. If this charm could buy a wife, then Tela knew its value, and felt that in the long journey into the unknown that they were about to make, it might be useful.

But Tela, Tree woman though she was, had reckoned without the trees and their just wrath. As she and M'Kato, two tiny insignificant black figures amongst the green giants of the forest, made their way north, the trees seemed to bend down their great arms and clutch at them, while up amongst their topmost branches raged the storm of their wrath.

Gone was the peace of the Tree Country, and in its place was a region of terror and alarm. The biting scorn of the trees seemed to lash at M'Kato and Tela like so many whips. The forest became dark and hostile, voices came out of it, threatening, condemning. But it was only Tela who knew the reason for this, and she, with Kundi's charm hidden carefully away in the bag of mealie meal that she carried on her head, kept silent.

When night shrouded the Tree Country, and a full round moon came up and hung behind the trees like a crystal globe, the very shadows that the trees cast were living things, hideous and leering hobgoblins that pursued them with pointed fingers and mouthing faces. And the air was filled with mysterious, menacing sounds. M'Kato became increasingly aware of them.

"You know the Tree language," he said to Tela, "ask them what they want of us."

But Tela prevaricated. These were not her trees, she said, she could not understand them.

M'Kato looked at the forest before them, dark, hostile and full of mystery; he felt that he could not go on. He said so to Tela, and Tela wished that it had been his tongue that had been cut off instead of his hands. It was not until a great tree-limb came crashing down beside her, that, palsied with fear, great beads of sweat on her brow and body, she told M'Kato the truth. Then, throwing herself face downwards upon the earth, she began to moan forth her repentance.

It was M'Kato, with the aid of teeth and toes, which he had learned to use expertly, who undid the bag of mealie meal and withdrew Kundi's charm. He laid it at the foot of one of the scolding trees, and immediately there was peace and quietness in the forest. Tela, in between her moans, said that the trees would tell Luala where to find the charm.

With the coming again of tranquillity in the forest, Tela's fear subsided; she rose from the ground, and the two went on again through glades of calm green beauty, their figures dwarfed into insignificance by the immensity of the trees.

WHEN M'Kato came at length to the Little River, some six moons or so after he and Tela had left the Tree Country, he spanned it with his eye. It was sufficiently narrow for a spent assegai to reach the other side, even though thrown inexpertly by a clumsy foot. He sat down upon the right bank of the river with a great feeling of thankfulness that now he could start upon his life's great task. Tela, who had been lagging behind for some considerable time, came up with her baskets of food and, making a fire, cooked a meal for M'Kato and herself. M'Kato indicated to Tela that at last their journey had come to an end; this was the river he intended to sit by, and she, Tela, could now get on with her gardening.

He did not tell her the reason why he wished to sit by the river; that was a secret between himself and Kundi. Even the witch doctors of the Tree Country had never sought to know it, and Tela was either too wise or too indifferent to ask. She merely looked about her for some fertile land to cultivate and plant; but near the river the soil was poor, so she had to go some little way from it before finding a suitable patch.

When it was found to her liking, she and M'Kato

erected a shelter of boughs which afterwards they enlarged to a hut of two rooms. M'Kato, by this time,
had become expert in the use of his stumps as well as
his feet, but the burden of the work naturally fell upon
his wife. But she was a strong woman and a cheerful
worker, and made no complaint.

When M'Kato went back to the river and took up
his post there, she hoed her land and made a garden.
The plants were sprouting in it by the time her child
was born.

Tela had come to know the women in the village of
Akesi, a day's journey by foot from the Little River, and
when her child was born, they came and stood round
her while she knelt upon the grass mat in her hut, and
wailed and shrieked with her in her pain. The birth
was a long one, and the women of Akesi attributed this
to the fact that Tela had married out of her tribe. The
Tree people were a thin, lithe race with small bones,
whereas M'Kato had the heavy bones and broad shoulders and thighs of his mother's race. When at length
the child was born, it was found to be a man-child of
fine proportions, but without the breath of life inflating
its lungs; it had been smothered in the birth. The
women carried the dead baby to the door of the hut, and
laid it there on a bed of dried grass. M'Kato, leaving
his seat by the river, came to the doorway of the hut and
stood there like a black statue, looking down at his dead
son.

He contemplated the child with a calm, inscrutable

countenance, bereft of any emotion. He remembered the time when he had stood in the shrine on the plain below Kundi's hut, looking at the crudely carved figures on the altar, and had involuntarily cried out the truth that he had felt. Now he looked down upon that which had been created with this mighty force, and he felt a little sorry that it had been wasted in this way. A dead child was all there was to shew for those nights of curious energy in the Tree Country.

He remembered Kundi's warning. "There will be many things to lure you away from your task, O Zulu, and one will be your desire for a woman. But remember this : every time that you take a woman, O my brother, you lose a little of that force that will bring you the fulfilment of your task. A man may create many things besides children but it is only we old, wise ones who know it."

M'Kato went slowly back to the river; he felt suddenly a great distaste for Tela, for all women ; in the future he would leave them alone, and go on with his work by the river.

While the women wailed and moaned about Tela long into the night, because her child had been born dead, M'Kato sat by the river absorbed in his own thoughts, and the furrow in his brow was deep like a wound.

After that Tela slept alone, and if it had not been for the fact that she was afraid of what the trees might do to her (having had one experience of their wrath already), she would have joined the women in the village of Akesi, and slept as they did, sometimes with one man, sometimes with another.

The people of Akesi were mongrel bred; they followed no moral law in their relations with one another, and disease was rife amongst them. They were a puny race of people, and their domain did not extend very far; they assembled together in a cluster of villages grouped about the main village of Akesi, but beyond these villages with their outlying fields of manioc their tribe did not go. The women were comely when they were young; they had a tinge of Arab blood in their veins, since in the days of the slave traders Arab slavers had crossed the Little River into their territory continuously. They wore bright prints and calicoes wound about their bodies, as did the Arabeezi women higher up in the Province Oriental, but these calicoes served rather to set off the full-breasted charms of the younger women than to hide them. The men of Akesi were skeleton-limbed and evil of countenance, neither warriors nor agriculturists, but adepts in witchcraft. They were a zoomorphic tribe, and in each of the five villages their animal fetish hung over the door of the witch doctor's hut—the whole skin of a male leopard. Many are the tales of the leopard men of Akesi that have come down to the sea. Old hunters still delight in the story of the leopard pack that routed a rogue elephant, right under the eyes of the Governor of the Province Oriental and two missionary explorers, who were passing through the district of Akesi just at the time a rogue elephant came in from the jungle breathing fire and flame and destruction. The Governor of the Province Oriental was an agnostic, and had lived for ten years in Africa, so the occurrence did not bewilder him as it did the missionaries. They never felt quite the same afterwards. It is a difficult thing to set to work to evangelise a country where men, without the slightest warning, could turn themselves into wild animals, and make a rogue elephant flee before them, trumpeting loudly with fear, and afterwards, in the twinkling of an eye, turn themselves back again into men, and resume the more peaceful occupation of squatting cross-legged in front of their huts, recounting to one another the deeds that had been done in Akesi in the brave days of old.

The Akesians kept amongst them a vestal virgin, that the most powerful witch doctor among them, K'Tooma, used in the practice of his craft. This virgin was always a young girl of another tribe, usually of some tribe from the banks of the Congo River. In the days gone by they had seized her from the Arab traders who had come to Akesi with their bands of slaves; but when the Mission was built on the hill by the Little River, and the slavers made a detour, they had to go farther afield, and bargain for her with some of the chiefs of the Big River. The virgin was never seen except at a ju-ju ceremony; she dwelt in a hut set apart from the village of Akesi, right in the middle of the jungle, and the women of Akesi once a day went to her and handed food through an opening in the wall of the hut. It was only K'Tooma who ever entered her house.

The vestal virgins of Akesi did not appear to live very long, for the witch doctor always seemed to be bargaining with some chief or other for one. When a vestal virgin died no one but K'Tooma knew what became of her body. It was never talked about in the tribe.

It did not matter, apparently, to what race the virgin belonged, for in the days of the slavers, the women they brought with them to Akesi had been gathered from many quarters — Wahuma women, large rawboned negresses from the West Coast, Orasavo women (stolen in the night, as no Orasavo chief will sell his women) and half-caste Arabeezi. Sometimes the witch doctor of Akesi had seized a woman of one race, sometimes of another ; the only thing of which he was careful was that the woman was a virgin. The witch doctors always hung about when the Arab slavers tested the women for their virginity. This they usually did when they made camp on the banks of the Little River ; it was their first halting-place in their long march from west to east. In the west they gathered their slaves, in the east they sold them, and the Little River was the demarcation line between the two.

After the building of the Marist Mission, slavers became chary of camping by the Little River ; they took their slave bands farther north or south. It was rumoured amongst the slavers that the kindly old director of the Mission on the hill was apt to interfere in their affairs.

Two days after his arrival at the Mission, Father Domenique had encountered a slave band passing from west to east. Looking down from the height of the hill at dusk, he had seen a great rabble crossing the Little River by raft. Two tall Arabs dressed in white herded the band, men chained together, women tied together with stout rope, followed by the usual rabble that follows every slave band, anxious for the pickings.

Father Domenique, pulling his old leather slippers up at the heel, hurried down the hill to meet the Arabs, anxious to have company at supper, and not realising their occupation.

He found the slavers courteous and educated men who were glad enough to accept the hospitality of the Mission on the hill. It amazed Father Domenique to find such men engaged in a nefarious traffic. At supper, when they had been mellowed by his uncle's good red wine from Pays Basque, he pleaded with them for the souls of the young girls tied together in the rabble horde that was making the night merry with song and dance down by the Little River. But the Arab slavers laughed : "How you Christians waste your pity ! The girls come with us willingly enough. It is only the men we have trouble with."

But Father Domenique shook his head in a puzzled, pitying way. All so young, all of them heathen, all of them unbaptised. "At least let me baptise them before you take them away," he suggested gently.

But the Arab slavers laughed until they shewed their even white teeth between black moustache and beard.

And after a while they went down the hill again like two ghosts in their long white robes, while Father Domenique stood by the window of his study, looking out sadly into the night. Its darkness was broken by the flaring torches of the slavers' camp, and its silence by wild laughter and ribald song. Round the camp-fires the negro rabble danced and sang and shouted, half-crazed by the palm toddy that had been served out to them by the slavers.

He saw the two helpers of the Arabs, huge, rapacious negroes from Sierra Leone, untie the women, and one after another throw them down on the ground ; he saw the women afterwards divided into two groups, one group pushed into the midst of the men half-crazed with liquor, the other taken away to some distance and guarded there by one of the huge negroes. These were the virgins ; the Arabs had said carelessly that a so much higher price was given for virgins in Abyssinia that it paid them to take care of the women ; they saw to it that, until they came to the slave market, the virgins slept alone. And apart from the noisy rabble, like a vulture watching its prey, stood the witch doctor of Akesi, calm, speculative, watching his opportunity, armed with nothing but his craft and his cunning. Would the virgin that

he took be better protected in his hands or the slavers' ?
Father Domenique wondered. He sighed gently ; it was
something past his understanding. Turning away from
the window, he crossed to the writing-desk, and seating
himself at it, by the dim and flickering light of a candle,
he wrote a letter to his bishop.

THERE was something of deliberation, stateliness, and dignity in the whitewashed Mission perched up on the hill beside the Little River. When it was built, labour-saving methods were unknown in Central Africa ; time was not economised for life was spacious, labour was cheap. The Mission, therefore, was built carefully and well, with due regard for fine work and good design. But it seemed strange that the dignity of the fine building should have so little influence upon those who dwelt within its walls. The stately purity of its whitewashed walls never put to shame Brother François' lewd tongue, never cured Brother Antoine of his over-indulgence in wine, never brought humility to the carping, critical Brother Paul, nor peace to the burning heart of Brother Joseph. Of all those who dwelt in the Mission, it was only Father Domenique who felt the well-built, dignified, white building as a soothing influence in his life.

The peculiar white dignity of the place was comforting to a heart that always secretly longed for the country of Basque. In the Basque country, there were low white *haciendas,* built when the Spaniards ruled beyond the

Pyrenees. There were mellow old monasteries with walled-in gardens, set out in a fashion more Spanish than French, with purple bougainvillæa drooping against a white wall, and crimson roses growing profusely in stone-bordered beds.

Thinking of one of these gardens, Father Domenique had planted bougainvillæa by the Mission wall, and had asked the same uncle in Pays Basque who sent the wine to send him also red rose bushes ; when, after a time, both the bougainvillæa and the roses bloomed exotically, his simple old heart was filled with great joy.

But he tried to keep all pride out of his heart, although it was difficult to do this with his rose bushes flowering so well. He set himself a penance or two, and said more frequently than ever the phrase by which he ruled his life, "Of myself I can do nothing."

Father Domenique had grown old in this belief. "My God doeth the works," he always asserted. But if he had thought to look down, with intelligent speculation, at the figure of M'Kato sitting upon the bank of the Little River, engaged with the secret business of his own thoughts, sitting there day in and day out, oblivious of the life about him and yet seeming to grow more and more a part of it every day, he might have had a doubt. He might even, perhaps, for a short space of time, have entertained the heretic belief that there were more Gods than the one that pulled the strings of the Catholic Church.

But Father Domenique never theorised upon any subject whatsoever ; he accepted what his religion taught him, sweetly, sincerely, and without question. His business in life was not to think or speculate, but to bring converts into the Catholic Church ; and because he had much patience, though a limited mind, he was successful in doing so at the Mission by the Little River, and at his death was given much praise by his bishop.

Certainly Father Domenique often thought of M'Kato at his post on the river-bank, but only with the zeal of the converter of souls, not as a questioner as to why he was there. He often spoke to the black man when he passed over the bridge on his mule, and tried to instil into M'Kato's mind the beauty of God's will.

But M'Kato never appeared to listen very attentively ; he always seemed wrapped up in his own thoughts ; they were like a cloak that he drew round to shelter himself from outside conversation. Yet Father Domenique was patiently persistent ; the time would come, he felt, when M'Kato would listen, and so, little by little, he tried to sow the good grain in the barren soil.

That was how he came to give M'Kato his rosary. First, he spoke to the black man, then he prayed with him ; at least, Father Domenique offered up an earnest prayer, whilst M'Kato gazed with quickened interest at the rosary that Father Domenique was fingering. Noticing his interest, Father Domenique, kindly, but with great personal sacrifice, as the rosary was his most cherished possession, gave him the beads. "Count the beads upon it, a prayer for every bead," instructed Father

Domenique earnestly; "the Blessed Virgin will hear them, and give you all that you ask."

M'Kato was very interested in the rosary. So this was the white man's fetish, and he counted the beads upon it, just as old Kundi counted the drops of blood that fell from a rooster's beak. He was very glad to have it. The rosary dangled across his legs, and M'Kato looked intently at the crucifix.

Father Domenique, seeing his apparent interest and thinking that the first seed had begun to sprout, hastened to explain the Passion. M'Kato nodded his head wisely. "God killed Him," he said, not very perturbed; he was used to the white man's ways.

The sweat broke out on Father Domenique's brow at M'Kato's irreverent and casual tone, but he had not stored up sweetness and patience in his heart all these years for nothing. He began again to explain carefully the facts of the Passion to the black man, but just at that moment a large fly came up and settled upon the habit of Father Domenique. Staying in his explanation a moment, he swotted it energetically with his palm-leaf fan. He was fortunate in making his kill. M'Kato asked instantly if the fly had to be killed because all other flies were bad.

There was a difference between flies and human beings, Father Domenique hastened to point out, shocked at the black man's impiety — Father Domenique, worthy and gentle old priest, had little sense of the ridiculous. But M'Kato could not see this; he shook his head vigorously in protest, but paying no heed to him, the good father went on with his discourse. During the Marist Father's recital M'Kato sat cross-legged and immutable, gazing into space. When Father Domenique had finished, uncrossing his legs, he said : "You must be God," and then re-crossed them again more comfortably.

Father Domenique nearly fell off his mule in his eagerness to combat this statement, but M'Kato repeated it.

"Why do you say that ?" asked the good father, very hot and flustered, and using the palm-leaf fan in its proper capacity.

"Because you like killing things," replied M'Kato, and then returned once again to his deep thinking, whilst Father Domenique, astride his mule, made his way up the steep hill to the Mission, perturbed and uncomfortable, and quite unable to go on with *his* thinking.

But Father Domenique was not one to give in easily ; the same sturdy spirit that had brought him out to Africa to grapple with the souls of the heathen, sent him back again to the river next day.

"Why," he asked the black man, "do you think that God likes to kill ?"

"You say that your God is powerful," replied M'Kato.

"Yes," answered Father Domenique firmly ; that was something on which he could not be baffled.

"If I were powerful, I should like to kill also," said M'Kato, and then, withdrawing himself behind the barrier of this thoughts, refused obstinately to say another word.

Father Domenique ambled away sadly on his mule, with the faint hope that another day M'Kato might prove more tractable. It was at least something, he felt, that the black man had not thrown away his rosary, but had hung it on a twig of a scrubby bush growing on the river-bank, just near where he sat. But afterwards Father Domenique was not so certain about this, when he saw M'Kato sitting there day after day, his gaze fixed upon the rosary. He felt distinctly uncomfortable, for he had an idea that M'Kato was not putting the rosary to the use for which it was intended ; he was not counting the beads for any good purpose.

It was the only time that Father Domenique felt any qualms about a fellow being, but he dismissed them quickly as unworthy of him, and set himself a penance which kept him out of his little walled-in garden for two long days.

M'Kato placed the rosary on the bush beside him in a convenient position for counting the beads. If the white man's fetish would help him in the fulfilment of his life's task, as Father Domenique had told him, he was very glad to have it, and would certainly count the beads upon it. He considered for a long time as to what way they should be counted, and decided that every time any unforeseen and unheralded event occurred in the vicinity of the Little River, something that might lead eventually to the one great event of his desire, then he would count a bead.

Soon afterwards he was able to count the first one,

when Brother Joseph left the Mission and slunk across the ford with hurried, frightened footsteps.

The tortured figure of Christ upon the Cross did not worry M'Kato. He had not a very clear conception of the good father's explanation of its meaning, but to him it indicated only one thing. After all the beads had been counted and fulfilment had come, that was what would be meted out to him as the white man's punishment. He knew, because he had seen figures like that before, hung from trees on the banks of the Kafue. Dark, swinging pendulums that blew about in the wind and were preyed upon by vultures — black men who had broken some white man's law !

BOOK II

ON the banks of the Little River, at the point where the settlement of Chembi had sprung into being so suddenly some little while before, torches flared in flaming red and orange splendour. They shewed, by their barbaric light, naked black bodies huddled together, pulsating with life, a score of faces like black pansies raising themselves from the soil, pressed together with that eager look of living upon them that is so often to be seen in flowers. Men and women, children of all ages, alive, black, naked, swayed together in perfect rhythm, chattering in one shrill monotonous tone, sweeping forward towards the river, and then drawing back as the cold water washed their feet.

Spotted yellow and white prick-eared dogs lounged about on the outskirts of the group, sniffing at this and that. And aloof and serene from the huddled mass of black palpitating bodies, was a group of Europeans, bareheaded, some in white drill suits, others in gold-braided uniforms, others again, the womenfolk these, in frocks of misty colours. Apart from these, again in a separate group, with their coifs like white-winged birds just come to rest, were the sisters from the hospital on the hill ; and beside them, but lost in the darkness, except for their white faces like so many round white globes strung up against black velvet, were the black-robed brothers from the Marist Mission on the hill.

Into this ill-assorted pageantry, the little snub-nosed wood-burning river-boat stolidly puffed her way. Coming slowly up river, with siren shrieking, she made for the shore where the torches gleamed, and dropped her gangplank there with a solid plonk that sounded above the high-pitched voices of the natives, the incessant bleating of the goats crowded on the lower deck of the steamer, and the orders shouted by the captain from his bridge to the engineers below.

Plonk went the gangway, and off it surged the life that had been cooped up on the boat for five long days. The captain first, in his white suit braided and buttoned in gold, stout, jovial, the creases of his fat little neck over-riding his stiffly-starched collar; then the passengers, limp, lethargic, permeated with the damp river breezes, walking languidly, stubbing their boot-toes on the cross-bars of the gangplank; lastly, the horde of black people from the lower deck of the boat, with their possessions: a bleating goat led by a string, some fluttering chickens in a cage, a nest of baskets, a fishing net. A chattering, giggling, pushing, pulling horde of people eager to be once again on shore!

Then on the shore, pandemonium; greetings exchanged between Europeans, greetings exchanged between negroes, the wailing of goats, the squawking of chickens that were already getting their necks wrung preparatory to the great feast that always graced the banks of the Little River on boat nights, and half-drowned by this pandemonium, the shrill, <u>attracting laughter</u> of the women at the drinking-booth, half-hidden amongst a group of palm trees.

Once a fortnight the little snub-nosed river-boat puffed her way up the Little River to Chembi, unloaded her passengers thus, and afterwards replenished her engine fuel from the piles of wood that were always in readiness on the banks of the river. All night long, on river-boat nights, a stream of black men walked up and down the gangplank of the boat, each with a basket on his head, filled with cut wood on going and empty on returning. With the first hint of dawn in the sky these baskets were thrown down, and the labourers curled up on the river-bank and took their sleep. An hour after sunrise they were on board the boat again, and she was puffing her way down river, her siren shrieking a farewell to the sleepy few who gathered on the banks to see her off.

The boat went no further up the Little River than Chembi, for higher up, just below where Lardi, the ferryman, plied his raft from bank to bank, white rapids foamed over rocks in the dry season, and in the wet season, spray from the chutes was thrown high into the air.

The coming of the river-boat was an event in the lives of the inhabitants of Chembi, black and white alike. Only one person seemed to take no apparent interest

in it, and that was the black man, M'Kato, who sat upon
the river-bank with a frown of concentration upon his
brows that was deep like a wound. M'Kato never
moved from his post on river-boat nights. Tela, he
knew, went down to the river-bank, and sold baskets of
fruit and vegetables to the *chef de bateau.* He did not
object to her going, because she made money by doing
so, and money was a useful commodity ; it bought a
great many luxuries at the trading-store, and kept Tela
from grumbling too much at his continued absence from
their hut. But he himself preferred to sit upon the bank
and watch from a distance the red glare of the torches
against the darkness of the night ; and the everlasting
chatter of the black people came to him like the sound
of surf beating upon some distant shore.

M'Kato had sat thus on the river-bank before the
wood-burning boat had come up river, before the settlement of Chembi had come into being to bring the boat
there, and he saw no need to alter his mode of life for
the curiosity of a few pitch torches and the excited
screams of the black people.

The settlement of Chembi was of mushroom growth.
There was none of the leisurely-built, stately dignity
about its houses that there was about the Marist Mission
on the opposite side of the river. But it was younger
than the Mission by some ten years ; Chembi was built
when lick-spittle methods of labour had come to Central
Africa.

In a few years, Chembi had grown to be quite a

caravanserai; to its market came everybody who had anything to sell, from traders in ivory to humble vendors of poultry.

The market was presided over by a fetish man, who settled all disputes between litigants, and settled them in his own way. There was a white man's law which said that such disputes were to be taken in front of the resident magistrate, but the fetish man never let things get so far out of his grasp. He was the equal, he considered, of any white magistrate in the settling of disputes, and as his methods were more direct and took less time than the white man's, the litigants were usually satisfied.

Father Domenique would often shake his head sadly over this market held in the town square every Wednesday. It was gay, compelling, provocative, the very antithesis of the cool serene atmosphere of the Mission on the hill. Brother François said of it that all the delectable commodities of earth were for sale there, but none of the spiritual delights of Heaven; but he did not say this in Father Domenique's hearing.

Everything from an elephant's tusk to an egg was bargained for there, the bargainers screaming one above the other in their bargaining. In one corner palm toddy was brewed and sold; in another, old Googli sat with his jars about him and offered them at two francs a piece. They were cheap enough at the price, because they were hand-made pottery jars, baked in Brother Martin's oven at the Mission, but old Googli did not sell many of them. Fetish men came up-river to Chembi upon occasion and bought them, and they did not haggle over the price ; but the white residents of Chembi did not buy his jars. Mrs. Alec Younghusband said that she would not have one inside the house ; they gave her the creeps, although she could not say why. They were big, ugly jars crudely wrought and queerly shaped. Father Domenique, with an eye for symmetry and line, asked old Googli one day why he made the jars so rough and ugly. Old Googli, after spitting before him, replied : "Can I alter the souls of men ?" But when Father Domenique sought to question him further, he said : "That is for you to do ; that is what you have come here for," and then lapsed into obstinate silence, from which he could not be withdrawn.

It was no wonder that Father Domenique shook his head over the Wednesday market, and actually went to the magistrate to see if it could not be abolished. But the magistrate would do nothing in the matter. "It brings trade to Chembi," he said.

"And much evil," sighed Father Domenique, who grew more convinced every day of the Devil's reign on earth.

BLACK GOD
By DORIS MANNERS-SUTTON

ONE of the great dramas of our day is the slow encroachment of reason and the commonplace upon the primitive forces of nature. Those who understand this crudely write melodramas of magic and the occult; but those who feel its subtle implications make books that have a singular fascination for the modern mind. They are the only ones who should be allowed to write of the dying mysteries of such continents as Africa. *Black God* is a story of two worlds, and both convincing. It is a brilliant picture of the black world of the upper Congo, where the trees talk to the tree people, where leopard men hunt in packs, where ju-ju is a perfectly sensible way of making life possible in the jungle, and where primitive man lives in the constant excitement which those feel who are still part of the unconscious forces of nature. On the bank of the Little River, M'Kato, the Zulu, sits for half a lifetime, dangling the stumps of his handless arms, an assegai ready by his agile toes, while he concentrates his will upon the white man who maimed him and who some day will be drawn there, by the force of thought, to his death.

Meantime, at the ford of the Little River, an ivory trading post grows under his eyes—a rational, trivial, ironical settlement of white men in the jungle which they can conquer but cannot understand. There is Father Domenique of the Marist Mission who loves all men, but roses more; and the Reverend Jones, who conducts revival meetings in rivalry with the ju-ju of the medicine men; and Mme. Boul-boul's Tavern, where the broken men and clerks keep out the tropics with drink; and nuns; and Arab slave traders; and M. Lafontaine, who is writing a history of the town and finally takes to magic himself so as to defeat the Black Master, and hold Africa for the whites.

And while M'Kato, waiting, sees without interest houses go up, and the steamer come, and Flore, the first prostitute, and automobiles—the blacks carry on their own emotional life unsuspected except by Trader Voss and M. Lafontaine. Old Googli, the cannibal, makes a pottery jar from the remains of Brother Francois when, insane with the tropic night, he attacks the sacred virgin of the medicine man, and is torn to pieces by a leopard pack in the jungle. The Black Master comes and goes, children are raised from the dead, the black god plays tricks upon the white man. It is a record of the primitive, struggling hopelessly with reason and the trivial, yet scoring its points, keeping its beauty and much of its terror.

And, like a silent chorus in a Greek tragedy, M'Kato sits on, counting a bead on the rosary Father Domenique gave him when Brother Joseph rushed through the river at night seeking a woman; counting a bead when Sister Marte loosed the mooring of the raft of the malicious ferryman, Tardi, and let him sweep over the rapids to his death; keeping a bead for the unquestioned time when his concentrated thought will bring the bloated English planter, who ruined his sister and cut off his hands, to the Little River where his punishment is ready.

Hence, in this excellently written, humorous, and yet sensational story of the Congo, one gets, in a series of flashes, an interpretation of a continent, an ironical yet sympathetic study of modern pioneering, and an acute and sensitive account of the primitive mind. There have been books like this in French. I know none to compare with it in recent English. It reminds one of Kipling, but if less vigorous and poetic, is far more ironical, and subtler than Kipling's Indian stories. And this woman writer has the gift of capturing personalities. It is extraordinary how many vivid portraits she has packed in not very many pages. Medicine men are her specialty, but her chiefs are remarkably convincing too, and so are the tropic-ridden white men, who seem stupid beside the savages, and yet are irresistible.

But what is best in *Black God* is its own odd humor, the humor of a writer too wise to laugh at the magic of the primitive or to be afraid of it; too shrewd to be taken in by the myth of the white man's burden; too philosophical not to see what his trivial presence means to the mysteries of the black god. Not recently has so much irony, so much beauty, and such a gallery of personalities been included in a story of concentrated revenge.

HENRY SEIDEL CANBY

BOOK-OF-THE-MONTH CLUB, Inc. . . 386 4th Ave., New York, N. Y.

PRINTED IN U. S. A.

THE coming of the river-boat to Chembi made a great difference in the lives of the brothers of the Mission on the hill. They were now allowed out of their cells after dark once a fortnight, in order to meet the boat when it arrived at Chembi; for there were sometimes brothers from one or other of the Missions on the Congo River, who had to be met and conducted up the hill to partake of the hospitality of the Mission for the night.

Father Domenique liked river-boat nights; it warmed his hospitable old heart to be able to conduct five or six strangers up to the Mission, to shew them his garden by the light of the moon, or on moonless nights, by the light of an oil lantern, which he carried round and held behind each flower to shew off its beauty, his black robe dragging in the dewy grass, and his old leather sandals flopping up and down at the heels with the eagerness of his steps. And then, afterwards, he would conduct them to his study, and over a well-cooked supper and good wine (served there instead of in the common dining-room) expound the virtues of the Mission.

In the wet season he had not now to rely upon the company of one of the brothers for supper, because there was always some traveller coming to or going from Chembi. Father Domenique was very happy after the settlement was definitely established on the banks of the Little River, despite the riotous market-place and other haunts of the Devil.

The brothers of the Mission liked river-boat nights also, each in his own way. Brother François cast sheep's eyes in the direction of the drinking-booth, where full-breasted native women in gay calicoes giggled and smirked as they served palm toddy to customers, who withdrew with them afterwards into the shadows cast by the palm trees at the back of the booth. Brother François would pass a sly red tongue over his dry lips when he looked at this booth.

Brother Martin, who had come to the Mission in place of Brother Joseph, had very different thoughts from those of Brother François : he looked eagerly at the boat steam-ing up to the torch-lit bank, calculating in his mind how many packets of screws and nails, or how many planes and saws would be on board her for his carpenter's shop. Brother Martin saw life only in the terms of his carpentering.

Brother Antoine thought of Father Domenique's Uncle in Pays Basque, and hoped that he had remembered to send more wine. Brother Antoine also cast sheep's eyes at the drinking-booth, but it was at the palm toddy that he looked, not at the women who served it.

Brother Paul liked these nights once a fortnight also, because they gave him some outlet for his spleen. In the cool serenity of the whitewashed Mission there was little for his narrow, carping, critical mind to find fault with, but down by the Little River, with the yellow torches flaring, the women of the booth smirking and giggling, and the crowd of black palpitating bodies by the water's edge swaying backwards and forwards with excitement, he could steep his soul in prejudice and intolerance. Brother Paul crossed himself hurriedly and shuddered when he looked in the direction of the drinking-booth. But he was not alone in his self-righteousness, for on the river-bank also stood the Reverend Llewellyn Jones, lean of figure and lean of mind. The Reverend Llewellyn Jones was minister of the Baptist Church and director of the Mission that had been established at Chembi under an agreement between the English and Belgian governments. His flock was small compared with that of Father Domenique, but then, as he pointed out in his letters to his Mission Headquarters in London, Father Domenique had had at least ten years start of him. "Only give me time," he would end each letter, "only give me time, and you shall have all the converts you desire."

The Reverend Llewellyn Jones was a tall man with a cadaverous face, a little yellow as to complexion, as if his intolerance had somehow affected his liver. He was married, and there were three small Jones children comfortably at school in England. Mrs. Jones was as short and stout as her husband was tall and lean, a simple-minded, kindly woman, who believed in God, her husband, and the right of the British Government to rule mankind. That their Mission had to be conducted under the protection of a foreign flag was a constant source of worry to her. When things went wrong she would say to her husband, with just a trace of irritation : "If we were only living under the protection of the Union Jack !"

The Reverend Llewellyn, although he did not actually say so, was entirely in agreement with her, and he was always careful to hint at this circumstance in his letters to Headquarters. "The converts have been as many as could be expected under the conditions that govern us," was a favourite phrase, intimating that if the British flag had only flown from the flag-pole in the centre of the town square, then more heathen souls might have been induced to "get religion" in the Baptist Mission, instead of attending Brother Martin's carpentering classes on the other side of the river.

It was not for want of effort that the converts of the Baptist Mission were fewer than those of the Catholic one, for both Mr. and Mrs. Jones were indefatigable workers ; Mrs. Jones, in particular, was an efficient organizer and a good teacher. The Women's Mission with its Bible class, its sewing guild, and its cookery school under her supervision, was a live unit, and she was as efficient a midwife as the Sisters of Mercy who ran the hospital on the Marist Mission hill.

But Mrs. Jones's peculiar delight was a wedding. She had been happily married herself, with real orange blossoms (sent specially by a cousin from the south of Spain), tucked away in her hair, and she wished that all women might have the same pleasure — yes, even the untamed black women of Central Africa. She planted orange trees in the garden of the Mission, and saw to it that every bride who entered the Baptist church had a sprig of the blossom fastened in the crimps of her black hair. Wedding-veils she contrived from mosquito-netting, and it was very effective when the mesh was fine.

On the requisition list to Headquarters there was always the item : "Mosquito-netting, white," and then added, in Mrs. Jones's neat, round handwriting : "Fine mesh, please." Headquarters, reading the requisition sheets, thought that the mosquitoes on the Little River must be unusually small ones, and sent the finest meshed netting obtainable ; so Mrs. Jones's black brides were always correctly dressed and a great success — a success, that is, until Bimbu, the gardener of the Mission, brought Biki into the church to be married.

Biki was a servant in the home of the accountant of the I.N.T. Stores ; she was a tall, comely girl and a good worker. She was not from Akesi or of any of the smaller villages near the Little River, but came from the basin of the Lower Congo. The accountant had brought her with him when he had come to keep the books at the Chembi Store. The Reverend Llewellyn Jones had noticed for some considerable time that Bimbu and Biki were often together on the river-banks at night-time, and when at last the girl's condition could no longer be ignored, he spoke to Bimbu about it. Bimbu, as well as being gardener at the Mission, conducted the Bible classes for serious students ; he had been with the Reverend Jones for some considerable time, and could both read and write. Like Biki, he did not belong to the country in the vicinity of the Little River, but was of the Bangala, and had received his education at the Baptist Mission at Kinshasa. Not wishing to lose his position as gardener, or to give up his Bible classes, Bimbu agreed to bring Biki to church.

Mrs. Jones, in a little flutter of good-will, decided that Biki must have her veil and blossom, despite the fact that the ceremony was somewhat tardy. But her good-will was a little shaken when, almost as soon as the wedding ceremony had been performed, Biki's baby was born in the church. Biki uttered a scream and began to tear at her clothes, and before Mrs. Jones could efficiently take the matter in hand, she tore them from her and kneeling on the red plush carpet before the altar, bore her child.

Afterwards it was wrapped up, whimpering, in the discarded wedding-veil by Mrs. Jones, tight-lipped and silent. The baby was a strong, fat, vigorous baby, but it was not a black child ; it had strongly marked and unmistakable European features. Biki never came again to the Mission, but Bimbu still continued in the garden and with his Bible classes for serious students ; and the little half-caste baby, as time went on, played on the banks of the river with other chubby specimens of black humanity, and being heedless of the colour of its skin, was as happy as they.

Mrs. Jones was always punctilious in saying : "Good morning, Biki," when she passed the girl in the streets of Chembi, and Biki would sometimes answer, and sometimes pass by with an impertinent giggle. Whenever Mrs. Jones encountered her she seemed to have a new baby on her hip, but they were black children, and apparently belonged to Bimbu, who appeared to wish to outrival the patriarch Jacob.

Just as the Reverend Jones had decided, after a long night of prayer, that Biki should once again be allowed into the fold, and at breakfast-table had suggested to Mrs. Jones that she should approach the girl again, she having lived serenely with her husband for some years and multiplied according to the Lord's command, Bimbu announced his intention of leaving his gardening job at the Baptist Mission, and going up the hill to help Father Domenique lay out his vegetable patch.

"But that will necessitate your joining the Catholic Church," protested the Reverend Jones.

Bimbu, stubbing a black toe in the dust, supposed that it would.

"After all your years with us !" reproached the Reverend Jones.

"Why do you want to leave us, Bimbu ?" asked Mrs. Jones, coming out at that instant on to the verandah

where the interview was being conducted, the Baptist
Minister in his verandah chair, and Bimbu stubbing his
toes in the dust of the garden path.

Bimbu answered without hesitation that the Catholic
Mission had offered him higher wages, two francs a
month more.

Afterwards in his study, the Reverend Llewellyn kneeling on his square blue rug, wrestling with the Devil cried
aloud in his agony : "For two francs, O Lord, for two
francs !"

THE REVEREND LLEWELLYN JONES had one sacred hour a day, and that was the hour before dusk, when he went into his study and wrestled with the Devil — not always the Devil in his own heart, but in the hearts of those poor black brethren who might come to him for aid. In this sacred hour he was always available for interview ; any of the Mission boys had only to come on to the verandah and knock at the study door, and out would come the Reverend Llewellyn, stern but kindly of countenance, ready to wrestle with the Devil.

"Let us pray," he would say after he had listened to a recital of the boy's sins, and then he and the black brother would kneel on the verandah matting, and the Reverend Jones would evoke the Heavens with a prayer suitable for the occasion.

If any of the boys who came to the Reverend Jones during this sacred hour was not in trouble, he was rather short with him ; his business was the saving of souls. Some of the Mission boys who had not lost their superstitious beliefs, thinking that, if they did not come to be prayed about, they would be evil-wished, in the way old K'Tooma did when people ignored his bones, invented their sins. One even went so far as to say that he had stolen the magistrate's goat, but the magistrate had no goat and the Reverend Jones knew this. But to make certain he cut the sacred hour short and walked over to the magistrate's house to enquire.

"Just a little trouble with one of the boys," he explained.

The magistrate assured him that he had no goat, never had had one, and never would have; he detested the things and always used tinned milk in his coffee; in order to prove this fact he stamped out into the back room of his house, and after fumbling there for a while, brought back a tin of condensed milk, opened and half-used, and shewed it to the Baptist Minister.

At supper that night the Reverend Jones was rather silent. He was thinking of a small cottage in a little West of England village, where wallflowers bordered a walk leading up to the door of a study, on which only sinners knocked who had properly sinned and were, therefore, worthy of being saved. When he said grace after the meal, he said it in an unnecessarily loud voice, "For this Thy portion we are truly grateful," which made Mrs. Jones uneasy. She had considered the fish excellently cooked, but the curry, perhaps—just a little too hot; she would have to instruct the cook again in the art of making curry.

The Reverend Llewellyn's methods at the Baptist Mission were the methods of a revivalist. He believed in the good old-fashioned way of song and prayer to help the heathen into the fold. Besides the services held in the

church, the sacred hour, Bible classes, and other activities,
he held prayer meetings occasionally on the banks of
the Little River. These were always well attended, and
when the Reverend Jones, in his rich Welsh voice, led
the meeting in song, the river was heavy with the great
surge of voices that arose in unison with his.

> Here we come to meet the Lord
> Hallelujah! Hallelujah!

shouted the men in frenzy, swaying to the rhythm of
the hymn until the sweat poured off their black bodies.

> Here we come to meet the Lord,
> Hallelujah! Hallelujah!

sang the women, clutching at their calico gowns, and
nearly tearing them from their bodies in their emotion.

Neither the men nor the women had very much idea
of what they were singing; they had been taught the
words in the Bible classes, but it was the heavy emotional rhythm of the hymn that appealed to them. Led
by the Reverend Llewellyn Jones they felt that they
could sing themselves to death by the river-banks, though
this was scarcely the end that the Baptist Minister was
anxious to achieve.

The sexes were always segregated in the river-bank
meetings, ever since that terrible and never-to-be-forgot-
ten incident of the first meeting. That was something
which the Reverend Jones had never reported to Headquarters; he could not think of it even without a visible

shudder, and he had spoken of it only once to his wife, and then in a hushed and awful voice.

A young girl too, such a very young girl, scarcely old enough for the sewing circle. In the middle of one of the hymns her piercing shriek had risen above the voices of the revivalists who were singing their loudest, and when the Baptist Minister had stopped the singing to investigate the matter, she had got up hurriedly from the ground and had made off into the bush, with the man following her. It had been with great difficulty that the Reverend Jones had continued the service. He felt it keenly that a young girl had been raped in the sight of God and the Baptist Mission. Ever after that the meetings were divided into two bodies, Mrs. Jones leading the women's voices on the one side, and the Reverend Jones the men's voices on the other, at a discreet distance apart.

No one objected to these revival meetings on the riverbanks. The Belgian Administrator regarded them with polite amiability ; Father Domenique shook his head over them, and was sorry for the black sheep that were being led into the wrong fold, but he took no action in the matter, did not even mention it to his bishop, for his own Mission was in such a flourishing state that he could afford to ignore the activities of his rival. Brother Martin, with his carpentering classes and his pottery oven, could draw more converts to the Catholic Church than all the songs and shouting of the Baptist people on the river-bank below.

K'Tooma, the witch doctor of the village of Akesi, felt that the Baptist Minister, was, to a certain extent, a dangerous rival, but K'Tooma knew in his heart of hearts, that, if it came to a show-down between them, he held in his box of tricks some that would oust the Reverend Llewellyn Jones from his place of medicine man of the Little River, if he were to use them.

Like the Baptist Minister, K'Tooma held his meetings on the banks of the Little River occasionally. But he waited till the moon was full, when it hung above the narrow river like a white glass ball, its reflection bobbing up and down in the rapids as they boiled over the rocks, then K'Tooma would come down to the banks of the Little River, chalk his magic circle there, and the dark, mysterious throbbing of the little-drums would summon his followers to the rites. K'Tooma, like the Reverend Jones, but with more deliberate speculation, was a good showman. The Administrator made no more attempt to check K'Tooma's ju-ju rites than he did to stop the Reverend Jones's meetings. It is doubtful whether the Administrator would have done much good if he had tried ; K'Tooma would merely have gathered up his box of tricks and departed for further fields, and probably evil-wished the Administrator into the bargain.

There is a story told of a Vice-Governor who came down from Stanleyville to issue an edict against ju-ju meetings on the banks of the Little River. He brought with him two native policemen, and when he returned to the Province Oriental, he left the policemen behind

to carry out his law against the witch doctor's magic.
K'Tooma did not hold his meetings while the policemen were about. He took a little trip down river, and
presently one of the policemen sickened and died of a
fever ; and the other, somehow, lost his reason, for one
night at the full of the moon he took off his uniform,
flung it into the river, and ran round and round in a
circle until he dropped down from exhaustion. When
he was found and carried up to the hospital for the
black people (which had then only been opened a day
or two, he being their first patient) he was found to
be mad.

After the death of the one policeman and the removal
of the other to the prison at Stanleyville (there being no
asylum) K'Tooma came back to Akesi, and at the next
full moon he chalked his magic circle again by the Little
River, and the drums beat out their summons to his
followers.

In a hut in the jungle some little distance from the
village of Akesi K'Tooma kept the vestal virgin that he
used in his rites. All that was known about this virgin
was what a boy who had "got religion" had once told
the Reverend Jones, and that was very little, merely that
she was kept secretly shut up in a darkened hut and
never allowed abroad except on those nights when she
was brought to the magic circle by the Little River.
What she did there, the boy could never be induced to
tell.

There was great curiosity about this vestal virgin at

Chembi, because every little while K'Tooma made an excursion abroad to bargain for one with a neighbouring chief. What became of the others, whether they were granted their liberty after a time and lived a normal life in the village of Akesi, or whether things more terrible than could be conceived occurred at those river meetings occasionally, was not known. Every time any of the white residents of Chembi attended a meeting of K'Tooma's, they saw nothing but the witch doctor, a picture of innocence, sitting beside a fire juggling some bones, and surrounded by a circle of admiring satellites ; the vestal virgin was never present, and there was apparently nothing about the meeting to which even the most puritanical of them could object.

The last vestal virgin K'Tooma had brought up river with him on the snub-nosed, wood-burning river-boat. She was a slim strip of a girl, with high, crisp hair standing up from a broad forehead, a Wahuma crossed with negro. She followed K'Tooma meekly off the gang-plank as if resigned to or unaware of her fate. The white men gazed at her with curious eyes ; they would have given much to have known what went on in her darkened hut in the jungle. Father Domenique gazed at her with much pity, remembering the time when he had watched the Arab slavers with their band of women ; but the brothers of the Mission regarded her indifferently, with the exception of Brother François, who looked at her with a kind of fearful curiosity, passing the tip of his red tongue across his dry lips.

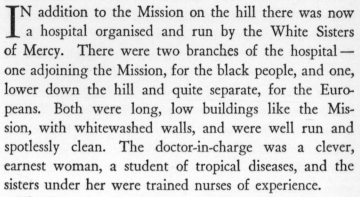

IN addition to the Mission on the hill there was now a hospital organised and run by the White Sisters of Mercy. There were two branches of the hospital — one adjoining the Mission, for the black people, and one, lower down the hill and quite separate, for the Europeans. Both were long, low buildings like the Mission, with whitewashed walls, and were well run and spotlessly clean. The doctor-in-charge was a clever, earnest woman, a student of tropical diseases, and the sisters under her were trained nurses of experience.

The European hospital was a boon to the white residents of Chembi, as, previous to its inauguration, any sick person had to go to Stanleyville for treatment, which meant a journey by safari, unless they were fortunate enough to be taken ill at the time when the river-boat made her fortnightly call.

The hospital for the blacks was always full of patients. With the invasion of civilisation had come sleeping sickness to the Little River, and also, there were many syphilitic cases from the village of Akesi. In the maternity ward the women of Akesi, under the care of nurse and doctor, had their babies on soft white beds, and were exceedingly uncomfortable and suffered more

pain than they had ever done when they had knelt on
the straw mat in their own huts. The little black babies,
instead of rolling naked and contented in the sunshine,
were now trussed-up in clothes, and slept in downy cots,
and gave vent to their disapproval of this unnatural
treatment in the usual manner of babies. But for all
that the White Sisters of Mercy did a fine work, and if
Dr. Forbeau's cures did not equal those of K'Tooma
down at Akesi, at least she could shew him points in
cleanliness and general hygiene.

The directress of the hospital for the Europeans, Sister
Mary Josephine, was a stout, middle-aged, Flemish
woman, a little short of breath on account of asthma,
which the doctors in Brussels assured her the climate of
Central Africa would speedily cure, but which she bore
with fortitude to her grave. She was a woman of intelligence and shrewd wit. She was of Irish extraction
on her mother's side, which accounted for her bright
wit, and her Flemish father had contributed the placidity
that hung about her like a well-draped mantle.

The spotless cleanliness of the hospital and the order
of the wards was due mainly to her gift for supervision.
The sisters under her, Sister Thérèse and Sister Marte,
were women of little personality. Sister Thérèse, the
elder of the two, was a tall, gaunt woman with a cat-
like tread ; Sister Marte was plump and small, with her
coif always a little awry on her shaven head. Both were
practical peasant women with no vision ; they were equal
to searching out the spiders that wove webs over night

in the corners of the wards, or to scrubbing the lockers
to a pitch of dazzling whiteness, or to attending mechan-
ically to the patients, under direction, but beyond that
their intellect did not go. It was Sister Mary Josephine
who was the driving force in the hospital, although no
one would have guessed it from her placid demeanour.

Underneath a manner that was as smooth and un-
ruffled as her well-starched bib, she hid an energy that a
lifetime of muggy, wet seasons in Central Africa could
not sap from her. Doctors came to the hospital, did
their three years there, and went thankfully home to
European civilisation, but Sister Mary Josephine stayed
for ever, growing more efficient and harder upon any
staff laxity every day. Sister Thérèse and Sister Marte
ran before her, and the black ward-boys were never
known to sleep at their posts.

Once a day Sister Mary Josephine, carrying a large
green-lined umbrella to shade her head from the sun,
descended into Chembi to purchase the hospital sup-
plies. She was always accompanied by one of the sisters
and a ward-boy carrying a large string bag. She selected
her goods with the same care and precision that the
housewives display in the market-places of every town
and village in her own land of Belgium ; and on Wed-
nesdays, when she walked through the native market,
the hub of business was perforce stilled for the moment,
so impressive was her large, white, serene presence in
the tangled, huddled mass of screaming vendor and
buyer. After her purchases were made each day, Sister

Marte or Sister Thérèse (whichever it happened to be), with the help of the ward-boy, would carry the goods up the steep hill to the hospital, while Sister Mary Josephine went to partake of a cool lemonade with Madame Voss, the wife of Trader Voss who ran the I.N.T. Stores. Madame Voss and Sister Mary Josephine were very good friends ; they had become acquainted when Madame Voss had spent three weeks in the hospital, suffering, as far as the doctor could see, from delusions. Madame Voss had a fondness for pottery, and besides buying many of the earthenware vases that were made at the Mission, she had at one time bought one of old Googli's jars. Old Googli spent most of his time on the banks of the Little River, making earthenware jars, fashioned from clay that he brought to the river-bank in a tattered old straw basket ; he sold these jars afterwards in the market-place for two francs apiece.

Old Googli belonged to a cannibal tribe at Pembi, famous for the fact that, in the red rubber days of the Congo, they had eaten thirteen men at a sitting, when one of the river-boats had gone ashore on a sand-bank near their village.

But for some reason or other Googli preferred to remain at Chembi and make his jars, although he went down river to see his own people often enough, and always returned from a visit to them with his basket heavy with clay, and for days afterwards would be very busy with his work on the river-bank. Perhaps it was the attraction of Brother Martin's pottery oven that kept him at the Little River, because the brother was good-natured enough to allow him to bake his jars in the Mission oven.

It was this stamp of sanctity upon them that induced Madame Voss to buy one, although the other white residents of Chembi assured her they would not touch one of the jars with a forty-foot pole. Old Googli brought more than clay in his basket when he came back from a visit to his tribe, they avowed. There were stories afloat about the doings of his tribe that were not pleas-ant for white ears, and although each and every white man asserted that he did not believe such goings-on, they never had more to do with old Googli than they could possibly help. They always had a feeling, when they came near him, that he was looking them over with shrewd speculation, and calculating the size and shape of the jar that they would make, if his tribe was ever lucky enough to catch them napping.

But Madame Voss bought a jar, pointing out to her husband, who threatened to throw the thing out of the house, that nothing evil could come out of the Marist Mission oven, and for a month or two it rested on the little table near the bay window in the living-room be-hind the I.N.T. Stores.

Then Madame Voss became ill, queerly ill. She was put to bed in a high fever, and for a week or two raved about a big black man who was standing over her want-ing to cut her throat. She was taken up the hill to the hospital, but all the doctor's skill and Sister Mary

Josephine's unceasing care could not cure her of her fever or her delusions. The black man was there, she said, always before her, bending over her with a knife, waiting to cut her throat.

One day André Voss took old Googli's jar and broke it into a thousand pieces; then gathering up the pieces with his own hands, he dug a deep hole in the garden and buried them three foot deep. A little while after that, Madame Voss regained her normal temperature and came home; she did not appear to remember anything about the black man with the murderous intent, and when she asked after the vase André Voss said that he had accidently knocked the table over one day and broken it. Brother Martin baked her another jar, as large as old Googli's but more symmetrical, and that one stood upon the little table in the bay window and brought harm to no one.

Every day on the verandah of the I.N.T. Stores, Sister Mary Josephine would sit with Madame Voss and discuss homely topics of interest to them both, such as the birth of Madame Voss's first grandchild, the delinquencies of native servants, or the difficulty of keeping food fresh in muggy weather. When the half-hour was up Sister Mary Josephine would rise, shake out her voluminous skirts, and raising her cream and green umbrella, proceed once more up the hill to the hospital. Life, she felt, as she leisurely climbed the Mission hill, flowed very smoothly in this reputed wild black country. Her white starched skirt swished about her as she walked, her coif

sailed like a ship in a breeze. Occasionally she wiped
her face with a handkerchief that she kept in the capa-
cious pocket of her skirt, together with her prayer-book
and rosary, but otherwise she never appeared to feel the
heat ; she went on her way, cool, serene and comfortable,
visioning, as she went, some extension to the hospital,
some added comfort for the patients, utterly oblivious of
the primitive life about her. The dark line of jungle
with its hint of hidden, mysterious things, the narrow,
yellow river with its crocodile-infested sand-banks, the
wild exuberant growth of flower and foliage, the men of
Akesi in their mangy leopard skins, the provocative-eyed
women in their gay calicoes, these things meant nothing
to her ; she climbed the hill to the hospital every day,
with as much unconcern as she would have walked up
the steep street from the lower to the upper town in the
city of Brussels.

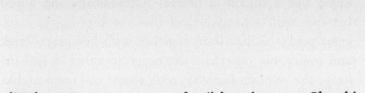

THERE was a portent of evil hanging over Chembi.
It had been there ever since the white eagle had been
killed on her nest. The killer had come and gone, but
the aroma of the deed remained. It hung over Chembi
like a dark cloud. Everyone was aware of it. Something
is going to happen, people said, looking up at the sky
apprehensively, as if expecting a thunderbolt or something of a like nature to fall upon them at any moment.
The portent of evil stretched across the river, through
the jungle, and over the plains to the village of Akesi.
K'Tooma felt it and crossed his bones in the fire, but the
flames refused to char them, so he knew the signs were
against him. This was something too big for conjuring.
He slept uneasily in his blanket at night.

While the white eagle was on her nest, said the Akesians, we had good luck; crops grew well, cattle were
prolific, and no woman went barren through the wet
season. K'Tooma should have looked after the bird;
that was his business. And if they had been able to find
another witchman as efficient as K'Tooma, they would
have put the neglectful witch doctor to death immediately. But witchcraft was dying out in the tribe, and
they had to think of the future of the race; it would be
nothing without its magic. So for more reasons than

one, K'Tooma's sleep was broken by unpleasant fore-bodings.

He had been down river bargaining for a vestal virgin when the white eagle was killed ; that, of course, was something of an excuse, and he made the most of it. Still, he knew that secretly his carelessness was being discussed among the elders of the tribe, and he was ap-prehensive.

For uncountable wet seasons the white river-eagle had sat upon her untidy nest in the rushes by the bank of the river, hatching out her young, her yellow eyes regarding the disorderly, riff-raff life of the river that passed before her with an implacable, baleful stare. She sat there and was never molested by the black people. She was part of the history of the Little River, the primitive, black savage saga of the narrow river. She had been there so long, in fact, that a legend had grown up about her. Storytellers told it in the market place, and chiefs over camp-fires at night.

The story went back to the time when a king reigned in Akesi, and the Akesians were accounted the greatest tribe in the land. The King's name had been Ouentizi, and he had had a daughter of whom he was very proud. She could conjure as well as he could, and that was say-ing something, because the king was proud of his clever-ness in this craft. But conjuring is not a woman's work, and too much of it is not good for anyone. Instead of marrying and settling down in a grass hut, baking mealie cakes, and bearing children, the king's daughter became restless. She refused suitor after suitor, although some offered as much as a hundred head of cattle for her. She was always dancing before the fire, throwing her arms in the air and stretching them outwards and upwards, as if she wanted to fly away like a bird. One day, however, she stretched her arms upwards thus when the magic bones were in the fire, and before she had time to realise it, she was soaring up to the heavens in the form of a bird — a heavy-winged white eagle. She soared over the village of Akesi, uttering terrified cries from her eagle's throat, but no one could do anything for her, because the two magic bones had charred away to ashes, and her woman's body had been consumed with them.

The king built her a nest in the rushes by the river, and the medicine men promised, if she would sit there and leave off her restless ways, to protect her down to their last generation. The white eagle, seeing that there was nothing else to be done, mated and sat upon the nest that had been made for her. She laid her eggs there and hatched out her young, and the witch doctors protected her nest from bird and beast and flying arrows, as had been promised.

This was the legend that was told about the white river-eagle, and every Akesian believed it to be true. They watched for the white eagle's return at the beginning of every wet season. If she were a day late they grew uneasy. Now the crops would fail, the cattle take a pestilence, and the women go barren through the rainy season.

But she always returned, sailing superbly across the plains, her piercing cries falling like a shower upon the earth, and behind her flew her mate, a smaller eagle of nondescript colouring. He stayed but little time on the river ; after a day or two he would be gone again, but the white eagle remained till she had hatched out her young and seen them well out of the nest, grey young fledglings trying their wings on the air. Then she would depart to the mountain regions beyond the plains, and the season of sterility would begin. The day the white eagle left the Little River dropped two inches from its banks, and the mealies and pumpkins began to dry on their stalks. The black men counted the seasons by the white eagle's coming and going. Seasons came and went, manioc grew high, cattle multiplied, and the women had their bearing pains. It would always be so, as long as the white eagle sat upon her nest, spreading the warmth of her maternity over the earth.

But one day the snub-nosed river-boat brought two sportsmen and their long train of bearers to Chembi, together with their equipage of guns, bird-lime, nets, and arc lights for dazzling the eyes of beasts at night. The sportsmen stayed at the white-elephant hotel, and grumbled at the lack of game that was to be found round about Chembi. Day after day they went out with their guns and returned without spoils. They laid their nets in the jungle, and spread their bird-lime by the drinking-pools, but the animals were wary. Monkey spoke to monkey, leopard to leopard, antelope to antelope about the strange apparatus of these two-legged creatures stalking jungle and plains. The beasts left their old haunts for the mountain regions, until such time as it should be reported to them that once more the water-holes and the jungle were free from snares. Since the coming of the white man to the Little River the beasts had become cautious and astute.

The black man and his ways they knew; he waged war upon them with spear and bow and arrow. It was fair fight; if he were fleeter than they, the spoils were his; but sometimes it was the other way about, and then a lion or a leopard would go back gorged to his lair, leaving the jackals and hyenas to snarl over some bones. But the white man's ways the beasts did not know, and they were afraid of him.

It was all very disheartening for the sportsmen, and they were talking of leaving the white-elephant hotel and journeying farther inland, when they spied the white eagle upon her nest. She was a fine specimen of an eagle, and would look well, stuffed, in a glass case in some museum. One of the sportsmen took aim, and because K'Tooma was away down river and neglecting his task of protection, the eagle fell from her nest into the river waters with a scarlet stain upon her breast, and a little pool about her was dyed crimson with her blood.

The sportsmen sent one of their bearers to retrieve the booty. The bearer brought the beautiful body with its ruffled white plumage to the bank, and the sportsmen, with pride, measured the span of the white eagle's wings.

They carried her home in triumph to the hotel, and set to work to skin her carefully and preserve the skin.

The residents of Chembi did not share their enthusiasm. They felt that a landmark had gone from the Little River. The eagle had sat there upon her nest through so many wet seasons.

"We'll have her stuffed and sent to the museum at home," said the sportsmen. "She's a fine trophy."

They were true sportsmen ; they delighted in killing. It gave them a feeling approaching ecstasy to see the splash of blood on the pure white breast of the dead bird. They could not understand the *garçon* of the hotel, an anæmic little Frenchman who felt sick at the sight of blood, rushing inside and shutting himself in the pantry when the sportsmen held up the limp body of the eagle for his inspection. For them there was no sight more perfect than a bird with the ruffled plumage of death, or a beast in its last convulsive death agony.

Everyone in Chembi breathed more freely when the sportsmen took their departure, crossing the river with their long train of bearers, and making eastwards for hunting-fields more prolific with game. But still the odour of their deed remained. It hung about in the air, and people could not forget the white eagle.

"On her nest too, with her eggs scarcely hatched out," the white men said, shaking their heads in disapproval.

"There will be no eaglets in this year's nest," said the black men in fear and indignation. It boded no good for the Little River.

BIBULA was in the backyard of the Younghusbands' house, plucking a fowl alive for dinner. Its squawks and cries could not be heard within doors, owing to the noise the vampire birds were making in the mango trees which grew in a shady line each side of the street. The birds screeched and screamed and flapped their wings as they dipped their long beaks in the ripe fruit, so the squawking of the fowl was drowned in this greater noise, and did not reach the ears of Mrs. Younghusband, who was in the living-room of her home, lying at ease on a cane lounge, while she read some six-months old English journal and thought over and over again: "Oh, how I hate this land, this hot, black, savage land."

Bibula sang as he plucked the fowl, but the song did not go well. It fell heavily upon the air, and the air killed it. Bibula shivered in his skin. It was an omen of evil. The air killed everything now, words, laughter, song ; they fell upon it heavily and died.

He tried a hymn, but the hymn went badly too. It was a hymn about Moses, and Bibula was rather doubtful as to who Moses was ; they had not learnt about him yet in Bible class. But still he tried the hymn.

Bibula was a practising Christian. He had been baptised, and knew a chapter of the Bible by heart as well as several hymns. Mrs. Younghusband wished that he had never been converted ; she disliked hearing him singing hymns about the house, although he always sang them with a kind of desperate cheerfulness that did much to rob them of their mournful quality. Still it was embarrassing for her to have a practising Christian in the house when she had ceased to be one herself.

"Boy!" called Mrs. Younghusband. "Boy!" But Bibula did not hear her on account of the vampire birds making such a to-do in the mango trees.

Mrs. Younghusband sighed and turned to her journal again. She thought regretfully of efficient English cooks who came at one's summons, and said : "Yes, ma'am," and "No, ma'am," whilst fingering their aprons. Bibula had been with her for three years now, and except for a few words of English which he had picked up with relish, he knew as little as when he had first come, and that was next to nothing.

"He knows nothing," Mrs. Younghusband always told her friends in despair, "absolutely nothing, and is unteachable."

But here Mrs. Younghusband was wrong. Bibula might have been lacking in knowledge of household matters, but he knew other things ; he knew more than his mistress in some respects.

Of the day in and day out events of the Little River, nothing missed Bibula. He could have made a register of births, deaths and marriages in Chembi as accurate as the one kept in the magistrate's office, yes, and added to it information that was not to be found in any register.

For instance, he could have told why Mrs. Young-husband's mouth had a bitter droop, and why the Lenotte baby had such an "English look"; why the cashier of the Banque du Congo Belge was found strung up to the rafters of an outhouse at the back of the bank, when his cash was correct to the last sou; what made M. Pelsot send his young wife back to Belgium when she had only been out three months, and what old Judge Picot said when he found a half-caste baby on his doorstep one fine morning. He could have told all these things and many more, but he did not; he locked the knowledge away deeply in his strange wild heart, and to all the residents of Chembi, and especially to his mistress, he was just that imbecile Bibula who never did a thing right, and was always amazingly cheerful about it.

But he knew, he knew. There were things that he knew also, not included in the phenomena of the actual, the real, but things half-hidden, half-guessed at. Mysterious things that came to him in strange ways, by queer messengers. A jackal running across the plains, a bird flying over the house, the wind shaking the handle of a door, all these things were signs, and Bibula could read them rightly.

He knew what was beyond every horizon, and the secrets the dark jungle hid; he knew who came and went on the waterways of the land, just as if the water-ways were mirrored before him; and he knew all the news of the Big River long before his master ever received it by letter. And now he knew that some dark and deadly evil hung over the Little River. He had breathed on the table knives as he had set the table for luncheon, but they had not sweated beneath his breath; an owl had hooted over the house at a midday hour, and now the very words he sang were swallowed as soon as he uttered them, by the big hungry mouth of the air.

Being a practising Christian, Bibula said the Lord's prayer twice over, but like K'Tooma, he found that this evil could not be cured by conjuring. There was nothing for it but to wait and see.

Some black women passing outside the fence caught his attention for the moment. They were carrying baskets of fruit on their heads, and one of the women walked wearily, lagging behind the others, heavy with the weight of her unborn child.

Bibula wagged his head sagely. "Walk a little faster, woman," he muttered, "your time hasn't come yet." This was a night of death, not birth!

Shadows began to creep into the backyard where Bibula plucked his fowl. The sound of the jungle trees came up to Bibula in long, eerie waves. He listened, but the fowl in his hands was squawking horribly. "Hush your noise!" he said, putting a hand over its head. He strained his ears to catch what the trees were saying, but they were only murmuring angrily together. Inside the house, in the coffin-coolness of the living-room with its shuttered windows, Mrs. Younghusband thought impatiently : What is Bibula doing ? If we are to dine to-night, then it is time he was in the kitchen looking after things.

"Boy !" she called. "Boy !"

This time Bubula heard the call, as he had subdued the cries of the fowl, and the vampire birds for the moment had ceased their scrabbling. "Coming, Missis," he answered, "coming," and putting the half-plucked fowl on the ground, he turned to go inside. The fowl, with a dazed squawk, revolved upon its legs dizzily, and then staggered away to hide its nakedness and agony in a corner of the yard.

The sun was going down behind the river like the inflamed eye of a leopard. The river ran on its way, smoothly, darkly, silently ; the trees stood beside it motionless. Bibula, listening again, could hear nothing. Well, sometimes the trees and the river had their secrets to hold. He pushed open the wire-door to enter the house. Then a sound arrested him, a sound that came suddenly and violently upon the air — the hoarse cry of a bird. Not of a vampire bird, but a cry from a more arrogant, fiercer throat. The cry was followed by another and then another, until they came down upon the distant plains like a shower.

Sweat stood out in great beads upon Bibula's forehead. He wiped it away with the back of his hand. It would be all right, he felt, if the night remained clear, but when he looked away towards the river, he saw that a mist was creeping up from it towards the settlement of Chembi on the one bank, and the dark line of jungle on the other. The white eagle was spreading her wings.

THE moon hung above Chembi, old and tired, a moon upon her back. Below the moon, the mist lay in a thick white pall, blurring the little town, until the streets grew mixed and distant; houses ran into one another, and were only saved from oblivion by their lighted windows like rows of stars fallen to earth. Through the mist came the raucous voice of a gramophone. By the river camp-fires burnt dully, the fires of the fishermen who had put out their nets before the mist had gathered; and the song of the women tending the fires rose like a low and bitter moan.

On the other side of the river was silence — the trees were silent, the creeping mist was silent, stifling everything in its shroud-like folds. The fire-flies were lost in the depths of its whiteness; the crickets with the fog in their throats, ceased their creaking; the monkeys sulked in the trees; and on the ground the jungle beasts crept about noiselessly — dark spectres in the whiteness. It was as if the jungle had died and the mist was its winding-sheet.

The mist reached up the hill to the Mission, and enveloped the long, rambling building completely; it hung low and heavily over the steep hill-path, and the two hospitals were completely blotted from vision. Never had there been such a fog on the Little River.

Through the mist on the hill, cleaving it apart, came a tall black figure, slowly, cautiously, descending the hill and going towards the jungle. It was Brother François in his long black robe, making his way carefully to the hut of the vestal virgin.

The hut stood there in the forest, a solid block of darkness against the white mist. Brother François when he reached it, kicked at the door with his elastic-sided boots, but it was well locked, with one of the padlocks that were sold in Chembi by the I.N.T. Stores. Brother François persevered, kicking harder and harder until at length the door gave way. The lock remained firm to the last, but the leaf-thatched door was flimsy and not proof against Brother François's vigorous kicking. Inside the hut was complete darkness; Brother François, gathering up his robe, stepped across the remains of the broken door, but he did not step far enough, for one of his boots caught in a portion of the thatching, and he went sprawling forward into the hut. His hand came in contact with soft warm flesh, and he could hear the heavy, frightened breathing of the wide-awake vestal virgin.

When Brother François came out of the vestal virgin's hut some hours afterwards the mist had grown thicker. In its density he lost his way; he wandered about in the jungle, going nervously from tree to tree, touching this

one and that as if for guidance, but the trees were hard
and hostile beneath his hands. Despite his nervousness
Brother François had a feeling of importance, as if he
had just accomplished some great deed, and therefore he
knew that he could not really be lost, it was only that
he was anxious to get back to the Mission before anyone
noted his absence.

But there was nothing about him but mist and trees ;
Brother François increased his pace to a run ; his direction was sound for presently he came to the marshy bit
of land by the river and then to the ford. He was perturbed to see through the mist that was now lightening
upon the river, the old black man M'Kato sitting upon
the bank, and wondered what he did there on a misty
night.

Up on the Mission hill, having awakened too soon, a
cock crew twice. Brother François, gathering up his
gown about him, sped up the steep path of the hill as
fast as his elastic-sided boots would allow him.

Over the river lay the rosy ribbon of a hot dawn. The
mist broke and hung in shreds and patches ; the houses
of Chembi came out of their obscurity and separated from
one another. Their windows were dark, like blind eyes
looking out upon the world ; no sound issued from their
doors. On the river-banks the fires of the fishermen had
mouldered away to ashes, and the singing women slept
beside them under blankets sodden with mist.

The fishermen sat in a long thin line upon the bank, patiently awaiting the sunrise when they would draw in their nets. On the other side of the river, the white Mission and the hospitals were like houses that a genie had conjured, just arising from his bottle of smoke. Inside the Mission Brother François sat on the hard straw bunk in his cell and carefully brushed the mud from his boots and his alpaca robe, in order that it should not be noticed at matins that he had been out of the Mission during the night.

That night, although the moon was still tired and lay upon her back, K'Tooma's drums rolled out in the village of Akesi. Trum, trum, trum, a-trum, they went ceaselessly hour after hour. "What the deuce is that old limb of Satan up to now ?" said Alec Younghusband in the settlement of Chembi. "He held his ju-ju rites last week at full moon, and now here he is at it again."

But no one in Chembi knew what K'Tooma was up to, and everyone was either too lazy or too indifferent to go down to the river-banks to see.

Where the chutes threw their white spray high into the air, K'Tooma had drawn his usual magic circle with the piece of chalk that Brother Paul had once used on the blackboard of the Mission School. This chalk had found its way to K'Tooma by devious means ; first, one of the school-children had appropriated it, and had afterwards lost it in battle to a child of K'Tooma's sister. But it was not without a struggle that the uncle had managed to get the chalk from his nephew ; in the end he had to resort to his witchcraft, until the nephew, becoming frightened, hastily disgorged the piece of chalk from his loin-cloth.

K'Tooma found the chalk useful for, previous to the coming of Brother Paul, he had made a paste of ground bones to smear upon the earth, which took up considerable time.

When the drums had ceased their beating, the young men of the village of Akesi gathered about K'Tooma's magic circle. They were nervous, excited, and the silence between them was ominous. With K'Tooma's appearance they seated themselves in a ring outside the circle of chalk, while the old witch doctor sat himself down by his fire, cast his bones and began his incantations. Hour after hour he chanted his weird song, while the bodies of the young men outside the circle became wet with great beads of sweat. One by one they rose and stumbled across the circle, and fell face downwards upon the earth, while K'Tooma continued swaying and chanting beside the fire.

When the dawn came, K'Tooma took off the mangy leopard skin that he wore about his shoulders and cast it into the fire ; the flames rose up and licked about the skin, charred it, reduced it to ashes.

K'Tooma took the red hot ashes, without apparent hurt to his hands, and cast them upon the sweating, trembling bodies of the men lying upon the ground ; then they rose up and departed, solemnly, silently, as if they had some great secret laid upon them.

K'Tooma, shivering a little in the chill of dawn for the loss of his leopard skin, went home to his hut and slept through the day, a sound and dreamless sleep.

SO many strange things happen in Africa that, when the vestal virgin's hut in the jungle was broken into, very little comment was made about the matter by the residents of Chembi. True, some coarse witticisms were indulged in on the verandah of Madame Boul-boul's Tavern, and the magistrate sat in his office at Chembi all one steaming hot morning, waiting for K'Tooma to come and make a formal complaint; but when K'Tooma failed to make an appearance, he let the matter rest and instituted no enquiry. After all, if K'Tooma desired to keep a convent in the middle of a steaming jungle, then it was up to him to see that it was properly guarded.

Who had broken into the hut no one knew, but there was a persistent rumour that it had been a European. The white men of the Chembi settlement were very eager in their denials of the deed, but as they did not over-protest the magistrate felt that he could not very well fasten the crime upon any one of them. The two religious leaders of the community, the Reverend Llewellyn Jones on one side of the river, and Father Domenique on the other, expressed different opinions about the matter. Father Domenique felt genuinely sorry for the girl, especially as she had disappeared and no one seemed to

know what had become of her ; K'Tooma, when he was
asked, maintaining a blank silence.

But although the Reverend Llewellyn Jones was outwardly shocked, and lifting up his eyes to the Heavens
called upon God to punish the sinner, in his innermost
heart he felt that just retribution had fallen upon
K'Tooma for practising such evil rites under the very
nose of a minister of the Baptist Church.

The village of Akesi was upset for some little time
afterwards, and the perturbed Akesians were distinctly
hostile towards the Europeans of Chembi. But gradually the clamour died down, and the men came again to
purchase their brass wire and salt at the I.N.T. Stores,
and the women brought baskets of fruit and vegetables
to sell at the house doors. It never came to light who
had been the sinner against the vestal virgin, so it appeared that the Reverend Llewellyn Jones's God was not
going to do anything about the matter after all. As for
the Akesians, they blamed their witch doctor. First, he
had neglected to protect the white eagle and so brought
ill-luck upon their heads, then he had left the vestal
virgin's hut in the forest unguarded, when everyone knew
that something evil was going to happen — even the
smallest baby in Akesi had felt it in the air and shivered
in its smooth black skin.

For a while K'Tooma had a bad time in the tribe, but
he gathered his satellites about him, and every night he
rolled his drums and juggled his sticks, and managed to

weather the storm without the loss of his head as he had feared at first.

It was some three months afterwards that Trader Voss, wandering on the outskirts of the jungle, discovered the body of Brother François, mauled, as if by a leopard, or more likely by many leopards, for the body was almost rent limb from limb, and shewed claw marks that one animal alone could never have inflicted. No one saw any connection between this occurrence and the one that had disturbed the village of Akesi three months before, except perhaps Trader Voss, who had been twenty years in Africa, and had come to have some sympathetic insight into its witchcraft. But he kept silent, for he had no love for Brother François (nor, as a matter of fact, for any of the "black crows" up on the hill, as he termed the Marist priests), and a certain amount of respect for the adroit old witch doctor of Akesi.

Trader Voss often walked by himself in the jungle; he liked its reserves, its silences, it was as if the jungle was deliberately holding back some secret that man might be the wiser for knowing. Many times he had sought to know this secret, but the jungle had always repulsed him, as if he were not of the chosen few who might see into its heart. He was now a middle-aged, corpulent man, and long years in the tropics had reduced his walking powers, but every day, at dusk, he left the I.N.T. Stores to wander away to the jungle and speculate there as to what went on in its dark depths. It was upon one of these visits of speculation that he found the remains of Brother François. Used as he was to horrible sights, having lived for so many years in Africa, he nevertheless felt his stomach turn when he gazed upon the mauled body of the Marist priest.

There was something deliberately revengeful in the mauling ; there was not a part of Brother François's body that had not been torn ; his clothes were rent in pieces and scattered upon the ground. And yet the leopards had left their kill, had abandoned it to the vultures. It was this circumstance and the fact that Trader Voss knew well that leopards never hunt in packs — they are solitary marauders — that caused him to rub his fat chin thoughtfully, and remember the many tales that he had heard of the zoomorphism of the Akesi tribe.

As he hurried, hot and perspiring, as fast as his corpulency would allow him, in the direction of Chembi, to carry the news of the tragedy to the Mission, he saw old Googli making for the jungle with his tattered basket of mud under his arm.

"Where is that old son of a gun going to ?" muttered Trader Voss between breaths, but he was too flustered then to give the matter more than a passing thought. Later, at the Mission, it came into his mind again, when the doctor drew his attention to Brother François's body, and stated that there appeared to have been the hand of man at work as well as the claws of leopards.

The brothers came down from the Mission with a litter and carried the remains of Brother François back to his cell. They arranged him as decently as they could under the direction of the doctor, and covered him with one of his own alpaca gowns. He was buried in the little cemetery behind the Mission as quickly as possible, Brother Martin working all night upon a coffin for him, as no one wanted to see the body more decomposed than it was already. Brother François had been missing from the Mission for two days, and the body, judging by its appearance, had lain quite that length of time in the hot, humid jungle. He was the first white occupant of the cemetery, and Father Domenique had to consider whether he should divide the land in two, one side for the white folk and the other for the black, or whether to bury them side by side. Finally, he decided to admit no distinction ; Brother François had died without the last sacrament and so was not eligible for consecrated ground. Besides, Father Domenique had never liked Brother François ; of all the brothers at the Mission, he had liked the lewd-tongued Brother François the least. Still, he put a bunch of flowers on the grave after the earth had been shovelled in, and set himself an extra penance, because he had plucked the flowers from his garden so unwillingly.

The Administrator held a short enquiry into the matter of the death of Brother François, and it was decided, at the enquiry, to put up a notice on the banks of the Little River, warning people not to wander too far into the jungle without arms, as the leopards were dangerous there. The Administrator sent a report to his govern-

ment, which was put away in some official pigeon-hole
and never read, and Father Domenique wrote sorrowfully
to his bishop. But neither mentioned the revolting circumstances of the body having been tampered with by
the hand of man ; that was something neither could understand or even wished to think about. It was only
Trader Voss who could have given some reasonable explanation of the matter, but when he was asked, looking
away to where old Googli sat on the river-bank making
a bigger and uglier jar than usual, he decided to say
nothing. He had no love for the "black crows" on the
hill.

A day or two afterwards old Googli brought his large
jar up the hill to the Mission, and asked Brother Martin
to bake it in his oven, and take special care of it. He
had made it to order, Googli said.

Brother Martin, as he put the jar in the pottery oven,
had a vague and uncomfortable feeling of having seen
it before somewhere, and not having liked it very well.
He went to the door of the pottery bake-house, and there,
with the tails of his frock-coat flying out in the wind, was
old Googli scampering down the hill, laughing himself
to death. Brother Martin did not know what was the
matter, but he guessed that there was something, and he
was rather short with old Googli next day when he came
for his jar. The old man carried it away carefully,
wrapped up in his coat which he had taken off for the
purpose. This coat had been given him by a passing
traveller, and was his most cherished possession ; he wore

it night and day, wet season, dry season ; it was green with age and ragged to a degree, but he was still proud of it. In taking it off to wrap up the jar in it, he shewed that the jar must have some special importance. Brother Martin asked what importance, but Googli only wagged his old head, and said K'Tooma had promised him four francs and a rooster for it.

MADAME BOUL-BOUL'S Tavern was on the outskirts of Chembi, some two kilometres from the
square where the flag-pole stood, without a flag. A recent innovation, it was situated at the beginning of a
grass-covered plain that stretched between the Little River
and the Big River (which was the Congo River, or more
correctly at this juncture, the Lualaba), and thus was
accessible to the residents of Chembi, and also to those of
Luakasi, a settlement on the Lualaba. True, the roads
from both settlements were bad, deviating into mere
kaffir tracks when they crossed the plains, but that did
not deter automobiles from traversing them bumpily.
There were three automobiles in Chembi, and five in
Luakasi, and these cars were always overloaded at night-
time going to the Tavern ; a two-seater held four people,
and a four-seater had once been known to hold twelve,
but that was a record. Those who did not have cars
went to the Tavern on bicycles, those who had no bicycles
stopped away ; there was a tacit understanding that,
below the bicycle standard, one would not find a welcome
from Madame Boul-boul.

Madame Boul-boul (that was not her real name, but
it served for the *habitués* of the Tavern to use ; it having

been given to her in a playful mood by one of them), was a Flemish woman of enormous proportions. The basket-making department of the Marist Mission had to make a verandah chair specially to fit her, and even then Brother Antoine made it a little on the tight side, so there was some difficulty about getting her out of it after she was once comfortably seated. People came to the Boul-boul Tavern to drink, to play cards and to hear Madame Boul-boul laugh.

She started with a hoarse chuckle which seemed to come from great depths, and this would gradually gain in force, until her enormous figure shook as if an earthquake were unsettling it. Madame Boul-boul sat behind the bar counter at the Tavern every night, in her huge basket chair, and laughed at least once during the evening. Monsieur Boul-boul — the very antithesis of Madame, lean, effeminate, clad in pink-striped pyjamas, which he wore morning, noon and night, probably under the impression that it was not worth while to change into day attire in such a climate and such a land — Monsieur Boul-boul lounged negligently against the counter at a little distance from his wife, and supplied a faint air of melancholy to the scene, in contrast with the voluptuous charms of Madame Boul-boul.

A white-livered, pasty-faced barman from Antwerp served the drinks, for Monsieur Boul-boul had never been known to do any work, and Madame had enough to do to sit in her chair and keep the accounts. In the background there were also a parrot and a very thin tabby cat

perpetually washing its face.   The parrot could say "Hail
Mary ! Whisky," and "Damn !" all in English, because
it had spent the best part of its life in Australia.   It had
belonged to a sailor, originally, who had for a time been
ill in a hospital in Sydney run by the Benedictine nuns.
There it had been a favourite of the Mother Superior, and
had attended chapel with her, where it had learnt one or
two prayers by heart, all of which it had now forgotten
save "Hail Mary !" ; sometimes it said this to the *habitués*
of the Tavern, walking from table to table, and drinking
out of the glasses of beer and what-not set before the
customers.

The parrot was almost as great an attraction at the
Tavern as Madame Boul-boul herself.   When the raucous-
voiced gramophone blared forth "Valencia" or "Tous les
tous," it would wag its head from side to side, and exe-
cute, on one of the marble-topped tables, a *pas seul* that
it had certainly not learned in the chapel of the Benedictine nuns.   The dancers would stop to watch it instead
of tap-tapping over the wooden floor, and the parrot was
satisfied ; like a spoilt child, it always wanted to be the
centre of attraction.

It was a garish scene at Madame Boul-boul's Tavern at
night-time, with the big hanging lamp flaring with its
untrimmed wick surrounded by a myriad of assorted insects all eager for a death by fire, the gramophone sending forth an incongruous medley of sounds, men and
women lounging over their drinks, and the green parrot
dancing waggishly upon a table.   Outside the Tavern

stretched the dark and soundless plain, and away in the distance, the hard edge of the jungle was etched fantastically upon the sky, the dark, immobile jungle of unseen voices and hidden things.

A perfect contrast in the mysteries and the certitudes of life! On the one hand the dark jungle hiding its mute, unknowable things, and on the other the precocious parrot, emancipated from its savagery, and dancing upon a table in front of men and women, whose voices rose and fell like the tides of the sea, speaking of commerce, of bargaining, of journeys made and to be made, of love, and hatred, and passion, and all things which make up the life of man. Each one gazing at the parrot, but seeing in it not a reflection of himself, grown out of the simplicity of the primitive into a mountebank acting his way through life, but merely the pert green parrot that old Admiral Delabouche had brought to the Tavern and presented, in an act of light-hearted gallantry, to Madame Boul-boul.

It was only old Admiral Delabouche himself who ever saw the parrot in this relationship, for sometimes, if he were asked his name and station by a newcomer to the Tavern, he would point to the parrot and say: "There you see me! A *charlatan* caught young in the nets of quackery."

Admiral Delabouche sat night after night at the Tavern, drinking whisky and playing dominoes, and seemed as much an intrinsic part of life there, as the barman or Madame Boul-boul herself. Although he was always called so, everyone knew that Delabouche had never been an Admiral ; the nearest he had come to an Admiral's hat, was a stoker's tam o' shanter, which he had worn in the French Navy when he was eighteen or thereabouts ; but he had that appearance. If he had been knee-breeched and his beard trimmed a little, he would have done very well for a Drake or a Hawkins, for he would have made a better Englishman than a Frenchman any day.

Admiral Delabouche claimed no nationality ; as he expressed it himself, he was content to be a citizen of the world. As a matter of fact he was of mixed blood, his mother of French nationality, his father a Scot — that combination of blood that is supposed to produce conquerors of the world. He himself had been born on the little island of Sainte Marie off the coast of Madagascar, and had been brought up in the old town of Antananarivo by Madame Delabouche, who owned the Cinq Francs Tavern there. His mother, early in her married life, had absconded with a planter friend ; and Delabouche's father, after he had drunk himself to death at the Delabouche Tavern, left, with his kindest regards, his personal belongings, consisting of his debts and his eight-year-old son, to old Madame Delabouche.

Madame Delabouche ignored the debts but kept the son ; in return for his bed and food, he made himself useful in the bar. After he left the Tavern at the age of sixteen or thereabouts, his son, having forgotten his real name, and Madame Delabouche being dead and therefore unable to remind him of it, took the name of his patroness, and hoped that the wicked old lady, looking up from Inferno, would not be displeased.

Perhaps in taking to himself her name he took also a little of her character, for he set out into the world with excellent wits to live upon, and in the years that followed used them to good advantage.

Between the day when he had set out from the Cinq Francs Tavern, and now when he lounged on the Boulboul verandah, much time had elapsed, and during that time Admiral Delabouche had travelled greatly, but not, we may take it, in the sedate fashion of a tourist seeing the world. He had been, amongst other things longshoreman, wharf rat, privateer, gunner, trader, hunter, cowboy, and thief; now he was merely old Admiral Delabouche, who bought and sold whatever he could lay hands on and then drank away his earnings at the Boulboul Tavern. Some saw in him merely a debauched old man, others a lost leader. But there he sat in the far corner, each night, playing dominoes with Monsieur Lutz until he had drunk himself so blind that he could no longer count the spots.

The friendship between these two men was somewhat extraordinary, for Monsieur Lutz had never adventured in his life. He had come out to the Congo, under protest, merely because his bank had sent him there, and he never ceased to regret the cheery *cafés* of his beloved Brussels, the well-paved streets, the orderly houses with their long mirrors, their plush-covered furniture, and

their four-postered bedsteads with goose-feather mat-
tresses. He lived in the Congo as one lives in exile, the
only ray of happiness in his existence being his nightly
game of dominoes with Admiral Delabouche. This
game he played with the same care as he gave to his
ledgers in the Banque du Congo Belge and he calculated
the pips much in the same manner as he added up a
column of figures. Admiral Delabouche, on the other
hand, played in a reckless fashion, and was constantly
having to be set right by the careful accountant. "Now,
my dear Admiral, it is not possible to place a six-five
against a seven-nine ; you see how it would be, it would
stop the game."

Then the Admiral would mutter, *"Sacré nom de nom,*
what observation you have, *mon cher* Lutz !" and put
the right domino in place.

The Admiral never got away with his cheating, if it
could be called that, for they played for such small stakes
(a centime a hundred), that it seemed scarcely worth
while for him to try it on, especially as he nearly always
won, the luck being mostly with him in the matter of
getting out first with his dominoes.

Perhaps it was just an absent-minded little habit, left
over from the days when he had thrown loaded dice at
a dollar a throw ; at any rate, it never made any difference in the friendship between the two men. What they
saw in each other no one could tell, but evidently they
saw something, because every night they sat together at
the Tavern, and played their game of dominoes, every

night with the exception of those when Admiral Delabouche was away on one of his trading excursions, or
when Monsieur Lutz had an attack of fever. Then the
one without the other was like a lost sheep, but curiously enough, it was Admiral Delabouche who always
appeared the more lost. Perhaps he was getting a little
old for any new adventure for, on the nights when
Monsieur Lutz was missing from the Tavern, he would
sit in his usual place and distinguish himself only by
drinking himself more blind than usual. When the
pasty-faced barman came to put out the lights for the
night, or rather for the day, as the dawn was always
breaking in the east before the Tavern lights were extinguished, there he would find the Admiral lying across
one of the marble-topped tables, dead to the world.

"Let him be," Madame Boul-boul would order with
good-natured tolerance, as she rose creakily from her
huge chair to go to her bed. "Let him sleep there, for
he has no one to see him home tonight."

CONVERSATION at the Tavern was nearly always desultory, being mostly confined to statements such as : "We have twenty bales of coloured cotton coming by the next boat," or "There are a hundred casks of palm oil for the *Prinz Friedrich* this trip," or perhaps, "A thousand kilos of bone we have in the store this month, good bone, too." It was only when the river-boat called at Chembi, and the tall young *chef de bateau* came out to the Tavern on a borrowed bicycle, that conversation ran to any brilliancy. The *chef de bateau* was a young university student, who had failed to get his *baccalaureat* because he had been too brilliant. Afterwards, a disgruntled and unsympathetic uncle to whom he was indebted for his education, bed, and board, turned him out into the world via a pastry-cook's, where he had to make himself useful helping the *chef*. One day, the *chef* and he having disagreed upon some knotty point in science, about which the *chef* knew nothing and was therefore inclined to be dogmatic, the young university student left the pastry-cook's in Brussels to work out his own destiny.

His working it out brought him to the Congo as *chef de bateau* of the *Prinz Friedrich,* one of the smaller of the river-boats of the *Navigation Maritime du Congo*

Belge; he made an excellent *chef de bateau,* with a light hand for pastry, but he never forgot his original brilliancy. On the deck of the *Prinz Friedrich,* as the boat steamed up river in the gathering dusk, when the hanging lamp was lit in the stern, and the passengers sat round the dining-table under its glare and partook of the food that he had prepared, he would lean against the door leading down into the cook-house, and give one of the brilliant orations that had failed him in his exam, because none of the examination committee had had intelligence enough to understand it. He did the same at Madame Boul-boul's Tavern.

"Here comes Monsieur Brown," the Tavern clientele would say, straightening up a little from their lounging, "now let us listen to what he has to say." And leaning negligently against the bar counter, in the same manner that he leaned against the cook-house door on the river-boat, and had in former years leaned against the blackboard at the Brussels University, Monsieur Brown would begin his discourse.

His name was Brune, but Mrs. Jones, a little nervously, being uncertain of her French accent, had once called him Monsieur Brown, and the name had stuck to him, as such appellations usually do in the outposts of the world. Monsieur Brown he was then, on the river — this young, over-grown schoolboy, who leaned against the bar-counter at Madame Boul-boul's on river-boat nights, recounting a philosophy that not all the making of pastry could ever take from him, whilst to him listened the

Tavern *habitués,* uncertain as to what to make of him and
his theories, and deciding, before he had finished, like
the examiners who had failed him, that they could make
nothing at all.

As well as arguments in philosophy, Monsieur Brown
brought to the Tavern a spirit of carnival; he was like
a young pierrot, standing under the lamp in his loose
white suit and the flowing black cravat, that he always
wore instead of a tie, a young pierrot who had lost his
cap but kept his gaiety. A *comédien* let loose from his
caravan, who at any moment might take to juggling
with balls as he now juggled with words!

Perhaps it had been this very spirit of gaiety, that sat
so well upon him, which had caused the examiners at
Brussels to be a little wary of letting him loose upon the
world with the stamp of their approval. Perhaps they
had sat in their chairs, long-nosed and disapproving, while
he had recounted his ideas, and had seen in him no
black-coated, pince-nezed professor, but a gay and youthful adventurer, strolling in a world to which they had
no access.

It seemed appropriate at Madame Boul-boul's that,
when he stayed in his oration for a moment or two to
wet his throat with a draught of beer, pandemonium
should break loose, that dancing couples should gallop
across the floor in a wild exuberance of spirits, that the
gramophone should sound more noisily than ever, and
that Madame Boul-boul, with her little black boot-button
eyes popping out of her head, should begin one of her

deep-seated chuckles, and the parrot dance fantastically upon a table. It seemed as if the oration of Monsieur Brown had been the prologue before the curtain, and afterwards it went up upon a scene of the most fantastic gaiety.

This illusion was heightened if the night were moonless, for then pitch torches were lit in a row outside the Tavern, to guide the automobiles from Chembi and Luakasi to their right destination; in their smoky glare, which put the light of the hanging-lamp to shame, but did not get rid of the ready-to-die insects, everything looked more theatrical than ever. The long white pierrot, waving his thin arms whilst he recounted his philosophy that life was all gaiety, and sorrow only a distorted image like the reflection in a convex mirror, and over in one corner Admiral Delabouche and Monsieur Lutz, bending over their dominoes, a little aloof from the rest, just as if they were the most important actors in the scene, the hero and villain hobnobbing together! The others, the mad dancers, the waggish parrot, the fat woman with the boot-button eyes, the effeminate Boulboul in pink pyjamas, the pasty-faced barman polishing glasses, being extras, all fitted into their parts quite nicely.

It all seemed right for this tall young philosopher with his extraordinary philosophy; somehow, all the madness in the world would have seemed right for him. There was always the feeling that perhaps the next time that he appeared it would be with a feather in his hat.

Monsieur Brown, out of apparently the crudest mate-

rials, managed to create an atmosphere Hans Andersenian
in the middle of a grass-covered plain of Central Africa ;
he was one of those rare souls who can make a fairy
story of his own life, and drag those about him into
it. It is scarcely probable that the people recognised the
parts for which they were cast, or that the young philosopher himself realised what he was creating. Rather
he waved his long, thin arms, saying : "Here is happiness
for those who want it," and a queer kind of fête arose
about him, to die away again when he went upon his
way, as he did when the dawn broke over Madame Boul-
boul's Tavern.

The Tavern clientele, although they were never able
to make much of the discourses of the youthful Monsieur
Brown, responded eagerly to the gaiety that he let loose
among them. For a few short hours on river-boat nights
those at Madame Boul-boul's enjoyed the strange sensation of being suddenly wafted away into another world,
where they were able to forget completely who they were.

The elderly Mrs. Younghusband, whirling in the arms
of a fair young Russian count, felt that she might go on
whirling thus for ever and grow younger with each
whirl ; and the tall, stiff young soldier husband of
Madame Guillet left off drinking beer at the twenty-
second glass, to lift his wife to his shoulder and prance
with her across the floor. And over in the far corner
old Admiral Delabouche absent-mindedly put the right
domino in place.

Monsieur Brown, looking on while he drank his beer,

would say : "Good, they have the froth, but I drink more deeply."

When the dawn appeared in the eastern sky, then the yawning barman went forth to extinguish the torches, and the play for the night was over. Other lights appeared on the plains, like a row of fire-flies in marching order — the company departing in their automobiles and on their bicycles. The youthful philosopher on his borrowed machine would be somewhere ahead, going back to the dark river, where the snub-nosed river-boat lay, pushed against the shore — the line of chattering labourers traversing the gangplank with baskets of wood for the last time — going back to his making of tarts, with life ahead of him like some lovely adventure.

WHEREAS in the days of old a king had reigned at Akesi, now two chiefs divided the throne between them, a civil chief, Muronga, and a fetish chief, K'Tooma. Between Muronga and K'Tooma there existed a feud as old as the hills ; it had been handed down from generation to generation of fetish chief and civil chief, ever since a king of Akesi had lost half his throne to his medicine man by his own carelessness.

They were secretly afraid, as well as jealous, of each other. The civil chief might have his warriors and his weapons, but the fetish man had his cunning and his magic bones.

Old Muronga had less power than K'Tooma, though he had more pomp. He had his state robes, his seraglio, his council of elders, and he could make a good display with his archers upon occasion, but what were all these compared with the conjuring power of K'Tooma ?

It was only once a year that Muronga felt that he could assume any sort of dignity, and that was when, at the end of the dry season, the beasts came in from mountain and jungle and plain to the river-lands, and Muronga led his warriors to the hunt.

The men of Akesi were not hunters by tradition ; they

went upon the hunting path only when hunger forced them — when, after a drought of six months, fish were scarce in the Little River, and their crops all but finished. It was then that they took down their round straw shields from the rafters of their huts, their spears from over the doorways, and gathered in front of the chief's residence to wait for the coming of the beasts to the river. Muronga sat in front of his hut in his blue robes of state, and about him gathered the archers and spearmen, the pick of his tribe ; no skeleton-limbed decrepit magic-makers these, but men whose naked bodies were as liquid and flowing as water, as strong as wind, as fierce as fire. As he gazed upon them, the old chief felt his heart bursting with pride. For once there was no fly in his ointment, for K'Tooma was never present at this ceremony, and so Muronga felt strong on that one day in the year, a strong king on a powerful throne, not an old man harried, on the one hand, by a cunning, rapacious medicine man, and on the other, by insatiable tax-gatherers of the white man's government. Muronga was of the old school ; he regretted the coming of the white man, and although outwardly friendly towards all Europeans, he harried the tax-gatherers as much as he dared. He brooded upon the good old days of Akesi, the days of his youth, when slavers came to the river, and traders in ivory who said : "A good trade or a stove skull," and kept their word. Then life was adventurous ; one could lose one's head if one wanted to, or quietly poison one's enemy without diplomatic interference.

He wished those days would come back again, but he knew that they never would. The white man was too firmly entrenched in the vicinity of the Little River, and he was an old man, an old man who dyed his hair, so that his followers would not notice his age and put him from the throne. There was nothing he could do about it except secretly collect the tax-gatherers' heads, whilst he sat upon his tottering throne waiting for his end.

But with his archers and spearmen about him, he forgot his age and his dyed hair, and drawing his grandchildren about him, he would boldly relate stories of his prowess on the hunting-path. There he sat in front of his hut backed by sky and distant plain, while the drums rolled out, the hunters sharpened their spears, and the women in one continuous circle, danced before him. Hour after hour they danced without shewing signs of fatigue; it was only when the mighty shout went up from the throats of the hundred hunters to say that the aminals were speeding over the plains towards the river, that they gave way, and falling face downwards on the earth, lay there as if they were never to move again.

From far away came the herds galloping across the plains, the buffaloes, the antelopes, the duiker and gazelles, lumbering rhinos, elephants jostling one another in their eagerness to get to the water. And when the drought had been exceptionally long, then came the giraffes, like some graceful jest, some fantastic fairy tale ; with their long necks in the air, their thin legs moving rhythmically, they loped over the brown plains. They came from very far indeed, from the great grass country a considerable number of kilometres from the Little River ; it was only when the season was exceptional and the water-holes dry in the grasslands, that they came to the river.

Directly the animals were sighted, the waiting Akesians started out upon their hunt. Led by the old chief, they crept on bent knees, with shield and spear lowered, through the dry grass of the plains. Gradually they spread themselves out into a gigantic circle, and when the circle was almost complete, the drumbeaters would go forth to drum the scared and frightened beasts through the one opening into the ring of crouching hunters. When the last animal was within the circle the hunters would close in upon them, and with upraised spear rush upon their prey.

The Akesians killed only for the necessity of eating ; therefore they hunted only as many beasts as they needed to feed their tribe until the rains came and the crops sprouted again. They were chivalrous hunters too ; after a kill, they would pray the beast's pardon, and explain at some length their dire need.

"O great brother," they would address the dead beast, "we are sorry to have killed you, but our wives wait by the cooking fires and their pots are empty. Let not your race hold it against us that we have killed one of you, for our need was great, our empty bellies cry aloud in their hunger."

This, of course, did not do the dead beast any good,

but at least it served to shew that the sentiment of the black hunters was not one of blood-lust and brutality.

If the beast were a lion, then the ceremony of asking pardon was prolonged by dancing, by hand-clapping, and general homage by the hunters to the dead King of Beasts. Finally, the old chief would take off his blue robe of state and throw it upon the body, and thus the lion would be carried home to the village of Akesi, with the pomp and ceremony of a funeral cortege.

All through the night the dancing would continue, by feast fires that sent their flames high into the Heavens, while the war-drums rolled ceaselessly a dirge for the dead king. Then the sound of the drums reached across the plains, across the river to the white settlement of Chembi, so when a lion was killed during the brief hunting season of the Akesians, very few of the residents of Chembi got much sleep.

THE drums disturbed the sleep of the residents on the other side of the river also. They penetrated to the cool dank cells of the Brothers in the Marist Mission, and caused Brother Martin to turn in his sleep and murmur, "Five hack saws, two cross-cuts, sixteen double-edged chisels, a dozen sheets of fine emery paper," as if he were making an inventory of his carpenter's shop. They made Brother Antoine toss and turn with a throat that burned for a draught of cool beer, and Brother Paul would lie awake and count their rumbling with vicious spleen. It was only Father Domenique who slept well and peacefully in his bed.

Of the White Sisters of Mercy in their well-ordered hospital lower down on the Mission hill, it was Sister Marte who was worried by the drums. Sister Mary Josephine said, "Those things which we do not desire to hear we do not hear," when they started beating, and Sister Thérèse put cotton wool in her ears. Sister Marte did not follow either Sister Mary Josephine's example or Sister Thérèse's, for the sound of the drums fascinated her. Even though they alarmed and disturbed her, yet she sought to listen to them.

For many a long day the drums had been rumbling.

First, after the vestal virgin had been raped ; then during
the hunting moon ; and now that the rains were late in
coming, the witch doctors set about making their magic
and the sound of the drums rolled out day and night
across the plains. There was no rest from them. Sister
Marte heard them as she went about her work, and at
night they seemed to roll and rumble through her very
dreams.

Sister Thérèse put cotton wool in her ears and refused to hear the drums of Akesi. She refused also to
hear Sister Marte when she spoke to her, and this was
irritating, for Sister Marte, without wool in her ears,
could hear both the drums and Sister Thérèse's sharp,
scolding voice. There was a great deal of bickering between them, which culminated, one day, in a violent
quarrel over the possession of a broom.

There was only one broom at the hospital, one good
broom, and Sister Marte wanted it to sweep out Sister
Mary Josephine's office, but Sister Thérèse was using it
in the ward, and apparently did not hear Sister Marte's
request for it.

Sister Marte repeated her request, but Sister Thérèse
stuffed the cotton wool farther into her ears and went
on sweeping. For some months a sense of resentment
against Sister Thérèse had been accumulating in the
usually placid breast of Sister Marte. It seemed that
Sister Thérèse was receiving all the favours at the hospital. It was she who helped Sister Mary Josephine and
the doctor when Madame Lenotte's baby was born, a

fine distinction, as it was the first white child born in the hospital; and frequently of late, Sister Mary Josephine had chosen Sister Thérèse to accompany her on her daily shopping expedition.

And now the broom! That was the culminating factor in Sister Marte's decision to leave the hospital — the only personal decision she had ever made in her life. The quarrel between the two women was short, sharp and violent, but Sister Thérèse, being the taller and stronger woman, kept possession of the broom. When Sister Marte found herself outmarshalled, she ran out of the hospital down the long steep hill towards the river — ran out just as she was in her white hospital clothes, with her coif well awry on her shaven head. But by the time she reached the river, she was sorry that she had not stayed to get a cloak, for the moon was covered with dark clouds and drops of rain were beginning to fall sparsely. The long drought had broken; Sister Marte, listening, could hear the swirl of the flood waters coming down river. The rains had come to the mountain regions first, and the Little River at its source was already overflowing its banks.

Sister Marte hurried to the ford. She did not wait to take off her clumsy shoes and stockings, or even hold up her voluminous robes, but waded through the ford waters that were already beginning to run less sluggishly over their bed.

When Sister Marte had set out from the hospital, she had only one idea in mind, and that was to get as far away as possible from the maddening presence of Sister Thérèse ; but now that she was safely across the river, with the lights of Chembi twinkling before her, she thought of making her retreat secure. The rains were beginning, and soon the river would be uncrossable by foot. But there was Lardi, the ferryman, and his raft ; he would still be there, waiting by the bank to take passengers across the river at a sou a time. Lardi feared neither rain nor wind nor flood waters. On Lardi's raft, then, Sister Mary Josephine would come to the settlement next morning to take Sister Marte home, home to long hours of penance and prayer, and the uncongenial companionship of a woman with cotton-wool in her ears.

Sister Marte peered about her, looking for the raft. It was moored a little farther down the bank, and Lardi was asleep upon its boards, with his ferry-pole in his hand.

The ferryman had often gesticulated and pointed at Sister Marte, behind Sister Mary Josephine's back, when they had crossed on the raft together, and she was more afraid of the misshapen, dwarfish figure than of any of the black men about her. But when she spied the raft she had courage enough — the courage of desperation, perhaps — to venture near it and take the mooring-rope from the tree branch to which it was tied. Sister Marte, with the mooring-rope in her hand looked about her furtively. The moon had come out from behind the bank of dark clouds, and she could see by its light that the river-banks were deserted — deserted except for the

still, squatting figure of the black man, M'Kato, on the
opposite bank, by the ford. But Sister Marte paid no
heed to M'Kato ; he was to her, just an inoffensive old
man, who always sat upon the river-bank, apparently
gazing at nothing. She hearkened again to the flood
waters coming down the river ; they were nearer now,
soon they would be upon Chembi, and they would sweep
Lardi's unmoored raft with them over the chutes — that
is, if Lardi did not wake up too soon. Sister Marte, with
the mooring-rope of the raft clutched almost to her
bosom, prayed that Lardi's sleep that night might be long
and unbroken.

WHEN the wet season began the Egyptian geese came south and nested by the Little River ; their hoarse cries and cackling voices came up from the rushes where they built their nests. The voices of the frogs in the marshland were more strident than before. At dusk through the tall grass on the river-banks, at a safe distance from the settlement of Chembi, the male hippopotami pursued their females with amorous gruntings ; and at night, on the little islands in mid-river that were rapidly being submerged beneath the rising waters, crocodiles roared of their love to a round, red moon.

When the hissing rain came up like a wall towards the river, then the love voices were stilled for a moment, the tall grass bent low, and the delicate flowers that bloomed amongst it were slashed into fragments. But there was always the fierce sun afterwards to stir the earth to passionate fruitfulness ; the orchids broke into a riot of colour, creeping vines that trailed their tendrils in the river-waters were covered with gold and purple flowers, a soft carpet of young green grass was spread upon the earth, and the dark, hostile jungle bloomed like a month-old bride.

At the beginning of the dry season the Egyptian geese

flew north again, the honk-honking of their hoarse voices
coming from a distance, like ghostly echoes through a
vista of years. Then the Little River ran narrowly on
its way, and through its yellow waters the rocks appeared, where, in the wet season, the chutes flung their
white spray high into the air. Then reappeared the submerged islands, on which crocodiles sunned themselves
in lazy groups, whilst in the rank yellow grass of the
river-banks, the male hippopotami skulked together, their
mates, heavy with their coming maternity, sleeping all
day in the jungle, and only lumbering up to drink at the
river when a yellow moon hung in the sky, like a parched
and withered old lady.

There were only two seasons of the year in the vicinity
of the Little River : the season of birth and the season
of death, the season of fruitfulness and the season of
harvest. They followed each other with regularity.
The rains came, the earth burst into a splendid bloom-
ing, there was lustfulness in all things. In the villages
the elders sat all day round fires, brewing a heady drink
from palm canes. The rains ceased, the lush grass by
the river-banks became dry and yellow, the swollen river
shrank, and the hot sun shone fiercely all day, purging
the swamp-lands of their fever. In the villages all the
palm toddy had been drunk, and men and women slept
apart.

Then followed the rains again and began the riotous
excess of the earth. But sometimes the wet season was
delayed. Then the land became drought-stricken, the

plains lay hot and arid under the pitiless sun ; grass, burnt to its roots, withered and died in a day ; even the jungle seemed parched and gasping for breath.

In the villages the maidens took offerings to the shrines and danced in a row before them. Their thoughts were : "O let the rain fall upon the earth and, in the darkness of the night, a groom upon my body."

Then if the rains still did not come, the drums rolled out and the witch doctors made magic.

This year, by the Little River, the rains had been long in coming. Each night the sun went down like a glowing coal, and the moon came up, shrunken and distorted like a crippled old woman. The maidens danced in their straight rows in the village of Akesi, and uttered their simple maiden prayer, but still the rains held off. The scorching sun poured down like a flood of fire, the earth was burnt, the river dried almost to its yellow bed, the streets of Chembi were thoroughfares of dust and refuse, and the houses took on a parched, cracked appearance. In the Mission garden up on the hill the flowers drooped to death, and no amount of Father Domenique's watering with his little tin watering-pot could save them. The drums of K'Tooma rolled and rumbled to no purpose, and the witch doctors grew tired and over-worked with their making of magic.

The Little River ran so low that the *Prinz Friedrich* could not make her usual fortnightly trip to Chembi. Goods had to be brought overland by bearers from Luakasi. All day long a thin line of bearers wound through the withered grass of the plains, some carrying cases of gin, some bales of cotton, some cases of Bibles. They chattered and laughed as they came on their way, and the usually soundless plains rang with their merriment. All the younger men of Akesi were pressed into this service of bearing, and the Akesians waxed rich for each bearer was paid a franc for his journey. The women of Akesi wore better calicoes and more bead necklaces in consequence, and the men sometimes ran to a white drill suit in imitation of the white men. In this manner the money found its way back again into the tills from which it had come and no one was any the worse off.

Madame Boul-boul's Tavern did a great trade in cool beer. The nights were hot and oppressive, and throats were parched. Each night the row of travelling lights on the plains grew longer, every available vehicle being pressed into the service of taking the white residents out to the Tavern for a "cooler" before going to bed.

The river-boat not being able to come to Chembi, the young Monsieur Brown was absent from the Tavern, so conversation there ran on dull lines.

"There were clouds in the sky at sunset tonight, the rains should come before morning."

"*Mon Dieu,* how much it is costing the company to have the goods brought overland !"

"Never seen the river so low before ; another week, and we'll be able to see its bed."

And Admiral Delabouche and Monsieur Lutz in their

corner intent upon their game. "Now, my dear Admiral, take care, a four-six will not match a seven-three."

"'*Cré nom de nom,* why must you always interfere, *mon choux.*" Thus they had it out with each other without any bad feeling.

This was Madame Boul-boul's Tavern, with the rains a month late : no brilliancy, no gaiety, no fête, not much of anything in fact, except a great and abiding thirst. Even the parrot suffered from it, and squawked peevishly when beer glasses were refused its inquisitive beak.

Then one night the rains came, unexpectedly, as the sunset had been cloudless and vermilion red.

Admiral Delabouche and Monsieur Lutz going home on their bicycles, somewhat later than usual, as the Admiral's thirst had refused to be quenched that night, were the only two of the Tavern frequenters who were caught in the great storm that blew up at a moment's notice. The tempest started when they were within sight of Chembi. Suddenly, without warning, the wind howled across the plains, and the rain followed the wind in great driving sheets of water.

"Now we are in for it," said Monsieur Lutz, ducking his head, and trying to obtain a more secure hold of his companion, as the Admiral was not very steady upon his machine.

But the drowning douche of cold water had sobered Admiral Delabouche. "Let us put on some speed," he said.

They pedalled their bicycles energetically, and came

to the river-bank and the beginning of the settlement of
Chembi. When they were passing along the bank they
saw, by the glare from the frequent flashes of lightning,
M'Kato sitting in his usual place opposite, cross-legged
and stolid, like some immutable black Buddha, unheedful of the storm that raged about him.

"I wonder what that old nigger does there, on the
river-bank," gasped out Monsieur Lutz, as he forced his
bicycle through the sheets of driving rain.

"He's up to no good," called back Admiral Delabouche, loudly enough to be heard above the noise of
the storm. "He's evil-wishing somebody, I'll be bound,
I've seen 'em at it before, on the West Coast."

The wind and the rain followed the two men through
the streets of Chembi, roaring after them round corners
and chasing them down the streets, but finally they were
safely indoors in Monsieur Lutz's tiny habitat. And
then, above the roar of the tempest, occurred a bigger
noise, a sudden crash followed by a long-drawn-out
demoniacal scream.

"What's that ?" asked Admiral Delabouche, seated on
the sofa in the living-room, and shewing a tendency to go
to sleep in his wet clothes.

"It sounded like a scream," Monsieur Lutz shouted in
return, as if he were still outside and had to make himself heard above the roar of the tempest.

"It's the water sprites at their tricks," chuckled Admiral
Delabouche, preparing himself for slumber again.

Perhaps old Admiral Delabouche was right ; the water

sprites must have been at their biggest trick of all — that of pushing old Lardi and his raft over the chutes to the perdition that he had so often jested over with his passengers; for next day his broken raft was washed up on to the bank of the Little River, several kilometres below where the deep and perilous chutes cascaded into unknown depths. His body was never found; the white men said that the Devil had claimed his own, and the black people asserted that he was still at his tricks deep down in the foamy depths of the Boiling Pot; they could hear his laughter rising above the roar of the chutes.

Certainly someone must have played a joke upon old Lardi, otherwise how did his raft come to be swept over the chutes, when before the rains came it had been securely moored to a tree on the river-bank? And if not the water sprites, then who? But that was something that never came to be known, for, self-preservation being the first law of Nature, Sister Marte, secure under the roof of the Baptist Mission, kept silent when old Lardi's fate was discussed, and M'Kato, beyond ticking off the event on Father Domenique's rosary, as he had ticked off many another before it, remarked not the matter in any way. If he had thought of it, he might have allowed himself the liberty of a chuckle for an enemy vanquished, for old Lardi had ever been a thorn in his flesh, but his thoughts were entirely concentrated upon another matter — the fulfilment of his life's great task.

THE doors of the Baptist Mission stood wide open so that anyone might enter, even though it was night-time. There was a light in the minister's study, for he was working there on the usual monthly letter to headquarters, but the rest of the house was in darkness. Mrs. Jones had had a tiring day (the cooking class always fatigued her) and so had retired to bed unusually early. Under one layer of cool linen sheeting she was sleeping peacefully, when suddenly the wire door of her bedroom flew open with a bang, and someone stumbled, almost fell, over the threshold into the room.

Mrs. Jones, waking instantly, called "Llew! Llew!" in a slightly shrill voice, and struck a match to light the bedside candle. By the flickering glare of the match she saw, standing in the doorway, irresolute and a little downcast, Sister Marte from the hospital on the other side of the river.

There was a moment's silence, during which the two women regarded each other steadily, then the match flickered and went out.

"Please come in and shut the wire door, so that it will not bang to and fro," Mrs. Jones said, as she lit another match. And Sister Marte, accustomed all her life to obeying a voice of authority, shut the wire door behind her with the needed care, and came slowly into the room.

By this time the Reverend Jones had come in answer to his wife's summons. "Just wait a minute, Llew," Mrs. Jones said to him. "I will rise and put on my dressing-gown. Here is Sister Marte from the hospital on the hill; perhaps she needs our help. Perhaps she has something that she would like to tell us."

Mrs. Jones rose out of her bed, wrapped a thin blue muslin dressing-gown about her body, thrust her feet into straw mules, and then looked expectantly towards Sister Marte. Sister Marte stood in the centre of the room, her coif a little awry, her fat, red face perspiring freely, her voluminous gown tumbled and disordered, but she had nothing to tell them except that she had left the hospital on the hill, because she had quarrelled with Sister Thérèse. This she repeated over and over again, in the flat, monotonous voice of one repeating a lesson.

It was extremely disappointing; Mrs. Jones, and perhaps also the Reverend Llewellyn, had been looking forward to some lurid details of secret life up on the Marist Mission hill. But Sister Marte would say nothing beyond the fact that she had left the hospital for good; and so saying, she took off her coif and threw it from her, leaving her shaven head bare and slightly ridiculous.

"Well, poor thing, perhaps she will tell us more tomorrow," said Mrs. Jones briskly. "Anyway, we must make her up a bed here for tonight."

It was to be applauded in the Joneses that they never questioned for an instant the right of Sister Marte to come to them in her trouble, whatever it might be, a quarrel with Sister Thérèse, or something worse. It was quite evident, by the state of Sister Marte's robe, that the quarrel had been a violent one.

The Reverend Llewellyn Jones was able to add, with stern approval, to his London letter that night, a post-script : "We have just had the most surprising proof of the cruelty and injustice of the Catholic Church, for Sister Marte, of the White Sisters of Mercy, who have a hospital on the other side of the river, has fled to us for protection." He fervently hoped that the matter would find its way into the London Press, and that the Catholic Church would get a good shewing up.

But apparently, when Sister Marte was gently questioned next day, there was nothing to shew up beyond the fact that she and Sister Thérèse had quarrelled over a broom, and she had left the hospital because of this.

She had chosen to call for aid at the Baptist Mission rather than any other house in Chembi for, knowing of the rivalry existing between the two Missions, she felt that the Reverend Jones and his wife would never give her back to Sister Mary Josephine, as doubtless the other residents, who were of her own faith, would hasten to do.

All day long Sister Marte sat in the Mission, gazing

out of the living-room window. Neither the Reverend
Jones nor his wife interfered with her in any way. They
allowed her to do exactly as she liked, and so she sat all
day on the window-seat, in her nun's robes but without
her coif, her head feeling cool and comfortable for the
first time in many a year.

Sister Mary Josephine did not come to see her, but
Father Domenique, when the rains lessened, rode over on
his white mule. The Baptist Minister saw him coming
and went out into the roadway to meet him. Briefly but
firmly he pointed out to Father Domenique that, while
Sister Marte was under his protection, no one from the
Catholic Mission would be allowed to visit her; he would
not have her annoyed, he said.

Father Domenique replied that he would write to his
bishop. "She has not asked to be released from her
vows," he pointed out to the Baptist Minister gently;
"her place is with us."

But the Reverend Jones could be very firm upon occasion. Sister Marte's place was where she wished it to
be, he answered Father Domenique.

The Administrator, when he was appealed to by the
Catholic priest, said briefly: "I wash my hands of
the whole concern," even before he had time to hear the
rights of the case. So Father Domenique wrote to his
bishop, but before the bishop's reply could be received
Sister Mary Josephine passed the Baptist Mission and
Sister Marte from her seat in the living-room saw her.

Sister Mary Josephine had been as usual to have her

glass of lemonade with Madame Voss on the shady verandah of the I.N.T. Stores, and over it said to Madame Voss : "So stupid of Sister Marte not to come back to the hospital. It was over a broom. We have only one broom at the hospital, one good broom, and both Sister Marte and Sister Thérèse wanted it at the same time. Sister Thérèse has very violent passions sometimes ; she has been set an extra penance for this affair. But there is too much work for her at the hospital now ; it is very stupid of Sister Marte to stay away so long."

"Perhaps if you just went past that way !" suggested Madame Voss, "Sister Marte sits all day long by the window of the Baptist Mission, looking out on to the street ; she would be sure to see you. Sister Marte was always very fond of you, Sister Mary Josephine."

"I will try it," Sister Mary Josephine said, "for we really need her help ; every bed is full at the hospital at present."

So Sister Mary Josephine, with the two wings of her large white coif carrying her forward like the sails of a ship, went past the Baptist Mission, and Sister Marte, half-hidden behind the chintz window curtains saw her. Instead of a stern disciplinarian, this large serene woman, so calmly indifferent to all that went on about her, suddenly seemed a refuge, a strength.

Sister Marte was afraid of many things in Africa, but most of all of the drums that rolled and rumbled incessantly in the village of Akesi. They irritated her, frightened her almost to a point of stupefaction. Perhaps more than all else, more even than her antagonism towards Sister Thérèse, these drums had driven her forth from the hospital. There was something sinister in their rhythm. They did queer things to Sister Marte, set her blood beating in her pulses until she could count the beats as she counted the rhythm of the drums ; they made her ill-tempered and quarrelsome. Just at the moment that Sister Thérèse had claimed the broom they had sounded almost in Sister Marte's very ears. Goaded beyond endurance by their evil beating, she had snatched at the broom. Afterwards, when she was flying down the steep hill towards the river, they beat behind her, driving her forward, wicked, sinister, inciting her to evil deeds.

Now that the rains had come the drums of Akesi had ceased their noise, for the witch doctors were resting thankfully from their labours, but they still rolled and rumbled in Sister Marte's ears — ghostly echoes of the drums she had listened to for so many months. They were fainter certainly in the daytime when she sat on the window-seat of the Mission living-room and gazed out at the dusty streets of Chembi. But at night-time, when silence fell upon the town, and there was no sound other than the barking of mongrel dogs and the singing of the women by the fishermen's fires on the river-bank, then they rolled and rumbled even louder than before. The atmosphere of the Baptist Mission brought her no peace from them, as she had hoped it would do.

Speeding down the Mission hill that fateful night of

her quarrel with Sister Thérèse, she had told herself that on the other side of the river the drums would not be heard. But she was listening to them still, as she had listened for many months.

And out in the street Sister Mary Josephine, calm, cool and stable, was passing along, looking as if she had never heard a drum in her life. Sister Marte, coifless, on a sudden impulse ran out of the Mission, and, catching up with the superb figure in white going through the street like a passing procession, said, gasping a little for breath : "Let me carry your basket for you, Sister Mary Josephine."

Sister Mary Josephine handed over the basket without comment, and together the two women passed out of Chembi towards the river-bank.

When they reached the ford, Sister Marte felt a sudden desire to confess to Sister Mary Josephine her heinous crime of sending Lardi to perdition ; but before she could utter more than a word or two of her confession, Sister Mary Josephine interrupted her : "You will get sunstroke without your coif, Sister Marte ; take my umbrella and hold it over your bare head."

Very meekly Sister Marte took the green-lined umbrella and held it above her shaven head and the opportunity for confession was lost. The two women, gathering up their skirts, splashed across the ford and continued on their way up the Mission hill in silence.

A month or two afterwards Sister Marte was sent back to her native town of Liège, and Dr. Forbeau, a keen student of Adler and Jung, recommended that she be released from her vows.

Sister Mary Josephine discussed the matter with her friend, Madame Voss. "Sister Marte was never fitted for a secluded life," she said. "She should have lived in the world and borne children, many children."

And so passed Sister Marte from the Little River, passed without knowing what an essential part she had played in its history, in its progress. Without her the building of a bridge across the river might never have come to pass, for Lardi's raft would have been adequate for the needs of the settlement for some time to come. But when no other ferryman came to take Lardi's place a bridge began to be spoken about by the white residents, and although it did not come into being till some considerable time afterwards, it was certainly old Lardi's death that was the primary factor in its being spoken about at all.

BOOK III

THROUGHOUT the land the black people were being pushed back into their forests. The white men had come, first in ones and twos, and then in their hundreds. Now they sat in the seats of power and the black people were lowly and humble in the land that had been theirs for countless ages.

The white men held the power by the waterways and in the settlements, but in the forests the black people were still supreme. There they walked naked and unashamed, and kept their magic. Wise men met over the cooking-pot, medicine men crossed their bones, and that one great, exact and infallible science, which had been their forefathers' since the beginning of their race, was theirs still. In the settlements by the rivers it was dying, killed by the scorn of the unbelievers, but in the forests it still lived and held the tribes together, so that they bred and multiplied. The elders clung to it as the last stronghold of their race. If their magic were taken from them, then they would have nothing at all; they would be at the mercy of the white people, for it was their only weapon against them. The old men sat in a circle round the witch fires, and thought heavily and with mistrust of the white man and his ways. One came today, two tomorrow, soon their shadow would be cast over the whole land ; their deforming influence would kill the things that the black men loved and reverenced.

The young men liked the white man and his ways ; they infested the settlements, they worked for him, they attended his schools. But the elders withdrew farther into themselves, and went to their forests where no white man dwelt, and where they could make their magic in peace.

Their magic told them of the coming decadence of their land, and they were sorrowful, for they loved their land and all things in it : flowers and animals, birds and trees, the fish in the rivers and the croaking frogs in the muddy pools. They felt no superiority to the other life about them, only the rich wonder of someone partaking in an amazing adventure. But they knew that if the white man came in his myriads this adventure would cease ; the white man would build up his own puny civilisation, and gradually the things they loved would die under the withering breath of his scorn.

They clung to their magic as the only thing that would save them. The witch doctors, who had, in days gone by, taken one apprentice and taught him their craft, now sought for two, so that their magic would live after them. But the apprentices were dull and sometimes a little contemptuous, thinking more of writing in a round hand upon a blackboard than looking into a witch fire and seeing visions there.

It was a hard time for the black people. It is sad to

see old and lovely things vanishing from existence, to have traditions trampled in the dust. But the power of the unbeliever is strong; dumb and confounded, the black men sat in their circles, wondering who was right, they or the white man. It was only the very old men and the witch doctors who knew, and they kept on with their conjuring, but grew more and more secret about it. In the darkened forests they made their magic against the oncoming rush of the white man, but thought is long, and vision is slow, and they were old. They knew it was all of no use.

Some, more brazen than the rest, openly practised their craft under the white man's scornful nose : K'Tooma with his rattling drums, old Googli making pottery jars from the genital organs of man, and M'Kato on the banks of the Little River, with his vendetta against Humphrey Brown. But they were close and secret about their methods of making magic, and no white man ever caught them at it. The first two made magic because they were adepts at the craft, and it was their profession. But the third, M'Kato, made magic because of his agony of soul.

At first, when the time seemed long as he sat by the Little River and results slow in coming, he would think of the swamps of blood in Northern Rhodesia ; he would think of the cries of M'Tessa as she was carried over the threshold of the white man's house ; and then he would think of her as he had seen her afterwards, pert, provocative-eyed, like the women of Akesi who crossed the river continually to go to the white men's beds. And that last thought was the worst of all; it would drive him back to his concentration instantly. But later, when he had come to almost complete immobility, and inactivity of all bodily senses, time ceased for him altogether. Day and night were no more to him than shadows that fell across his post by the river; seasons came and went without his awareness. The vision of the pert M'Tessa then passed from him entirely; it is doubtful if he would have shewn any recognition if she had suddenly stood before him.

So there M'Kato sat on the river-bank, through the black man's seasons and the white man's years, patiently making a magic that would take the best part of a lifetime to bring to fulfilment.

M'KATO looked withered and dried, like a bough that had lost its sap. He was not an old man, but he had the appearance of great age. The flesh had fallen away from his bones; he was now skeleton-limbed like the men of Akesi, and his once massive shoulders sagged as if under some heavy burden. The white residents of Chembi always referred to him as "That funny old black man, M'Kato," thinking that, in their way of counting, he must be nearing the eighties; but as it happened he was only half that age. His long vigil by the Little River had piled the years upon him.

While he sat on the river-bank his wife, Tela, neglected and disgruntled, worked in her vegetable patch and sold fresh vegetables and fruit to the residents of Chembi. She was always well-dressed in bright calicoes, but she was as withered and old, almost, in appearance as M'Kato. There was no savour in her life; for many years Tela had slept alone. She was a Tree woman, and the Trees forbade her to go to another man, but she often looked longingly at the women of Akesi who forded the river to go to the white men's houses in Chembi. She worked in her garden day in and day out, and developed into something of a scold. When M'Kato came to his hut for food or rest, her nagging tongue soon drove him forth from it again. He took to sleeping by his post near the river and thus Tela was left more alone than before.

Tela was continuously jeered at by the women of Akesi for being childless. They brought their children to shew her, they poked their babies almost into her face. "Look at this one, see what a fine child he is !" or "See how big my child has grown, a fine man he will be !"

And Tela would feel secretly sorry for herself, although she never indicated this to any of the women. The bitterness of being childless became a thorn in her flesh, and gave her no peace night and day. The manioc grew and flourished under the cultivation of her hoe, the mangosteens were more prolific in her garden than elsewhere, the pumpkin vines were always heavy with fruit, but Tela herself was unfruitful.

She sought out K'Tooma for his advice, but surprisingly he had none to offer, even though she brought a basket of her choicest fruit with her.

"Your husband," he told her, "has much work to do by the river."

"Of what use will be this work of his when it is finished ?" demanded Tela petulantly, "does he make baskets there by the river, or weave cloth, or catch the silver fish upon a line ? No, the moon comes, the moon goes, and there he sits with his thoughts, while I sleep in the hut alone."

K'Tooma regarded the great basket of Tela's fruit

thoughtfully. It was good fruit, luscious and large.
"Leave me that basket, O Tela," he said, "and I will send
my sister's child, Lindi, to help you with your garden ;
perhaps M'Kato will then come home."

Tela left the basket of fruit, and next day Lindi came
and hoed with Tela in her garden. But M'Kato did not
come home to sleep at his hut, although he knew about
Lindi being there. Lindi often walked through the
streets of Chembi with a basket of fruit on her head,
crying her wares, and passing him sitting on the river-
bank, would swing her hips provocatively at him. But
M'Kato took no notice of her, although she was a young,
buxom woman, as Tela had been when he had first
taken her to wife. In the early days of his coming to the
Little River, M'Kato had exchanged the first fruits of
Tela's garden for an assegai, and with this he practised
assiduously, until he was able to throw it with his toes
for quite a good distance. The day that he managed to
throw it across the Little River was a red-letter day for
him.

People said when they crossed the river : "What can
that old nigger be doing with his assegai ?" But when
they asked M'Kato, he merely pointed out to them that
he was throwing it across the river, and as that had been
previously apparent to them, they did not get much satisfaction from their questioning.

After the ferry was swept away M'Kato was left in
peace by his questioners, for the river was turbulent for
some time, and the white men did not attempt crossing

through the ford. Of those who dwelt on M'Kato's side
of the river only Father Domenique ever troubled about
him, and he had long since ceased to ask him questions,
contenting himself with merely a few words of cheer,
and a whispered prayer when he came near the black
man.

Of all the residents on the right bank Father Domenique felt the loss of the ferry most ; he was once again
thrown upon the resources of the Mission for a supper
companion. Brother Martin came the most often to his
table, but Brother Martin, although a good carpenter
and a worthy man, was somewhat dull of intellect, and
Father Domenique found his company a little heavy.

He wrote regretfully to the uncle in Pays Basque, and
the uncle with his usual good nature, sought out friends
who had some influence in Brussels, and so the machinery
was set in working order for obtaining a bridge across
the Little River.

Sister Mary Josephine also helped in the matter. At
first Sister Mary Josephine had not been perturbed by
the loss of the ferry. She sent her ward-boy to buy
chickens and eggs and vegetables in Akesi, and so was
independent of the markets of Chembi. But as time
went on, she began to miss her morning chat with
Madame Voss over the cool lemonade, and also as it
was difficult to bring patients across the Little River when
its waters ran high, the white residents took to having
their fevers in their own homes. Sister Mary Josephine
saw herself sitting with idle hands in a hospital full of

empty beds. She wrote about the matter to her sister, who was Mother Superior of the Convent of the Precious Blood in Brussels.

The Mother Superior did her best (there were many daughters of government officials in the school attached to her convent), but she succeeded only in advancing a little the good work that had been done by Father Domenique's uncle. It was not until the two black women who claimed to have been resurrected from the dead came to Chembi, and took Papa Grandeau away with them when they left, that anything definite was done in the matter. The story of the resurrected women got into the daily newspapers of Europe, and Government officials in Brussels found, when they came to look a second time over the correspondence urging the construction of a bridge across the Little River, that they did know something of the Little River after all, and as it had received great prominence of late in the morning press, it might be as well to build a bridge across its waters.

PAPA GRANDEAU was the bureau clerk at the white-elephant hotel. His name was Jacques Lemoine Grandeau, but everyone called him Papa, or perhaps, out of his hearing "the old one." He was a little old man, with white hair and the beard of a prophet. He stroked his beard continuously with fingers that trembled a little when speaking to clients, and was unnecessarily meticulous in the recommendation of a room.

"Yes, yes, monsieur, a single room on the ground floor. There are many vacant, we can accommodate you well. No. 28 ? No, my dear sir, do not take No. 28, for it is next to the bathroom and the cistern refilling itself will keep you awake all night. No. 36 now, a nice room, though the mirror is cracked, and it has no chair. Or 38, a cool room, but no view !"

He looked after everyone in a kindly, inefficient way, on the whole making a great muddle of his job. "If it wasn't for the fact that he's related to one of the directors, I would have got rid of him long ago," the Hotel manager always explained to clients. "But there you are !——" and he would spread his hands in an eloquent Gallic gesture, which conveyed the fact that it was unfortunate, but the directors of the company which owned the white-elephant hotel had to be taken some notice of.

Papa Grandeau had a history. He had once been Lieutenant Jacques Lemoine Grandeau of the King's Cavalry, but that was thirty years ago. He was, then, not so very old, despite his white hair and beard. A lieutenant, say at twenty-eight, and add thirty to that and you get fifty-eight. But men age quickly in the region of the Equator. The passing of the dashing young lieutenant into the aged bureau clerk had, to be sure, taken all of thirty years, but then what is thirty years — not sufficient surely to bring about that trembling of the hands, that intense whiteness of the hair, that peculiarly vacant, childish expression of the eyes ? Lieutenant Jacques Lemoine Grandeau should now, by rights, have been General Grandeau, waxing the ends of his moustache a little, in imitation of the Germans.

Jacques Lemoine Grandeau had come out to the Congo in the 'eighties, with an exploring party of fourteen men. These white men, with a hundred or so native bearers, had gone into the interior of the Province Oriental, the region just above Stanleyville, then unexplored, and of the fourteen white men, Lieutenant Grandeau was the only one who returned. As for the bearers, no one knew what became of them (it was surmised that they had left the party long before tragedy began to overtake it), for young Grandeau came back to Stanleyville alone. Unkempt, starving, ill with a burning fever, he stumbled into the old Arab town (then just renamed Stanleyville after the intrepid explorer Stanley) at the close of a long, hot day, and was taken into the home of an Arab trader there, and cared for until his fever had abated.

He told the trader that he had been lost in the Great Forest of Silence, that he had been ill there, and almost starved to death, that all his companions were dead, and he had left them, unburied, in the forest. Then he sank into merciful unconsciousness from which he did not recover for many weeks. After that there was a period of convalescence in Europe, and then young Grandeau dropped out of the public eye for some time. He turned up again in the Congo some years later, as inspector for the I.N.T. Company. He had left the army, it seems, and the influence of some obliging relations had obtained for him this inspectorship. But he did not keep the position long ; in a month or two he was down at the coast again, waiting for a boat to Europe or another position to be found for him. Evidently the relations did not want him back in Europe, for another position was found, but the same thing happened again, happened, in fact many times over. Jacques Lemoine Grandeau drifted from position to position, now clerk in this trading-store, now accountant in that, inefficient and muddling his job, until finally he was given notice to go despite the influential relatives.

And now the final stage of bureau clerk at the Hotel Blanc, where, owing to the scarcity of clientele, he could do no harm, even if he did no good.

That was Papa Grandeau's history, briefly stated. He would tell you more of it himself, if you appeared interested. He was always ready to talk of his life, and especially that part of it connected with the ill-fated expedition. He seemed to gain some secret satisfaction from relating over and over again the tragic history of that exploring party; and if his account was a little disjointed and rambling, it was none the less interesting, and none of the horrors were left out.

When clients appeared, as they did at extremely long-spaced intervals, and he wrote their names in the hotel register, his conversation would always, somehow or other, turn upon that expedition made so many years before.

"No. 49, monsieur? Yes, a quiet room, no noise at all, as it is an inside room. Perhaps you like silence, monsieur; for myself, I prefer a little life about me." And then, his fingers shaking a little on the pen-handle as he entered the number of the room in the ledger before him: "Have you ever walked on soft spongy ground until your feet sank into it and yet made no sound? There is ground like that in the Great Forest, lying north and west of the lakes. Do not go there, monsieur, it is an evil place. A forest of trees and black spongy soil. No animals live there, no birds, no insects — there is only a great darkness and a great silence."

And then perhaps in answer to an enquiry. "Yes. I have been there, monsieur, many years ago, with an expedition. There were fourteen of us. I left the others in the forest, the Great Forest of Silence."

Then again if the client was not in a hurry, and few were who came to the Hotel Blanc, he would relate the history of the expedition, from the time of its setting out from Belgium up to the third week in the Great Forest west and north of the lakes. He never got beyond the third week in the forest; there his voice would falter and sink away into silence, and his eyes take on that peculiarly vacant expression that is characteristic of the mentally unhinged.

"We walked in the forest for three weeks, we counted the days, and tied knots in a piece of string so that we should remember them. Nasta and Goearts only lasted the first week; they died of a fever which quinine and strychnine could not cure. The second week Dupois went mad.

"Have you ever known of vines, monsieur, that come and grip you and drag you down, down, down into spongy mud—great, clinging, crawling vines that wind about your body when you sleep? After we lost Van Brunt to these vines we did not sleep well at night. We sat huddled together, every now and then cutting, chopping, fighting the vines to keep them from enveloping us. We had no fire, the wood was too damp in the forest to make one. We just sat in the darkness and fought the vines.

"They say the forest is haunted, monsieur. The black men believe that the spirits of the dead dwell there. *Qui sait?* We saw no ghosts, but always following us, as we moved forward through the obscurity (for the forest was almost as dark in the day hours as at night), was something. We felt it—felt its breath sometimes on the back of our necks. But we could neither see nor hear it. Pilsot died of fright; he was young, a mere lad, twenty or thereabouts. This is not a land for babes, monsieur. If I might say so, one lives too near to life on the Equator, and when one is young, one has need of a little illusion, is it not so ?"

"No, monsieur, we buried none of them. How could we in that spongy soil ? The black mud swallowed our implements, drew them out of our hands, and if we had not let them go we would also have been dragged down into the mud. So we left them lying on the black earth, our comrades, their eyes open and staring up at us. What else could we do ? And presently the mud would cover them.

"We went on thus for three weeks. Twenty-one days. Yes, we still counted the days, and made knots on our piece of string. And then we felt the shadow, the phantom behind us, grow into many shadows, many phantoms. They were near . . . so near. . . We started to run, but they ran behind us, these phantoms, and we felt that at any moment they would overtake us. Ghosts, spirits, shadows, phantoms, call them what you will, we fled before them into the darkness. And then . . ."

It was here that Papa Grandeau's voice would trail off into nothingness. He would become enigmatical, or suddenly remember his duties as hotel clerk, or merely sit and stare in front of him with eyes that looked as if they would never see anything any more, as they had once, perhaps, seen too much.

Beyond this point in the narrative Papa Grandeau would never go. If he were pressed, if he were recalled to himself, then he would obligingly start the story over again from the very beginning where the expedition had set out so gaily from Antwerp. And the listening hotel client would be left with mouth agape and a cold chill of horror in the region of his spine, to wonder how much of the story was true, and if the ill-fated expedition had actually happened.

If he consulted the hotel manager about the matter afterwards he was never any the wiser, for the manager knew nothing about Papa Grandeau's past ; and besides, it had all happened, if it had happened at all, thirty years ago, and he had only been out in the Congo some four years. There was a forest, somewhere north and west of the lakes, and hunters who came to the hotel spoke ill of it ; but whether this was Papa Grandeau's forest, the hotel manager could not say. For himself, he never went exploring ; he had enough to do to mind the business of the hotel and make it pay, which it never would do with so few travellers upon the river.

So the hotel client would have to remain unsatisfied, and he either forgot Papa Grandeau and his expedition then and there, or continued to puzzle over the account

of it, according to his turn of mind. If it were introspective, then it was quite likely, what with the phantoms and the clinging vines and the black, spongy mud,
that if he got any sleep at all that night, it was broken
by very unpleasant dreams.

TWO women came to the Little River, two black women in calico robes like shrouds, who claimed to have risen from the dead. They had a score or more of followers, all of whom vouched for the authenticity of the women's story. They had watched and waited by the side of the dead women, they said, until finally, one day, they had arisen, gathered up their death-robes about them, and announced their intention of going through the land as prophets, telling of the wonders of the world of the dead. They came from Kongola on the Lualaba River, and were making their way to the lower basin of the Congo.

They held meetings on the banks of the Little River, and gathered more followers about them. They claimed to be able to give everyone a glimpse of the Life Beyond, as they had discovered the secret of slipping in and out of the body whenever they chose, and it was a secret that could be passed on, taught to disciples.

K'Tooma looked askance at their activities. He could bring the dead to life himself if he had a mind to, but it was an expensive undertaking. He had tried it once, but the "dead," whilst awaiting their resurrection, had eaten him out of house and home. He was not minded,

however, to sit by silently and watch these women taking all his followers away from him. He set up a rival
camp of resurrection, and between the two camps and the
excitement they created, the Little River was for a time
in an uproar.

The white residents of Chembi regarded the goings-on
in both camps with amusement; but when a dead child
from the village of Akesi was actually brought to life
by one of the women, they began to be a little wary of
the proceedings, and the Administrator set about finding
a means of suppressing the meetings and driving the
women from the vicinity of the river. This child, having died in the Mission hospital on the hill, had been
carried down from there by the father and, unknown to
the Mission people, taken to the resurrectionists.

The women worked upon him with passes and incantations, until the sweat poured from their bodies, and
after a short space of time, he sat up and started playing
with his black toes, apparently as alive as he had been
before his sojourn in the Mission hospital. For a time,
he seemed to remember nothing of his few hours away
from the body, and then he began chattering of a huge
forest with gigantic trees, trees many times larger than
the ones in the jungle near Akesi.

This conversation of the child (he was a boy about
six years old) was repeated and repeated amongst the
black people, until finally, by the channel of domestic
servants, it reached the ears of the white. They were
horrified to discover, after a day or two, that one of

themselves, Papa Grandeau in fact, was attending the meetings of the black women on the river-bank. He was drawn there, doubtless, by a desire to hear more of this mystic forest where the soul went after death, thinking it might resemble in some way the forest he had known, the Great Forest of Silence, north and west of the lakes.

After the resurrection of the child the meetings of the women were more crowded than ever. Here was tangible evidence that their claims were true. Even the Mission converts came to hear the women preach, and the Missions on both sides of the river saw their attendance falling off, carpentering classes and saving-one's-sins through song and prayer are poor things of interest compared with the supernatural. Letters went to Headquarters in London and to Father Domenique's bishop, and for once the two missions were in complete accord. They saw with amazement their own story being taken right out of their hands, practised, and even improved upon in some respects, and they could do nothing in the matter.

It was through the Mission sources that news of the resurrectionists came to the newspapers of Europe. The Press thought it a good story and so played the matter up. One enterprising paper even went so far as to send a special correspondent out to Africa to investigate the affair. But he never got further than the West Coast, for by the time he arrived there all excitement was over.

The women had drifted away from the Little River, and a new law had been passed, enabling Administrators to disband any resurrection meeting instantly. But one extraordinary piece of news he did obtain for his paper, and that was that, when the women left the Little River, they had taken with them, in their train of disciples, Papa Grandeau.

The old bureau clerk had dressed himself in a long calico robe, put sandals on his feet, and followed in the train of the resurrectionists. He spoke at their meetings, and like the little boy who had come to life by the Little River, he told of a gigantic forest where the trees grew six times as large as any jungle tree yet seen, a forest of great silence, where the souls of the dead dwelt.

Papa Grandeau had at last found an audience large enough to please him and attentive enough to appreciate all that he said. He was happy, completely and entirely happy for the first time in his life.

Papa Grandeau figured as a front page story in one of the daily newspapers of Europe for at least two mornings, under such sensational headings as "Can the dead live again?" and "A voice from beyond." After that, he passed into the *oubliette* of all journalistic sensation, and was heard of no more. But during his brief notoriety he had at least put the Little River on the map, so to speak. Much to his surprise, the Administrator of Chembi woke up one morning to find that his letters of recommendation about the bridge were having some

notice taken of them after all, that, in fact, tenders had
been called for the bridge, and were now under consideration by the government.

The Little River was then subsiding from the uproar
of the past few months. K'Tooma, who for a time had
resurrected obliging satellites at the rate of two a day
(though it had cost him a pretty penny to do it, as each
of the resurrected had demanded a rooster for his services) had retired again to his hut at Akesi, and his less
noxious and less expensive juggling of bones.

The black women in their shroud-like garments had
passed on down the river, singing and chanting as they
went, and once again the two Missions held out hope
of putting their own "resurrection" story across.

A lot of their converts had been lost, for the cortege
of the women was greatly augmented when they came
to leave Chembi, and sadly did the Mission people view
the great caravan of people, with the two women in
white in the lead, cross the plains in the direction of
Luakasi on the Big River. But they had courage and
perseverance, these Mission people, and turning with a
sigh from watching the last of their renegade converts,
they told themselves that in tomorrow there was another
day.

After a month or two of consideration of the tenders
submitted for the building of a bridge across the Little
River in Central Africa, the Belgian Government decided
to accept the tender of an English firm of engineering
contractors, principally because this particular firm had

given instructions to its agent in Antwerp to be free with a certain sum of money that had been placed at his disposal for such occurrences. Notice was sent to the Administrator of Chembi that the bridge would be built almost immediately, and a letter was also received from the firm of engineering contractors who had undertaken the work, Messrs. Smithers, Smithers and Chicot, stating that they were sending one of their firm, "our Mr. Chicot Brown" out to the Little River to report upon transport facilities, and they would be greatly obliged if the Administrator would give him every assistance possible.

News flew through Chembi that a bridge was to be built across the Little River, a bridge of iron, a bridge of permanent worth. Now their settlement was progressing indeed, thought the residents ; soon they would have the railway there.

M'Kato heard of the event of the bridge and remained unmoved. He had seen a town built and a ferry swept away, and he could see a bridge arise in place of that ferry with equanimity. He now scarcely ever spoke, Father Domenique might come and question him, travellers might stop and make inane remarks and black urchins dance derisively in front of him ; whereas once he had spoken, answered questions, beaten the urchins away with his arm stumps, now he neither moved nor spoke. He had achieved, in the long years of his vigil, complete immobility. M'Kato regarded long and earnestly the rosary which hung beside him on the scrubby bush. Many of the beads had been counted, but yet a few remained. He had counted the beads on Father Domenique's rosary with infinite care, always weighing and balancing in his mind whether any event which happened on the Little River was worthy of a counted bead. Now he had come to within four beads of the cross. Yes, the end was very near. He knew no emotion when he thought of the fulfilment of his task, for excitement, emotion of any kind, had long since passed from him, and in its place had come a sense of power and security. It was with this sense of power and peace full upon him, that M'Kato counted a rosary bead for the news of the building of a new bridge; the next he counted when Flore, the courtesan, came to Chembi, and two remained.

FLORE, the courtesan, came to the Little River by the river-boat, the *Prinz Friedrich*. She was a large, fair woman, with flaxen hair (not so flaxen at the roots as elsewhere however), like a cream magnolia in full bloom which the hot wind had already begun to wither a little. She was, apart from the tall orchids growing in the grass by the river, and the little walled-in garden of the Marist Mission, the most exotic thing in Chembi. But although Flore was a flamboyant *cocotte* savouring of the road houses outside Johannesburg, yet there was something large and generous and satisfactory about her. Looking at her, one realised how it was that Brother Joseph had at last come to peace in her arms. And this was what brought Flore to the Little River; to deliver Brother Joseph's dying message to Father Domenique, that he regretted nothing because he had at last found peace.

But Father Domenique felt a little doubtful about this; he would have felt much more satisfied about Brother Joseph's soul, if Brother Joseph had sent his regrets about the roses, but seemingly the brother had had no regrets. It was all most puzzling to Father Domenique, and he regarded Flore with a mild and fatherly curiosity.

Flore had found Brother Joseph in a little Tavern at Lourenço Marques. He was helping the Portuguese barman wash and polish the glasses, but he was ill, dying on his feet, from hunger, from fever, and a blood that burnt too hotly in his veins. With characteristic generosity Flore had taken him home with her to her hot little apartment overlooking the sea. There she nursed him back to a semblance of health, and under her care and attention he lived for another year or two. In the end he died in her arms, with the fire burnt out of his blood and his soul at peace. He wanted Father Domenique to know this, he told Flore, and with his dying breath had given Flore minute instructions as to the whereabouts of the Marist Mission on the hill beside the Little River.

Flore, in keeping her promise to a dying man, found herself one day, after some three months of travel, at Chembi, looking across the river to where the white Marist Mission stood, in all its stately dignity, on the summit of the hill.

But the Little River flowed turbulently between, and there was now no ferryman to take passengers to the other side. Flore crossed the river by foot. A woman who had adventured in the *cafés* of Lourenço Marques found the crossing of a swollen river little to make a fuss about.

Father Domenique received her in his cool study, and was courteous and kind to her, even though he was fully aware of her profession. She made no secret of it. He heard Brother Joseph's message with sadness, and sighed a little for a brother who had died without the last sacrament, however much he had felt at peace in the courtesan's arms. When Flore was about to go, he said to her : "Would you like to see my garden, mademoiselle ?" and taking down a large key which hung on the wall of his study, he led the way out of the Mission building, across the hot school yard, to the little white gate leading to the walled-in garden.

Flore liked the garden. The cool sanctity of the Mission had irritated her, used as she was to the loudness and lewdness of Taverns, but the garden was bright and colourful, and she had always loved flowers. Father Domenique picked a large bunch of white stock and gave them to her ; she thanked him profusely, though she would have preferred the orange and red cannas. Father Domenique was a little childish about some matters ; he thought that the white stock would be cool and sweet in her room, and perhaps lead her back into the ways of prayer and saintliness.

"You will stay perhaps for some little time at Chembi ?" Father Domenique asked Flore, as she was leaving the garden.

Flore thought it possible. She had not expected to find such a large settlement by the Little River, for Brother Joseph had spoken only of the Mission.

"Ah, but we have progressed since then," Father Domenique told her.

The director of the Marist Mission was a childish old man, and a little wilful. He looked round his garden pathetically ; no one had ever appreciated it in quite the same way as Flore.

"Perhaps," he suggested, "you would come and see me again."

Flore laughed good-naturedly. "You can't reform me, *mon père,*" she said.

"I was not thinking of that," replied Father Domenique in his quiet way. "I was thinking merely that you liked the garden so much — there are so few gardens in Chembi — that if you cared to come and sit amongst the flowers at any time, I would be pleased to have you, and it would not," he sought for a suitable phrase, and then added, "disturb the Mission at all."

"Well, you are a quaint one," answered Flore. "I thought at first that you would not receive me."

"We learn to be tolerant here in Central Africa," Father Domenique assured her.

Flore shrugged her ample shoulders, and went out the garden gate with her bouquet of sweet-smelling stock. But she came again to the Mission garden ; she came often, and a strange friendship grew between the courtesan and the gentle old director of the Mission.

The manner of Flore's living was never brought up between them ; only once did she ever refer to it, and that was when she said a little bitterly : "What chance did I have, thrown out of home to work in a factory when I was fourteen ?"

But Father Domenique did not pursue the subject ; instead he called her attention to a new bud that had appeared on one of the Gloire de Dijon bushes. He shewed her also, a little regretfully, the spaces left by the rose bushes that Brother Joseph had destroyed. "I have never been able to fill them, my dear (he called her "my dear" quite naturally as if she were some young relation). "I have written several times about the matter to M. de Conçot" (that was the uncle in Pays Basque) "but he grows old; his memory is not what it was. He has promised many times to send me some more bushes, but they have not come as yet. And I can scarcely mention such things to the bishop."

Flore laughed a little. Never had she come across such a simple and unworldly man as Father Domenique. She took up a protecting and motherly attitude towards him, as if she would ward off from his grey hairs any knowledge of the world that would serve to make them greyer. She wrote also to a friend in Johannesburg, and after some few months, a parcel of rose bushes, all neatly packed in sacking and straw, arrived for her by the *Prinz Friedrich*.

Father Domenique was delighted, and he planted the new bushes with his own hands, placing the soil tenderly about the roots of each, while Flore held the bush in place.

When she left that day, Father Domenique gave her one of his rare and beautiful smiles. "You are making my life very happy, my child. Come again, come again," he said, "do not make your visits rare."

FLORE was also a great success at Madame Boul-boul's Tavern. Flore was the very soul of Taverns, having spent the best part of her life in them. At Madame Boul-boul's she fitted into the scheme of things as if she had always been part and parcel of the place; she sat every night at the corner table next to where Monsieur Lutz and Admiral Delabouche played their game of dominoes, and drank vermouth in little sips. Sometimes one or other of the men from the settlement of Luakasi or Chembi would come and sit with her, and pay for the vermouth, and afterwards for a whisky or two. Flore could consume whisky better than any Scot; she drank it neat, and preferred the fiery liquid that Madame Boul-boul stocked for the benefit of Admiral Delabouche and other old-timers in the Congo, to the milder brands that most of the Tavern *habitués* favoured. The women who came to the Tavern ignored Flore, but the men, without exception, were pleased with her inclusion in the Tavern life. Apart from her calling Flore was a good sport. She was witty and gay, and helped to keep alive a little of the carnival spirit that the youthful Monsieur Brune brought to the Tavern on river-boat nights.

The young philosopher and Flore were instantly

friends. Two strange, bohemian souls thrown together by chance in the midst of a black, untamed land, they found each other congenial. Flore was also friendly with old Admiral Delabouche in a genial companionly way ; they had much in common, for was not Admiral Delabouche also the very soul of Taverns ? One night they matched each other whisky for whisky, but it was Admiral Delabouche who was led away by his friend, Monsieur Lutz, before the end of the evening, whilst Flore went home, not seeing the world any more rosily, in the Administrator's car.

Flore was more friendly with the Administrator than any one. After a time she was recognised as his mistress and had an established place in the community. The ladies did not ignore her quite so much then, for sometimes their husbands desired favours of the Administrator, and Flore was a good-natured go-between. Flore did not live at the Administrator's residence (after all, appearances had to be kept up), but had a room on the first floor of the white-elephant hotel, which was quite appropriately named the Hotel Blanc.

This hotel had been built on the bank of the Little River, in the hope that the passengers by the *Prinz Friedrich* would spend the night there instead of in their hot little cabins on board the boat. But the passengers always preferred to spend the night at Madame Boulboul's, and to cross the plains again in the grey hour of dawn to their hard bunks on the *Prinz Friedrich*. Then they would sleep the long hot day through, with the boat

moving slowly down river to the melody that the pole-
boys sang in her bows, as they prodded their long poles
in the river, searching for treacherous sandbanks or snags
of papyrus that might impede the progress of the boat.

Sometimes a big game hunter stayed at the Hotel Blanc,
sometimes an official sent to Chembi on a visit of inspection, but if it had not belonged to a syndicate it would
never have managed to keep open its doors with so few
clients. There was another hostel for travellers at Chembi,
but as it was in the low quarter of the town, and was run
by a Syrian who was called Mahomet Abdul, though it
was doubtful if that was his real name. Admiral Delabouche lived there, and so did some Arab traders who
bought and sold goods in the Chembi market, but an
official, a big game hunter, or a trading-store clerk never
so much as put his nose inside the door.

One or two Assyrians had come to Chembi. In the
usual way of these people, they arrived one day and the
next were to be seen hanging their eternal carpets and
silk shawls outside a shop door. The Administrator himself did not know how they managed it. Perhaps a servile, ingratiating Assyrian would come to his office one
morning with a pile of hundred franc notes, ready to
buy all the trading licences that the Administrator could
sell, and the next morning, while the Administrator was
still thinking the matter over, the black women were
crowding to buy gaudy shawls from the Assyrian's
bundle. After that, what could the Administrator do,

but weakly take the pile of hundred franc notes and grant the licence ?

The women of Akesi liked the Assyrian shops, and made most of their purchases there ; they became more fully and gaudily dressed, and even indulged in cheap perfumes and soaps. The women at the drinking-booth by the river wore high-heeled shoes, and smothered their black skins with rice powder, in order to do more business. All these things were signs of progress no doubt. In the matter of a few years Chembi had grown from a scattered collection of houses to a flourishing settlement. There were two missions, two hospitals, a bank, an hotel, a market square, a town band, and a fair-haired courtesan. It could almost be called a thoroughly Christian community.

Flore added greatly to the prestige of Chembi. It was something for the Administrator to have a white mistress, and such a genial, lively, good-natured mistress at that. Chembi felt, in this respect alone, greatly superior to the other settlements which graced the banks of the Congo waterways.

Chembi had once been fearful of losing Flore, but that was in the old Administrator's time. Flore, after delivering Brother Joseph's message to Father Domenique, looked about her for a friend of sufficient standing to make it worth her while to remain in Chembi. But the Administrator, the bank manager, and the directors of the trading-stores all had their wives with them and did

not need a mistress.　But then, just as if by a special act
of Providence, when Flore spoke of returning to Lourenço Marques, the Black Master came to the Little
River, and shortly afterwards the Administrator was
found with his throat cut in the bathroom of his own
house.　(Although it might appear somewhat irrelevant
to mention these two incidents together, actually it is not
so, for there was some definite connection between them,
as anyone can see who has chanced to read the journal
kept by M. Lafontaine, the magistrate's clerk, of the daily
happenings at Chembi).　This necessitated a new Administrator for Chembi, and after the passing of the
Black Master from the river, he came, a man, who, being
somewhat younger than the former Administrator, and
having left his wife behind him in Belgium, certainly did
need a mistress, and seeing Flore, gay and gracious, at the
Boul-boul Tavern, cast his eyes upon her.　And so Flore
came to have an established position at Chembi, and river-
boat came and river-boat went, and none carried her
down river on her way back to Lourenço Marques.

As it was undoubtedly the Black Master's visit and its
attendant circumstances that kept Flore at Chembi,
Chembi should have been grateful to the Black Master,
but Chembi was nothing of the sort.　When he disappeared from the Little River after his brief reign there,
the residents of Chembi sought to forget him as speedily
as possible (especially those women over whom he had
obtained something of an ascendancy with his sorcery
and charms), and succeeded in doing so very well.　For

a year or so after his disappearance, if his name were to be mentioned, say at the Boul-boul Tavern, or the Residency, or even over the counter of one of the trading-stores, it did not call to mind anything more than a vague recollection of the man. Ah, yes, a big negro, who sold charms and things, was all that Chembi could remember of the Black Master, and his reign upon the banks of the Little River.

But there was one very definite record of his visit and that was in M. Lafontaine's history of Chembi. In the last entry, entitled *A Survey of the Black Arts,* there is a critical commentary on the Black Master and his sorcery, and as the information appears to have been obtained by M. Lafontaine at first hand, by close observation of the Black Master and his cult, it is doubtless true and worthy of some attention, both as a record of the man's visit and a study of his arts.

M. LAFONTAINE'S history of Chembi was written in the form of a diary, and was called *Observations on, and the Progress of White Civilisation in Central Africa*. It was written clearly, concisely, with no nonsense about it, as became one who was a government clerk. A cold, dry chronicle of events as M. Lafontaine saw them day by day, and night by night, from the window of the magistrate's office where he was chief clerk, or from that of his own home, a squat little wooden bungalow not a stone's throw away.

Every evening, when M. Lafontaine left the magistrate's office, he hurried home to take down the thick black-covered exercise-book from the top shelf of the corner cupboard in his living-room and make an entry in it. He had no idea what was going to become of this diary eventually. He thought of leaving it, perhaps, as a legacy to his grandchildren (as yet unborn, his only child, a daughter, being still at school in Brussels) or of presenting it to the archives of some museum. Unfortunately there was no museum in his native town, and his ambition did not aspire to the archives of the National Museum at Brussels or Antwerp; something smaller and more intimate he would have liked, some place where the custodian took a personal interest in all manuscripts, and dusted them with his own hands. He liked to think of his diary being handled carefully, and read occasionally with due appreciation.

"Ah, yes, this was written by a man who went to the Congo in the early days. A valuable history ; it shews how we have progressed in our colonies. For example, 1927, October 30, talk of a railway being built from Kongola, 1929, January 16, electric-light poles erected at Chembi."

M. Lafontaine took extraordinary care to be exact in every detail, and he tried always to keep his own thoughts and opinions out of the diary, but sometimes they crept in unawares and gave a flavour of philosophy to it, of which Monsieur Lafontaine was totally unaware.

One extract read :

In observing the wild life about one, one is struck by the boundless vitality displayed, in direct contrast with the ever-increasing Robot-like creations of the white man. The dances of the negroes, the leaping of the animals in the forests, on the plains, the restless energy of the myriad insects in the air at dusk, the exuberant growth of vine and foliage in the jungle — in all these is displayed the same amazing vitality ; nowhere in nature does one find fatigue.

And another, this entry of the latest date :

There are black clerks in the stores who write in tidy round handwriting and column figures with agility. Automobiles travel on the dusty streets, and there are electric-light poles lying in the gutters ready to be erected at any moment. Chembi might be said to be progressing, expanding ; already the plains are being encroached upon for the erecting of more houses. But the jungle remains untouched. Men appear to be afraid of the jungle, few care to enter its depths. . .

Here Monsieur Lafontaine had laid down his pen. "Men appear to be afraid of the jungle. . ."

The introduction of the jungle into his diary somehow disturbed the even tenor of Monsieur Lafontaine's writing ; for a night or two afterwards, he could not settle down to it. After he returned from the office and had partaken of supper, the hours that he usually devoted to the recording of the day's events in the black-covered exercise-book, were devoid of inspiration. It was as if the jungle, looming darkly outside his window, forbade him to say anything more about it.

He returned from the office on the third night, with the determination that tonight there was to be no more waste time ; he would continue with his usual care and austerity the writing of Little River history. He would leave the jungle entry unfinished, and begin upon the traffic in intoxicants and their influence upon the black people. He had just come from bailing out of jail his cook-boy for the third time that week. The cook, having gone to the hotel for his master's beer, had drunk half of it on the way home, and had been promptly taken up by a native policeman, who must have been hovering in the vicinity when Mwengo was partaking of the beer, unless he had challenged him afterwards as he passed through the town, and insisted upon smelling his breath.

Monsieur Lafontaine, after paying the cook-boy's bail, and promising to come into court next day and say a few words on his behalf, felt that the subject of intoxicants would be an excellent one to comment upon that evening in his book, and so went home in a tranquil frame of mind.

It was the end of the wet season, and a breath of drought was already driving in from the plains. The grasshoppers creaked away in the short grass by the roadside, and in the swamp-lands by the river, the frogs croaked in hushed voices of their vanishing love-dreams.

From the river, purpling in the gathering dusk, rose up scarlet-winged flamingoes, in a long streak of sunset against the pale sky. Now the rains were over, they were going back to the eastern lake where they lived, ate, and died in a little incarnadined civilisation of their own, visiting once a year rivers and other lakes, like so many Rotarians on holiday, taking leave from their business for the moment, in order to see the world. Night came across the plains ; the darkness grew softer, more mellow, dropping down upon the river like a curtain of thick-piled plush. Insects circled in the air and flew in at open doorways, to dash themselves to death against bright lamp-globes. An owl too-whooed in a melancholy voice, and somewhere on a tree-bough in the jungle against a round yellow moon, an old monkey sat, telling stories to scornful youngsters of past and better days in the forest.

But, in Chembi, in the living-room of a squat wooden bungalow, M. Lafontaine sat writing his history of the Little River. In his thin, sloping handwriting he wrote :

It is evident that the use of intoxicating liquors would have a very demoralising effect upon the negro. As it is now, with the sale prohibited to any black person, the negro manages to obtain liquor surreptitiously.

But later, much later that night, after he had gone to bed and was sleeping calmly between cool linen sheets, the hot, exotic scent of the jungle came right up to the town of Chembi. It pervaded the streets, and found its way into the little wooden house where M. Lafontaine slept, and disturbed his dreams. He saw a river flowing darkly, and a moon above it fiery red. He saw the gleam of fishermen's fires in the velvet darkness and heard the wailing song of the women about them.

"A big fish, a big fish,
    They have caught a big silver fish like the moon."

Where purple-flowered vines covered the river-banks with their trailing foliage, black women dipped their babies in and out of the water. On the far plains, animals galloped like the passing visions in some weird fantasy. The old chief of Akesi sat in front of his hut, with his archers and spearmen about him, and throb-

throb, throb-throb went the hunting-drums. Women danced, a goat squealed, chickens fluttered and squawked in cages. All the turbulent, unbridled, crazy things came to upset his dreams. And M. Lafontaine, awaking in the cold, clear light of morning, had a feeling that he had lived through the true saga of the Little River in his sleep, and that now he had forgotten it again.

He left his bed and went to the window ; pulling aside the window curtains he gazed out into the street to see if the white topee was still playing its mountebank part.

Grey, flat-faced and ugly were the houses of Chembi in the too-clear light of morning. The dust came up in little clouds, raised by the breeze that was passing through the streets. In the gutters, like fallen soldiers in white tunics, lay the electric-light poles ready at any moment to be erected. Dogs were barking all over the town. A sleepy cock crowed in the Baptist Mission fowl-house. The young Russian count, who worked in the A.M.T. Stores, and the wife of M. Pinquot came up from the river, walking close together and hand in hand. Through the streets, in single file, like a procession, came the black women, who had slept in the white men's beds. Dong, dong, dong went the Marist Mission bell for prayers. And away in the distance, etched against the light sky, was the jungle of which man was afraid.

M. Lafontaine, going to the corner cupboard in his living-room, took down the thick black exercise-book in which he was writing his book, *Observations on, and Progress of White Civilisation in Central Africa.* Opening it at his last entry, he carefully ruled out with red ink that which he had written the night before. In its stead, in his thin, old-fashioned hand-writing, he wrote : "It is not the jungle of which man should be afraid but his fellow-man."

IF convention had not required that M. Lafontaine's daughter be provided with a dowry, it is certain that M. Lafontaine would not have chosen a colonial life. In his native land he would have been, perhaps, a librarian or a schoolmaster, who retired early from his profession and spent the rest of his life amongst the musty remains of pig-skin covered volumes. One could imagine him in an old-fashioned house with pointed gables, at the end of a narrow street, in some little town. Inside the house everything would have been neat and orderly — chairs with stiff, high backs and carved elbows at each side, high cupboards and old oak chests all going crick-crack, crick-crack, as if they had stiff joints like rheumatic old people.

But Madame Lafontaine (since deceased) was an ambitious woman, who wished to see her daughter married well, and for that a dowry was necessary, a dowry of the dimensions that no schoolmaster's salary could ever provide. The salary of a magistrate's clerk in the Colonies, however, was twice that of a home-keeping teacher or librarian, sufficient indeed, with careful management, to provide a *dot* that would marry a daughter into one of the best families. Madame Lafontaine, when her daughter was some few months old, set about finding such a

position for her husband. M. Lafontaine, being a con-
scientious father, placed his dreams behind him, and took
the colonial position when it was found for him, making
no moan about his fate afterwards, and only vaguely
regretful for the pleasant and peaceful life that he had
missed.

That he took a certain amount of interest in Colonial
life was evinced by his attempt at writing a history of the
settlement of Chembi ; but though at times he seemed to
have illuminating flashes of insight into the shoddiness of
life in this settlement, he never became quite at home
there. He was an exemplary citizen, but he always
seemed to hold himself a little aloof from the rest ; he
was regarded in the settlement as something of a recluse,
especially after the advent of the Black Master.

The Black Master came to the Little River and left it
again, all in the space of a few months. He reigned
there for a brief period, and then disappeared as completely as if he had never existed, to be forgotten by all
almost immediately. By all ? No, for M. Lafontaine
remembered him ; he had cause to remember him to his
dying day. After the end of the Black Master's brief season of power, he withdrew himself entirely from the
social life of Chembi ; he went no more to the Boul-boul
Tavern, and spent longer and longer hours upon the
writing of his diary. Old friends sought to rouse him
out of himself ; they would drop in casually after office
hours, but he was always engaged upon making an entry

in the thick black-covered exercise-book which contained his diary, and appeared to dislike being disturbed.

He could never be induced to talk of the Black Master, even during that period when, just after his disappearance, he formed the main topic of interest in the conversation of Chembi.

M. Dechaineaux, the manager of the Banque du Congo Belge, tried him, Trader Voss tried him, as well as one of the directors (then passing through Chembi) of the white-elephant hotel, indeed all those who had been interested in the expulsion of the Black Master from Chembi. But he merely agreed with them, "Yes, it was a good thing that the man had gone, a very good thing. It had all turned out quite satisfactorily," whilst impatiently tapping with his pen upon the exercise-book, as if he wished the conversation to end there, as he must get on with his writing. They thought it curious, as he, being in the magistrate's office, would keep the file of records about the man, and thus must necessarily know more about him than they did. But try as they might, M. Lafontaine could never be drawn out upon the subject of the Black Master.

The coming of the Black Master to the Little River was an event, but an event that, at the time of his coming, passed unnoticed. He must have come to Chembi by the river-boat, and landed quietly amongst the teeming throng of black people with their crying babies and bleating goats, for the citizens of Chembi were suddenly aware

of his presence in their midst without realising how he
came to be there. He was a fine figure of a man, a tall,
upstanding negro from the Gold Coast, suave, educated,
clad always in immaculate white. He had been educated,
he said, on the Continent, and it appeared that his education had been good, for he had a sound knowledge of
the classics. But this knowledge did not apparently stop
him from dabbling in the black arts of his own race, for
he made and sold charms. Love charms, he said they
were, and many of the black women of Akesi bought
them, and even some of the white women of Chembi.
Senhora Fernandez wore one openly upon her neck, but
then the Senhora could scarcely be termed white in the
true sense of the word. She was generally supposed to
be Portuguese, but there was a healthy doubt ; her skin
was more coffee-coloured than swarthy, and her hair
might have had a suspicious kink in it, if it had not been
so carefully oiled.

This tall negro who sold charms called himself the
Black Master, a master, he explained, in the art of love.
And so he became known on the Little River, too well-
known in fact ; from arriving unobtrusively by the river-
boat and living quietly at Mahomet Abdul's hostelry, his
presence came to be felt in Chembi. He seemed to domi-
nate the Little River. His tall, well-set-up figure was
everywhere. He was no ordinary nigger ; there was, as
a matter of fact, something a little unwholesome about
him ; the atmosphere seemed debased, polluted, like
mixed blood, when he passed. People in Chembi grew

uneasy about him, and spoke of his removal, but there was no actual reason for it. He preached no doctrine, stirred up no strife ; the love-charms he sold seemed to be harmless, but day by day he became more aggressive. He grew contemptuous of the white women whom at first he had coaxed to buy his charms ; he laughed insolently at the white men as he passed them in the streets. He openly boasted that he was soon to become a power in the land ; he would be the next Administrator of Chembi, he said, and after that Governor of the Province.

Several of the residents of Chembi demanded that the Administrator deport him ; they even went so far as to send a petition to the Governor of the Province Oriental, to this effect, but the Governor replied that the matter would be referred to Brussels. That, of course, meant considerable delay, whilst the Black Master's presence was becoming more and more intolerable. The captain of the *Prinz Friedrich* brought news of him from down river ; he had passed through other settlements and had done no good there. He seemed to be possessed of some extraordinary power, especially over women, yet no definite charge could ever be brought against him. There were rumours enough about his ways on the Little River, but they were all based upon surmise and could never be proved. Senhora Fernandez's name was coupled with his, and it was said, that, like K'Tooma, together they held ju-ju rites at the full of the moon. But accuse the Black Master of holding ju-ju rites, and at the next full moon he would be lounging on Madame Boul-boul's

verandah, drinking vermouth and beating time with
his large hands to the rhythm of the dance music. He
was as slippery as an eel ; there was nothing to be done
but watch him closely. The Senhora had brought him
to Madame Boul-boul's, in the days of his first coming to
the river. The other clientele of the Tavern did not like
his presence there, but they could not openly object. He
came in a little yellow car which he drove with the ease
of long association ; he was as well-dressed, if not better,
than any of them, and his manners were delightful. He
seemed to keep his aggressiveness for the open street ; at
the Tavern, he was a courteous, simple-minded gentleman.
The *habitués* of the Tavern shrugged their shoulders and
put up with him ; his huge black presence put some of
them off their drinks at first, but they soon became used
to him.

M. LAFONTAINE, strolling through the main street of Chembi, encountered the Black Master. The man was walking with his usual insolent bearing, and laughed openly at M. Lafontaine as he passed. M. Lafontaine's gorge rose; the man was nothing but an insolent braggart, but some deeper instinct told him that the man was more than just that. He was unwillingly impressed with a sense of the negro's power, his importance upon the Little River. Hitherto he had been contemptuous of the man and his charms. In his opinion he was a long-winded braggadocio, and his charms merely harmful to foolish women; but encountering him in the street, and the negro keeping to the footpath and leaving M. Lafontaine to take to the roadway, he had to revise this opinion. The man's charms, his sorcery, might be a lot of nonsense, but the man himself was a menace; he was not without personality, force of character, and doubtless he had a better (or a worse) reason for being at Chembi than just to sell his love-charms. M. Lafontaine saw him as a danger to the white civilisation that was being built up by the Little River. The man was frankly black, and his name, the Black Master, seemed to indicate power, leadership, and things perhaps even less savoury.

Let him have his way by the Little River, and the civilisation that they cherished there would be swept away, all the work of the pioneers would go for naught ; M. Lafontaine's diary, even, would be useless, for Chembi, as a white settlement, would be no more.

M. Lafontaine thought deeply about the matter as he walked towards his home. He walked slowly and meditatively, and several times passed his small bungalow before finally turning and entering its doorway. On his third time through the streets of Chembi, at the corner of one of the intersecting byways, he saw the Black Master's tall upstanding figure in the distance ; he was leaving the settlement and going towards the marshes.

It was almost dusk and seemed a strange hour for anyone to visit the marshland. The man would have to be watched, got rid of, in fact. Some of the residents of Chembi had already held a meeting about the matter and talked of direct action, but that was dangerous with the new laws for the protection of negroes ; something more sly, more subtle, was required. The man must be frightened from the river. All negroes were superstitious ; perhaps his superstition could be worked upon in some way.

As M. Lafontaine entered his own doorway, he turned to glance back to where the marshlands lay, brown and deserted, outside the town boundary. But this night there were dancing lights upon them. The lights were more than just the lumination from a colony or colonies of glow-worms. They flared and flickered, flamed up

and then died down again, and were red and yellow and
blue by turns, according to whether their flames were
ascending to the Heavens, burning steadily, or merely
sinking away into the brown morass. It was more likely
that they were the uncertain light of fires lit upon the
damp earth.

M. Lafontaine called his house-boy and pointed to the
lights. He had never seen them before on the marshes,
he said. What were they ? But the boy appeared too
frightened to reply. He would go and investigate the
matter, M. Lafontaine announced briefly, but the house-
boy's hair rose in fear. He begged his master not to go
near the marshes ; bad things went on there, he said.
He knew, but he dare not tell.

What did he know ? M. Lafontaine demanded.
Were the lights anything to do with that new black man
who had come to the Little River, the man who sold
charms ? But the boy obstinately refused to answer.

The Black Master had been heading in the direction
of the marshes when M. Lafontaine had seen his figure
in the distance. It seemed significant. M. Lafontaine
went into his house. It was a bad business altogether ;
he shook his head over it, and he was more convinced
than ever that the man (he could not use the term Black
Master even to himself, for the words stuck in his throat)
was both a nuisance and a menace. It was evident that
now the black people were frightened of him and his
works. He had to be got rid of, although M. Lafontaine
was not able to see at the moment how it was to be done,

not under the existing law anyway. It would have to be done under the old primitive law of the end justifying the means, if it was to be done at all. The other residents of Chembi seemed incapable of acting — acting in such a manner, at any rate — as instanced by their dilly-dallying after the meeting on the man's expulsion. It might mean that he would have to act individually in the matter, M. Lafontaine felt ; that is, if the danger continued.

He neglected the usual entry in his diary that evening to sit with his head in his hands, cogitating upon the matter. He had once, when a boy, gone into the methods of the necromancers of Italy in the fifteenth century. One, Pietro, il Diavolo, had intrigued him immensely, for he had made his enemies disappear in a surprising and unaccountable fashion. Pietro, il Diavolo had not been scrupulous as to the methods he had used ; he had gained his name by his oft-repeated maxim : "When you want to oust the devil, you must use the devil's ways."

M. Lafontaine remembered how he and some school-boy companions had tried out Pietro, il Diavolo's rites, or what they could make of them, in the garret one wet afternoon. They had been fairly successful in their efforts, and had succeeded in frightening themselves rather badly. In his mind's eye he saw the garret, hung about with dusty cobwebs, and ill-lit by a broken skylight. A rooster was there, hanging head downwards from a rafter, and a wooden crucifix, painted black, swung to and fro from its beak. In a ring sat the schoolboys about a fire that burned badly because the shavings were damp.

He saw the same schoolboys shortly afterwards, running for their lives through the village streets, their eyeballs bulging from their sockets with fear. It had all been a lot of nonsense, but certainly they had produced —well, one could call it results.

M. Lafontaine left off ruminating upon the past and came back to the present, the actual—the menace, for instance, of the man called the Black Master. He remembered again the queer rumours that were afloat about him, of his power with women, the Senhora Fernandez, his name had been openly coupled with hers ; but now it was said that the Administrator's wife was impressed with him, that he visited her occasionally at the Residency. He thought that, in a case like this, Pietro, il Diavolo's maxim seemed very appropriate, could be acted upon in fact. He disliked disturbing the peaceful and well-ordered condition of his life, but it seemed a public duty. He decided that he must once again make a study of—well, Magic (he disliked the word immensely) but go into it more thoroughly than he had done as a schoolboy, for now he had a definite purpose in view, an end that had to be achieved.

THE affair of the Black Master did not assume any serious proportions until the Administrator was found one morning in his bathroom with his throat cut. Then the residents of Chembi remembered the Black Master's boast, and an uneasy feeling came upon them that perhaps there might have been something in it after all, especially when the Black Master removed his baggage from Mahomet Abdul's to the Residency, seemingly with the full consent of the Administrator's widow. He seemed to have obtained a complete ascendancy over her, and was seen with her everywhere, until her brother-in-law came from the Lower Congo and took her, some said by main force, with him down river to his home.

The Residency then was empty save for the Black Master, who lounged on the front verandah for the best part of the day, and otherwise seemed to make himself thoroughly at home there. The magistrate issued an order of ejection, and M. Lafontaine served the notice in person. The Black Master received him with courtesy, thanked M. Lafontaine for his attention, offered to shew him round the garden where the dahlias were just coming into bloom, and quietly tore the magistrate's notice in two. M. Lafontaine came away more than ever impressed with the man's personality, his power.

M. Lafontaine had, for some time, been pursuing his investigations into Magic. He disliked the business greatly, but he saw very clearly, as he left the Residency, that he must see it through to the bitter end. His investigations took up a great deal of his time ; he now very seldom wrote in his diary at night, and also he asked for several afternoons off from the office, during which he made expeditions to the village of Akesi, to the hut of K'Tooma, the witch doctor. He always came away from these visits with a greater distaste than ever for his self-imposed task.

At first K'Tooma had politely intimated that he was powerless to help him, but afterwards, when M. Lafontaine had produced a handful of silver coins, he had changed his views and expressed a willingness to be of some assistance. Later K'Tooma came frequently to Chembi to buy at the trading-stores, and the store clerks wagged their heads over the amount of his spending ; he seemed to have suddenly become enormously rich.

On one of M. Lafontaine's visits to his hut K'Tooma gave him a charm, a weird arrangement of cock's feathers and human hair. M. Lafontaine gingerly carried it home in his coat pocket ; he hated the thing about him, for it seemed alive to his touch. This, he told himself, was imagination, but still the idea persisted. He put the charm on the mantelshelf of the living-room, and when his house-boy saw it there next day he left the house hurriedly, and nothing M. Lafontaine could say or do would induce him to return.

After that black men rather avoided him ; they appeared afraid of him for no apparent reason, and he had great difficulty in getting a house-boy to work for him at all. He had to offer the most exorbitant wages, and then they did not stay very long.

At night, instead of writing in his diary, he drew designs in coloured chalks upon the living-room table, but he was always careful to rub out these patterns if he heard the step of any of his friends coming to his house, though he seemed careless enough about his house-boy seeing them.

Meanwhile the residents of Chembi were waiting for the Governor of the Province Oriental to send a posse of soldiers to eject the Black Master from the Administrator's residence. But it seemed that it was not going to be so easy. One morning the magistrate said to M. Lafontaine, upon his entering the office : "Hark ye, that nigger is up to no good ; he went to the Administrator's office this morning, and demanded the correspondence. The clerks turned him out bodily, by force, and he was rather badly mauled. There will be trouble over it, for he has already lodged a complaint with me about the matter, and you know the law here ; the complaint will have to go through."

M. Lafontaine nodded. That afternoon he sent the Black Master's complaint through with the other correspondence to Brussels. It was quite safe to do so, he felt, for by the time the letter reached Brussels the Black Master would have left the Little River. M. Lafontaine had now finished his investigations into magic ; he felt quite sure of his knowledge, and was prepared to act upon it. That afternoon he closed the office earlier than usual, and went to his home ; his house-boy having left in his absence, the place was deserted.

M. Lafontaine felt that it was better so, and set about making such preparations as were necessary. By the time he had finished, dusk had fallen, and a full moon was rising above the hard line of jungle on the other side of the river. Away where the marshlands stretched, brown and deserted, along the river-bank, lights were dancing, as they had danced now for many a night. M. Lafontaine had watched these lights for some considerable time, but as yet he had not ventured near enough to know their cause, although he could make a fairly shrewd guess as to what they were. But now, going out of his house doorway, and closing the door sharply behind him, he turned his steps in the direction of the marshland. He was going to the patch of dark, dank morass to obtain a closer view of the lights upon it ; for that, and other things which he refused to think about, as he stepped briskly through the streets of Chembi.

He felt very calm and confident of success, and noticed with approval how the black men ran from him as he passed. But although he walked at a brisk, even pace, and his thoughts were positive and serene, on his thin, sensitive face was the expression of one who is suffering acute pain. He had, certainly, suffered greatly in the few weeks that were just past, but that suffering had now left him, although his face still bore traces of it. He had not realised that his agony of mind would mark him so, until that morning when he had looked into the mirror at shaving-time. He had promptly turned the mirror to the wall, so that he should not see himself again. It was better so, for the face that had peered at him from the looking-glass had not been his — there had been something almost negroid in the intensity of its expression. He had always been just a little vain of his good looks, but he knew that they had been destroyed for ever. If he came through the ordeal that was ahead of him, it would be with his identity impaired; he felt that he would be no longer Hyacinthe Lafontaine after his encounter with the Black Master and his satellites on the marshlands.

But now that feeling was passing and, as he strode along, he was becoming once again the magistrate's clerk with correct, if slightly pernickety ways — that is his inner self, but the shell, the body that encased his spirit, would never be the same. He thought that he might cast it from him later on and go free, leaving the wrecked body to be inhabited by a spirit of a different quality — one definitely more evil than his own.

As he drew near the marshes M. Lafontaine heard noises that fell strangely upon his ear. In the mating season the marshes were always eerie with the cry of birds, for curlews came to the swamps at dusk, and the tall, solemn secretary birds, but this was not the mating-season, and the noises that reached M. Lafontaine were from other throats than those of birds. When he came within the rays of the dancing lights, which he had guessed rightly were fires burning upon the morass, he could see that black men were huddled together in one gigantic ring, and that they were all chanting and clapping their hands in a rhythm that was wild, exotic, and meant to stir the blood.

In the centre of these men stood the Black Master, a handsome enough figure with the fitful light of the fires playing upon the ebony of his naked body. There was something hung about his neck, upon a long chain; it swung out from his body as he swayed to the rhythm of the clapping men. M. Lafontaine wondered if it was a crucifix, and if it was painted black, like the one they had used that time in the garret. He wondered also if the Black Master saw him, for he must have been a conspicuous figure, in his white suit, with the glare of the fires upon him.

It mattered little if he did. Suddenly he felt a great contempt for the man and his pettifogging love-charms; they were as nothing beside his greater and more powerful knowledge. He stepped into the circle of swaying black bodies and began to chant, but he chanted in perverse rhythm, against the black men, against the powerful negro who was swaying in their midst.

THE next day M. Lafontaine was absent from the magistrate's office; he was absent for several succeeding days, and when he came again he stated briefly that he had been ill. This was borne out by his appearance, for he looked wan and haggard, as if he had had many sleepless nights. The magistrate suggested a short holiday, but M. Lafontaine obstinately set about his work; a holiday, he asserted, was the last thing that he required, for it would give him too much time in which to think.

During the day M. Dechaineaux, the manager of the Banque du Congo Belge, stopped M. Lafontaine in the street. Had he heard the news? The Black Master had disappeared; the posse of soldiers had come from Stanleyville, but they had found the Residency empty. It was certain that the man was not in Chembi. Doubtless he had become frightened and had left the Little River; one hoped, for good, said M. Dechaineaux.

M. Lafontaine agreed.

It had all turned out very satisfactorily; they were rid of the man and without much trouble.

Again M. Lafontaine agreed.

They were celebrating his departure that night at the

Tavern ; was M. Lafontaine coming ? But the magistrate's clerk shook his head. He thought not, he had some work to do, writing up his diary as a matter of fact ; he had neglected it of late.

He parted from M. Dechaineaux rather abruptly, and went on down the street. Yes, he told himself, it had all turned out very satisfactorily, that was the correct word to use. M. Dechaineaux had been a little doubtful about the Black Master's possible return, but M. Lafontaine knew that he had indeed gone for good. The last time he had seen the man his satellites had been tearing him limb from limb.

M. Lafontaine wondered if he had not acted rather precipitately in the matter, now that the posse of soldiers was there. But upon consideration he concluded not, for although the soldiers might have ejected the Black Master from the Residency, and perhaps, even driven him from the river, his power, his influence, would have remained. Now that was broken for ever. There would never be his black rule upon the Little River, white civilisation would go on, progress as it had always done, and M. Lafontaine could continue to record it in his diary.

But, when he came to write in his diary, he found that he could not do so. His mind was disturbed, and the subjects he chose seemed irrelevant, out of keeping with the state of his feelings. He had a distressful sensation that, despite his triumph over the Black Master, white civilisation for him had been overthrown ; his mind was filled with black, primitive things. He could not even record properly that the eiectric-light poles had been put up in the streets of Chembi, though he tried to do so many times, and at length succeeded in making an unusually curt entry about the matter. But there were other things that he could write, he found after a time, savage, exotic things, which took much thinking out before they could be written down in the manner in which he was accustomed to write, dry and impartial — a mere chronicle of facts. He had to spend a longer and longer time with his diary to do this properly. Friends dropped in upon him, but he was always at his writing, and seemed to resent their coming. He now looked after himself entirely, as no house-boy would enter his bungalow. The black men eyed him askance in the streets when he walked abroad.

White men came to regard him curiously, too ; he felt vaguely annoyed about it, and more and more withdrew into his bungalow, and stayed there with closed doors. Rumours began to circulate about him, unpleasant rumours ; it was said that the Senhora Fernandez was frequently at his house at night-time, and after her open association with the Black Master that was not pleasant. When the magistrate spoke to M. Lafontaine about it, he did not deny the charge. The senhora, he said, was a clever woman. He liked her company.

M. Lafontaine's hours at the office became fitful, and when spoken to about it he did not mend his ways. Finally, after not having seen him for several days, the

magistrate called at his home, and upon getting no reply
to his knock, opened the door and entered the tiny house.

M. Lafontaine was seated at the living-room table, apparently engaged upon writing in his diary. Over the
table, suspended from the hanging lamp, hung a dead
rooster, and from its beak, swung a wooden crucifix,
painted black. But when the magistrate glanced curiously at this crucifix, he saw that the figure upon it was
not that of the Christ, but of a woman, contorted and
swaying grotesquely upon her hips.

The magistrate laid his hand upon his clerk's shoulder.
"Lafontaine," he said sharply.

M. Lafontaine looked up from his writing. "I cannot
make an entry," he said in a tired, querulous voice, "I
have written nothing for days." Then after a long
period of hesitation, he spoke again. "I feel that my
skin is turning black," he said.

By the next river-boat came a clerk from Leopold-
ville to relieve M. Lafontaine of his duties in the magistrate's office, and M. Lafontaine went home on leave to
Belgium. The residents of Chembi subscribed his pas-
sage money between them, as it was found, when his
affairs were looked into, that he was practically penniless.
Every franc, even, of the *dot* that he had been so carefully putting by for his daughter had been spent in some
unknown and unprecedented manner during the preced-
ing few weeks.

The diary M. Lafontaine was writing was left in
Chembi ; he seemed to have taken such an aversion to

it that it was deemed best not to pack it with his other belongings, but to leave it in the Administrator's office, where, later on, it would be useful as a reference book for anyone who wished to know something of the early history of Chembi. It was never much sought after in this respect, but in after years one or two investigators of Magic consulted its pages, and perused with judicious care the last entry of all, which dealt with the Black Master and his craft. It was interesting, they said, but not infallible. And it was a pity that it was not complete. It would have been interesting to know what was the outcome of M. Lafontaine's association with the Portuguese woman, Senhora Fernandez, if she gave away any secrets to the magistrate's clerk, and if, above all, she told him the meaning of the combination of the tail feathers of a cock with a woman's hair, for that was a puzzle which had employed the minds of investigators of necromancy for many centuries.

THE last entry in M. Lafontaine's diary, although it was entitled a "Survey of the Black Arts," did not deal with Magic in all its branches, but only with that cult particular to negroes, or those of semi-negro origin, which is known as *ju-ju,* the blackest of all the arts grouped together under the one broad name of Magic.

This entry was written in M. Lafontaine's usual dry and impartial style, and ran as follows :

Prevailed upon, not by the advice or suggestions of my friends, but rather by the fact that it appeared to me a public duty, I have engaged myself upon a most difficult task, which is now completed. I have made, during the past few weeks, a thorough investigation of the black art of ju-ju.

I wish that those who may read this could know how unwillingly I undertook the task, as then I might the more readily escape the imputation of a black mind, which will doubtless be said of me, when I have shewn what power and potency lies in this black man's craft. There have been many books written upon the subject of sorcery, especially during the fifteenth century in Europe, when necromancy flourished amongst the French and Italians, but all these books are more or less imperfect, incomplete, for they do not explain, in so many words, just how the power used by the necromancers is developed. It has been left for me to add this touch then to the knowledge that we already have, and so bring the records of the Black Arts, I shall not say to completion, for there is still much more that I have to learn, but at least out of the sphere of the supernatural to a comprehensive science, that can be grasped by an ordinary mind.

One Pietro, il Diavolo, a necromancer of Italy in the time of the Medici, records the fact that it is a very simple thing to take away a man's soul, and in despair afterwards, he will either commit suicide, or his body will crumble to dust, for a body without a soul is a vacuum, and a vacuum, above all else, is abhorrent to nature. I have obtained information from one K'Tooma, a witch doctor of the Akesi tribe, living about four kilometres from the Little River, that this is also a common practice in these parts and these times. K'Tooma states that he would be very willing to demonstrate this art upon the person of Muronga, the chief of his tribe, with whom he is always in bitter feud, but Muronga is wily, and will not use the women of his seraglio who are under his, K'Tooma's, thumb.

The deduction must be made, then, that this drawing of the soul away from the body is accomplished by a woman, or perhaps, women, under the mesmeric sway of someone well versed in the black arts. Probably the action takes place at cohabitation.

Soon after my obtaining certain information from K'Tooma, and working out the only possible solution of the matter, an excellent illustration of this practice occurred in Chembi. For some time there has been among us a negro calling himself the Black Master. This negro is a seller of love-charms and such-like symbols of the devil, and made, upon his arrival, the open boast that he would be the next Administrator of Chembi. It is now but a few weeks since our Administrator committed suicide, and the Black Master lives at the Residency in close commune with the Administrator's wife. It is rumoured that even before the Administrator's death, he had gained a certain ascendancy over her and was doubtless her paramour. In the light of what has already been written, the Administrator's death cannot greatly be wondered at, however much it may be regretted.

THE Black Master was a man of remarkable personality. I speak of him in the past tense, for since writing the above, the Black Master is no more, his presence no longer pollutes the atmosphere of the Little River ; he has become the victim of his own black craft.

One was always impressed, upon encountering the man, by a sense of his extraordinary power ; he was, to all intents and purposes, Nietzsche's Superman, and seemed to hold a sway, for no apparent reason, over all who came in contact with him.

It is interesting to note how his power was developed, and to surmise to what use he intended it should be put.

It is customary amongst the Arabs, I believe, for the chief of a tribe to keep in his tents a great number of virgins, some two or three hundred perhaps, and to use these maidens upon public occasions of festivity, to give proof of his strength and powers of endurance to his followers ; he de-flowering some ten or twelve virgins without fully performing the sexual act.

This, according to ancient Arab writings, tends to develop power both of will and physique in the performer, and is executed solely for that purpose.

But it seems that there can be even a deeper meaning to this rite when it is performed amongst the negro tribes. By dint of bribery, and also as K'Tooma has a distinct enmity for the Black Master, being jealous of the man's power, and wishing him to depart from the Little River, I elicited from the Akesian witch doctor that the de-flowering of virgins was used by the Black Master at his ceremonies, but the virgins were afterwards kept for other uses, instead of, as in the case of the Arabs, being retained as concubines in the chief's harem. What uses he would not say, but wagging his head wisely, he announced that the power to create was a mighty power, and when it could not create, when it was debarred, by some imposition placed upon it, from its proper work, it turned upon itself and destroyed.

Is it then that in the de-flowering of virgins without permitting them the satisfaction of creation, their creative force, in a disgruntled and dissatisfied intensity, begins to destroy ? But destroy what ? Is it not possible that under hypnotic influence this unsatisfied urge could be directed to destroy in whatever manner the hypnotist indicated ?

This surmise is open to argument, but after observing the Black Master and his methods, I have come to the conclusion that this is not only possible, but is actually the method by which ju-ju obtains its power and potency. It was undoubtedly the method used by the Black Master in his rites on the marshes by the Little River, I having personally witnessed one performance of such rites at last full of the moon.

The Black Master, through K'Tooma, purchased during his stay at Chembi some fifty or more virgins. These he deflowered before an audience of his satellites, five, six, sometimes even a dozen during one ceremony. Thus the Black

Master was enabled to strengthen his own personality, impress his followers, and have a force of creation or destruction at his disposal to use at will.

But what was the object in performing these rites ? What was the Black Master's idea in becoming a power in the land ?

Undoubtedly besides being a conjurer of no mean order, he was a man of unbounded ambition, and possibly saw in himself a potential ruler of all Africa. It was his open boast that he wished to break white civilisation and white domination in Africa. It fell upon me, as a white man interested in seeing civilisation built up in this savage land, to break this negro's sway, and remove his dangerous presence from the Little River for ever.

As I have stated before, I was helped in this by K'Tooma, the so-called witch doctor of the Akesi tribe, who, as soon as I shewed that I had a little knowledge of his arts (pitifully little at the time, merely what I had obtained when a schoolboy, through reading books taken by stealth from my father's library), indulged me with more, perhaps in fear that I might use my knowledge against him if he failed to help me, or perhaps out of jealousy of the Black Master.

K'Tooma gave me a charm which, he asserted, if thrown into the ring of the Black Master's satellites, would cause consternation amongst them, and bring about the Master's downfall. I took the charm reluctantly, and found it was made of a woman's hair and feathers from a cock's tail. The meaning of this singular combination I cannot fathom, and K'Tooma says that if he told the charm's secret its power would be gone for ever.

I took the charm with me to one of the Black Master's

rites, but I did not entirely rely upon it to bring about the man's destruction ; there were other things that I knew, things of which I will write later.

When I approached the marshlands I saw that the big negro was in the centre of a circle of his satellites, with his women grouped about him, and they were all chanting and swaying together in a wild and excited rhythm. I already knew that if this rhythm could be broken, if the singers could be out-chanted, then, when the Black Master was performing his rites, his potency would fail him, and he would be left powerless and ridiculous, to suffer the scorn of his followers.

It pains me to record that it was necessary for me to join in this obnoxious ceremony of ju-ju, but as I had a public duty to perform, I had to sink all personal distress and use, as Pietro, il Diavolo would have said, the devil's ways to oust the devil. With this thought in mind, I stepped into the ranks of the Black Master's satellites and began to chant against them.

Here there was a break in the narrative, as if made by distress of mind, but after a few days it was taken up again, and recorded as matter-of-factly as before.

I hope that I may never have to go near the marshland again, for when I think of that dark, dank morass even, I live again through the ghastly scene of the end of the Black Master.

It was even as I had surmised, a perverse rhythm destroyed the negro's potency ; he failed in the performance of his rites and fell, a ridiculous heap, in the centre of his stage.

K'Tooma's charm, thrown upon his crouching body, gave the impetus for the rising of his followers against him, and they literally tore him limb from limb.

Here again there was a break in the narrative, but after several days, M. Lafontaine wrote again.

It is strange how I have become imbued with the desire to know more of the secrets of ju-ju. It should be sufficient that the Black Master has departed this life and will trouble us no more, but it seems that the odour of the man's personality has remained, like a rotten fruit that, although fallen from its tree and buried deeply in the earth, yet leaves its perfume all about. A great curiosity comes over me every now and again to know more of his pernicious craft. There is a woman here, one Senhora Fernandez, who was said to be one of his accomplices. I think that I shall call upon her, and see what I can hear, using the knowledge which I have already acquired to extract more.

Then again the next day :

To-day I went to the home of Senhora Fernandez on the outskirts of Chembi. She lives alone and is attended by no servant, so that when I came to her door and knocked upon it, she opened it to me herself, and stood peering out at me in a suspicious manner. She is a tall, sallow woman of a somewhat mean appearance, and she seemed to resent my coming, until I said to her : "The tail feathers of a cock and a woman's hair, what is their sum total ?" Then she opened the door widely and asked me to come in.

Here the entry ended, beyond it there was nothing but a series of designs drawn waveringly upon the paper, as if with a feeble or unwilling hand, shewing beyond all doubt that M. Lafontaine's mental agitation was such as prevented his continuing the journal.

[To the next chapter's text, faintly visible through the page]

THE Black Master had gone and serenity once more reigned upon the Little River. Over the settlement of Chembi passed the sun and the moon alternately. The bank enlarged its premises, the electric-light poles went up in the streets and at night every house glowed like an orange against dark foliage. Clerks weighed bone and rubber in the stores, totted up their ledgers, and went home thankfully at six o'clock to have a sundowner. Yvette Pinquot said, as she rouged her lips and prinked before her mirror : "Happiness must be snatched or it is lost." Champagne came down in price and the town band played in the square on Sundays, with instruments slightly out of tune.

The building of a bridge across the river from a talked-of possibility became a certainty, for the representative of the engineering firm of Messrs. Smithers, Smithers and Chicot, of Birmingham, England, was already on his way to the Little River.

So the Progress of Civilisation, which M. Lafontaine had long ceased to record in his diary, went on, and life presented only this one conundrum : "What action can positive and persistent thought have upon the lives of those within the radius, so to speak, of this thought ?"

Trader Voss asked this conundrum one night at the Boul-boul Tavern, but no one could find a suitable reply to it. True, the parrot put its head on one side and said : "Whisky !" three times, with a very cunning air, and old Admiral Delabouche woke up sufficiently, from a half-drunken slumber, to say : "I've seen 'em at it on the West Coast," and then went fast asleep again, snoring heavily.

Neither of these two replies being in any way satisfactory, Trader Voss was left to find an answer for himself, and he spent much time and thought upon the matter without coming to any conclusion whatsoever. This conundrum had first occurred to him one night during his usual constitutional along the river-bank to the jungle. For many a year he had speculated as to why the old black man sat upon the right bank so engrossed with his own thoughts as to be, apparently, oblivious of all that went on about him ; and he had always had the uncomfortable sensation that there might be more in M'Kato's presence there than first met the eye. He had been known to remark more than once, *á propos* of Monsieur Lafontaine's diary (which M. Lafontaine, before becoming a recluse, had read aloud occasionally to a chosen few of his friends) that if anyone could write the history of the Little River, it would be that old black man who sat on the river-bank day in and day out.

But no one knew exactly what Trader Voss meant to infer by this, and he himself was a little doubtful— doubtful until that evening when, upon passing M'Kato in his usual place, looking more than ever like Omnipotence personified, it had come to him, in a sudden flash of acute perception, that between himself and this man, between the little settlement of trading-stores and iron-roofed houses, lying at his back, there was some definite connection. What connection he could not say.

But as he moved forward towards the jungle, rubbing his fat chin with his hand—a gesture he always used when perplexed—he wondered if perhaps they in Chembi, with their progress and their electric-light poles, their town band and their bridge-to-be, whilst building up white civilisation beside the Little River, might not after all be merely puppets in the hands of some inexorable power moving surely, involuntarily, but inevitably towards a predestined end.

The figures that peopled Little River history passed before his mind's eye in one long, exotic array : old Admiral Delabouche, Lardi, the ferryman, Brother François, Sister Marte, Madame Boul-boul, Father Domenique, the lean-jawed Llewellyn Jones, Papa Grandeau, the Resurrection Women in their long white robes, Flore, the courtesan, the Black Master—all stepping smartly to a tune called by some unknown piper. Who was this piper and what was the tune he called ?

Trader Voss, gazing at the still, squatting figure of M'Kato, with its immutable, inscrutable countenance, felt inclined to cry aloud : "Look you ! here is sorcery, bigger sorcery than you have yet known. You were afraid of the Black Master and his petty boasts of power, but you missed seeing the real power over you, this silent old black man on the river-bank. *He* is the Artificer of your lives. *He* is the Master Builder of Chembi. Watch him well, for his thrall is upon you !" But had Trader Voss cried this aloud there would have been none to hear except the vampire birds making their nightly scrabble in the ripe fruit of the mango trees ; and afterwards, when he sat upon the verandah of his own home trying to work the matter out to some definite conclusion, the disquieting sense of sorcery that he had felt upon him in M'Kato's presence left him, and he was able to reduce the matter to the bluntest and most matter-of-fact of questions, the one that he put later on to the clientele of Boul-boul Tavern, and to which no-one could find a suitable reply.

And much as Trader Voss cogitated upon this conundrum, he could find no answer to it, nor will he find one for some time to come, not until that grey morning, perhaps, when seated at his breakfast-table, partaking of his coffee and rolls, he hears his name being called outside his open window, called in hurry and great agitation :

"Voss ! Voss !"

Trader Voss heaves his corpulent form out of his chair and goes to the window. Yes ; here he is, and what of it ?

What of it ? Has he not heard of the tragedy on the river-bank ? The red-faced Englishman, who arrived last night by the *Prinz Friedrich,* has been thrown into the Demon's Boiling Pot. And Flore has been taken to the hospital on the hill bleeding to death from a bullet wound in her breast, their own Flore in whom they have so much pride.

The newsvendor leaves Trader Voss's window then, to hurry along and relate this extraordinary piece of news at other windows, at *all* the windows, in fact, of Chembi, for Chembi has witnessed many spectacular events, many tragedies, but never such an event, such a tragedy as this.

By the time Trader Voss reaches the river-bank, for he is slow of movement, all Chembi is there before him, gazing curiously into the foaming waters of the Demon's Boiling Pot.

But not so Trader Voss. Some instinct tells him to look elsewhere, and he directs his gaze to that spot just above the ford, where the black man, M'Kato, has sat for so many years.

But the old black man's place is empty. From the scrubby bush near to it Father Domenique's rosary swings about in the wind. But M'Kato is not there. Neither is he on the other bank with the excited throng of people by the Boiling Pot.

Trader Voss passes his hand over his chin in great perplexity, and stands there looking across at the empty place and the scrubby bush for some considerable time. He stays there until Father Domenique splashes through the ford on his white mule and comes up the river-bank and stands beside Trader Voss.

Father Domenique has never sensed Trader Voss's dislike for the Mission people, and speaks to him confidingly, as a child might speak :

"I could take it back now, do you not think so ? It was given me by a friend, a boyhood's friend who was very dear to me."

Trader Voss comes out of his reverie then, and finds that Father Domenique is speaking to him of the rosary blowing about on the scrubby bush. He answers nothing, and Father Domenique goes on :

"It is strange, my dear Monsieur Voss, I have often had a thought when I saw the old black man counting the beads that he was not, perhaps, counting them for any good purpose. A foolish thought, and one for which I have set myself many a penance. Now the old man has gone, and I can take back my rosary."

Trader Voss answers Father Domenique in a somewhat irrelevant manner, as he turns away from the river-bank to go back to his home.

"There is mystery in us and around us," he says. "We are close to something which we do not understand."

Trader Voss walks through the streets of Chembi to his home, slowly and thoughtfully. Away from the river-bank there appears to be a great silence, and in the silence a bird calls as if it were announcing the morning which has long since reddened the sky. The house-boys are shaking out mats on the pavement ; Baptist converts are walking up to the Mission School ; chickens, let loose from some fowl-house, are idly picking at the grass on the roadway.

In the streets of Chembi life appears to be going forward in its ordinary way, but Trader Voss feels that he has his feet set upon a pathway of great adventure.

But all this is before time. The bridge has not been built across the Little River, nor has the tragedy happened that the building of this bridge called into being. We are only at that part of Chembi's history where the bridge is being talked of, and the Administrator expects, by every boat, the representative of Messsrs. Smithers, Smithers and Chicot. Terrible firm with such a name! He can make nothing of it, except the "Chicot," which could be pronounced in a soft French way.

WHEN Messrs. Smithers, Smithers and Chicot, Engineering Contractors of Birmingham, England, decided upon sending a representative to the Little River in Central Africa to report upon transport facilities, prior to their sending engineers and workmen to construct the bridge across the Little River, they chose the youngest and most incompetent member of their office staff, mainly because he was related to the junior partner of the firm.

This young man was Humphrey Chicot Brown (his mother had been a Miss Chicot), and he was the son of Captain Humphrey Brown, who owned a plantation on the Kafue in Northern Rhodesia. Humphrey Chicot Brown (he was always known as Chicot to distinguish him from his father) had never been out to Rhodesia. His mother, delicate in health, did not live at the plantation. Sometimes she spent a little time with her husband at one of the coastal towns of South Africa, Capetown, or Durban, during the season, but the best part of each year she spent in England or on the Continent.

Chicot had been carefully and correctly reared ; he had passed through public school in much the same manner

as other English boys, vaguely and rather puzzled at
first, but coming out at the end with two firm convic-
tions : that England was always right, and that one must
play the game no matter what occurred. Oxford afterwards only heightened this conviction. Then his mother
made the mistake of her life in sending him to an
engineering school abroad. There he discovered new
ideals and a vague restlessness of spirit. He mixed with
strange companions who forgot to shave and scorned
beer, so by the time he had entered the firm of which
his uncle was junior partner, he was a thoroughly un-
settled young man, who had no idea as to what he
wanted to do with his life and a sneaking conviction that
perhaps it was not worth while doing anything at all.

"Wants backbone, that is what is the matter with
Chicot," growled his uncle, and when the opportunity
came to send someone to the remote region of the Little
River in Central Africa, the elder Chicot decided upon
his nephew. "Do him the world of good," he silenced
all opposing voices. "He'll get all this socialistic nonsense knocked out of him, when he gets among the
niggers."

So young Chicot Brown sailed for Africa by way of the
Cape. He journeyed leisurely by train through Cape
Province and the Transvaal, and then through the two
Rhodesias to his father's plantation.

"That's the best thing you can do," Mr. Chicot had
advised him previous to his starting out upon his journey. "Your father will know better than anyone how

to get to this river. He's been in Africa now thirty years
or more, and he'll be able to shew you the ropes if anyone
can. Go to him first, and get his advice."

The truth was that, knowing his brother-in-law as he
did (he didn't wonder that his sister always preferred
living in Europe), he had no doubt that he would imbue
his son with some anti-socialistic ideas more quickly
than a continent of niggers.

Father and son had not seen each other for seven
years ; it was just so long since Humphrey Brown had
been in Europe. They met on the station platform at
Broken Hill, and each was a little disappointed in the
other. Over a whisky and soda, which both felt they
needed, they took stock of each other. Son saw a big,
bluff, red-faced, elderly man, inclined to corpulency, with
bleared eyes and a hard mouth ; father saw a tall, thin
young man with fair stubbly hair, a mouth that curved
like a girl's, and a chin that was weak but obstinate.
Neither liked the other very well, but they were both
willing to concede the toleration of relationship. Humphrey Brown took his son home with him to his plantation on the Kafue, and there the two lounged through the
days that followed on the wide front verandah of the
house on the hill, trying vainly to get used to each other.

Then Chicot began his preparations for his long journey north. He pored over maps and made calculations
about transport and equipage. "I've a great mind to
come with you myself," Humphrey Brown said. "I'm
by no means in my dotage yet, and I've never seen that

part of Africa. They say it is going ahead wonderfully."

Chicot was partly relieved, partly dismayed ; his father, he knew, would be a great help on the journey, but somehow Chicot could not feel at ease with him. There was something sinister about Humphrey Brown, sinister and cruel. He was like a king who has ruled too long and run amok with his power. Chicot noticed how the plantation labourers slunk about in his father's presence with servile dread. He could not understand it at first, but after he came across old Cheteba he understood all things, and felt sick at the pit of his stomach in consequence.

Cheteba was a decrepit old black man who sawed wood all day at the back of the house and brought it in basket-loads to the kitchen for the stove. Chicot stopped him one day and asked him some question, not because he thought that the old man would be able to understand him, but because he wanted to be friendly with and well-liked by his father's servants. The old wood-cutter turned his face up to him, and opened his mouth. Chicot saw then that he had no tongue ; his mouth was just a red, mutilated gap.

He questioned his father about the matter at dinner that evening. Humphrey Brown laughed loudly. "He talked too much, that was Cheteba's one fault. A missionary came here and Cheteba got religion, and afterwards he talked too much about the affairs of the plantation, so I taught him a lesson. Now he doesn't talk at all ; he just saws wood and is thankful to do it."

Again Chicot felt that sick feeling in his stomach. He turned from his father with loathing. "I'm leaving the plantation tomorrow," he said, in a low, choked voice.

His father laughed again. "All right, son," he said, "and I'm coming with you. After you've been a little time in Africa, you'll get used to these things — you're young and raw at present."

But neither Humphrey Brown nor his son set out from the plantation next day, because that night some of the labourers tried to escape, and for several days afterwards the plantation was in a disordered state. Humphrey Brown felt that his presence was necessary to quell any uprising that might occur, and Chicot stayed out of a fearful and morbid curiosity, and yet loathed himself for so doing.

THE long December evening passed off quietly in the house on the hill beside the Kafue swamps. Humphrey Brown sat on his verandah smoking his pipe, while his son nervously pored over maps in the living-room, marking out his route to the Little River, whilst thinking about the cruelty that he found was meted out to the labourers on his father's plantation. He felt it incumbent upon him to do something in the matter, but he was undecided as to what he should do. This indecision was characteristic of him ; he had been reared to follow blindly in the wake of old traditions, and now that he had come to despise those traditions he was left with nothing upon which to base his conduct.

Brute force, authority, the power of the strong over the weak, he brooded upon these things, with the maps laid out on the table before him. His father thrashed the labourers at sundown for their pettifogging faults, and they were expected to stand up to the flogging like men, and work next day with sore and aching backs. But could his father be blamed for this ? Was it not rather the social system under which they lived, a system which permitted the power of the one over many, that should bear the blame ?

Chicot felt resentment, weak, useless resentment against his father, the social system, and mankind in general. There was nothing he could do about it, however, for he was not the stuff of which leaders are made. He turned to his maps again, and marked heavily the name of the Little River, which he found in the Belgian Congo, after considerable searching. He felt a peculiar distaste for the journey ahead of him, a premonition that out of it could come only disaster.

In the labour quarters of the plantation, somewhere behind their huts, the black labourers gathered together and talked in simple language of their own affairs, of legends of their race, of hunting in the forests, and of the great sad swamps that stretched away from the plantation for many miles, and brought death to those who tried to escape from the rule of Humphrey Brown. They spoke in low voices, almost whispers, when they told one another of the great bridge that now spanned the swamps, over which the white man's fire carriage passed every other day. If one could get to that bridge, climb up its steep posts — they were strong and would stand the weight of a man's body — and then crawl along the bridge to the land far beyond the sad swamps, out of the reach of Humphrey Brown's long arm!

They spoke thus round their fires, but their words were dull and hopeless, leaden like the mists that rose off the swamps at dawn. But Luenti, the young wife of one of the new labourers, interrupted their talk, flaming, youthful, fierce-eyed.

"Are you all cowards that you stay here to be beaten each day by the white man?"

"He beats us because our work is not good," said one of the older men, who had worked on the plantation for a number of years.

"Why then do you not work better?" demanded Luenti with excellent logic.

"We would rather be beaten than please him," answered one of the younger men, groaning a little as he laid himself down by the fire, for his back was sore.

"Ah-ha — cowards all of you, sons of the jackals that slink behind all other beasts in the forest, that grab their food from the lion's paw when he is not looking, sooner than kill for themselves, for they are afraid. Less than the very jackals are ye who would call yourselves men!" Luenti spat the words fiercely from her mouth, and then lapsed into silence, her breast heaving with scorn and indignation. The talk of the men began again. If only one could reach the bridge, the bridge with its stout posts! It was the dry season, the swamps were low; one could wade out to a great length and then swim, but the weeds would drag one down. Somewhere in mid-stream there was a current free from weeds . . . the night was dark, there was no moon . . . the dogs were asleep in their kennels. . .

At some midnight hour Chicot, in bed but not asleep, heard a great commotion outside, and rising, went out on to the verandah to see what was happening. Humphrey Brown was already there, buckling on his revolver belt over his pyjamas. And in the pitch darkness, somewhere down where the swamp waters might begin, dogs were barking, and lights were flashing this way and that.

"What is it ?" Chicot asked.

"You leave this thing to me," returned his father shortly, and striding down the house-steps, was lost in the darkness.

A little while afterwards the commotion by the river ceased, the lights faded away, and Humphrey Brown returned to the house. "It is all right now," he told his son curtly, and then added by way of explanation, "Some of the boys tried to escape, but they didn't get very far."

It was true, they did not get far. Chicot saw them next day, when, at sunrise, with the swamps glowing like some gigantic ruby, he walked along the edge of the waters. There they were, the black men who had tried to escape, their heads like so many ghastly black water-lilies floating on the surface of the rosy waters.

Some of the men were not yet dead, as evinced by the little disturbed pools of water about their mouths ; others had burst their eyeballs in some gigantic strain that they had subjected themselves to.

"Traps," Lensi the head-boy told Chicot, coming upon him on the banks of the swamps and seeing him apparently interested in the outcome of last night's proceedings. "The B'wana had put steel traps in the swamps, and the black men had been caught in their large and hungry jaws."

"Better to stay here and work for the B'wana," added

Lensi with an evil grin. Lensi was a partially-educated Barotse, who had worked for many white men in his time, and he had always found it better to tolerate the white man's ways than go against them.

"But they are not dead yet, some of them," Chicot said eagerly, "they might yet be saved."

"Better to let them die so," said Lensi. "It is not a bad death, better than to be put upon an ant-hill. Ants are nasty things. Have you ever seen black ants swarming on a body, B'wana?"

Chicot made no reply.

"B'wana named Kelly," went on Lensi comfortably, "came here — oh, a long time ago now — and one of the boys threw a stone at him, a stupid boy, but B'wana Kelly had looked at his wife. What is a wife? One can buy another one for two cows or a white man's suit of clothes. B'wana Kelly took the stupid boy and put him on an ant-hill."

"But he could have got away from the ant-hill," said Chicot Brown.

"B'wana Kelly tied him there," answered Lensi imperturbably.

A day or two afterwards, Humphrey Brown and his son set out upon their journey to the Little River, but there was constraint between them. They found no pleasure in each other's company, and avoided each other as much as possible.

"The young fool," thought Humphrey Brown, "I'll knock the nonsense out of him, if I have to tan his hide."

Chicot's thoughts were confused and indistinct, but sometimes, when he glanced at the red, bloated, cruel face of his father, he fingered the revolver in his belt nervously, as if he would like to use it and yet was afraid to do so.

BAKALI was a fat man, round of face, and rotund of body. A fat, equable, good-natured man, who never beat his wives. He sat last in the line of fishermen who graced the banks of the Little River at night-time, and he always caught the fewest fish. Bakali was slow in pulling up his lines ; he liked to sit on the bank and twiddle his black toes on the brink of the water, and think what a blessing it was to be away from his hut where his wives scolded and quarrelled all day long. Nights on the river-bank were peaceful, for his wives stayed at home and slept then, worn out, perhaps by their daytime bickering.

In thinking contentedly thus with his round head nodding forward on his fat chest, he was not alert enough to pull up his line directly a fish bit. He paid for his contentment next day, however, when his wives looked in his fishing-basket. Bakali had stood ill-treatment from his wives for a long time, but even a fat man's patience can give out, and one day he went to consult K'Tooma, the witch doctor of Akesi.

"Beat them," advised K'Tooma heartily. "Beat them."

"But they beat me," Bakali pointed out dejectedly.

"Then you must give me two of the fish you catch each night, and I will do something for you."

"But sometimes I don't catch two fish each night," Bakali answered.

"Then I can't help you," said K'Tooma, "you are a poor fisherman."

Bakali left K'Tooma's hut and trundled up the long hill to the Marist Mission. It was in the broad hour of noon and sweat stood out in great beads upon his fat body. At the Mission he put his case before Brother Antoine. He wanted, he said, to sleep at the Mission during the day hours; by night he fished, but during the daytime he wanted to sleep, and he had heard that there were no women at the Mission.

Brother Antoine was a little puzzled, but he thought that he would strike a bargain with the old fisherman. "You must bring two of your fish here every day for Father Domenique's dinner," he told Bakali, "then you can sleep in one of the outhouses, and attend mass when Father Domenique wishes it."

Bakali left the Mission in great disappointment. "I don't catch two fish every night," he told Brother Antoine.

"Then you are an idle and worthless fellow," said Brother Antoine, and turned him out of doors.

A day or two later Bakali crossed the river to the other Mission. The Reverend Llewellyn Jones received him on the verandah just outside his study. He knew the old man by sight; he had often seen him fishing on the river-bank.

"Well, Bakali," he said genially, "what is the trouble?"

Bakali again stated his case. He had nowhere to sleep, he said; he would like to sleep at the Mission during the day hours.

It seemed a strange request, but still, as it meant another sheep for the fold, the Reverend Llewellyn considered it.

"You must attend the Bible classes, Bakali," he said.

Bakali made no protest; he could as well sleep in a Bible class as anywhere, he thought.

The matter was arranged, without the Reverend Llewellyn asking for the fish that Bakali could not catch. But just before the old fisherman took his departure, the Baptist Minister said: "Now, Bakali, you must bring your wife to church; we like all our people to be married in the sight of God."

Bakali did not wait to hear more; his fat sides shaking with terror, he sped down the path leading to the gate of the Baptist Mission. He had not much idea of what the Reverend Jones had actually said to him, but he knew that it had been indicated that he must also bring his wives to the Mission, and that was far from what he wanted. There was no rest, no peace, for him anywhere, he felt, as he hurried out of the gate and forgot to pull it to after him. One Mission wanted his fish, and the other his wives. They were a strange lot, those Mission people.

Outside the Baptist Mission gate he collided, in his

frantic efforts at speed, with Admiral Delabouche. The impact had no visible effect upon the Admiral, but it sent Bakali rolling on the ground.

Admiral Delabouche looked on with amusement while the fisherman picked himself up, and rubbed the dust of the roadway from his limbs.

"Mille tonnerres!" exclaimed the Admiral, "if you had not just come from the Baptist Mission, I would think that you had seen a ghost, but they couldn't keep a ghost there without baptising it out of countenance. What is your hurry, you old rogue ?"

Bakali said that the Mission wanted his wives. Admiral Delabouche threw back his head and laughed till the street echoed with his mirth. "Go up the hill to the other Mission," he advised, "they won't want your wives there."

He had been, said Bakali, and they wanted his fish.

Admiral Delabouche laughed again, loud and long. *"Mon Dieu!"* he cried, "this is the best joke I have heard for many a long day, I must go and tell it to my friend, Monsieur Lutz."

The fat, rotund Bakali, rubbing one foot tentatively over the other, regarded Admiral Delabouche with speculative eyes. Here was a jolly white man ; perhaps he might help him in some way.

Once again he stated his case, while Admiral Delabouche listened with an air of cynical amusement.

"Bien!" he said at length, "your wives are very small beer, as the English would say, but if you would like to

come along with me and sleep in the nigger's outhouse at Mahomet Abdul's I shall make no objection."

And that was how it came about that Bakali, the fisherman, became attached to Admiral Delabouche, the adventurer. It was the beginning, too, of Admiral Delabouche's restlessness and discontent with his present mode of living. For Bakali, in an access of gratitude for his now peaceful days, and having nothing to give away but the fish that he wanted for himself, gave away some of the secrets of the Monkey Men who lived in the dark forest beyond the ridge of blue mountains at the back of Akesi. He inflamed the Admiral's curiosity to such an extent that he decided to adventure further than the collection of villages just outside Akesi, where for some considerable time he had carried on his trading operations; go on, in fact, to the Blue Mountains, and the land of the Monkey Men which lay beyond, and see for himself if the tales that Bakali told were true.

Strange things went on in the land beyond the mountains, according to the old fisherman, for the Monkey Men were powerful. When a Monkey Man came out of his dark forest into one of the villages on the plains, the villagers fled from their homes. Bakali knew all about the Monkey Men, because he had been born within sight of their forest, and he was more afraid of them than he was of his wives. But he liked talking about them so long as they were nowhere in sight, and he was never tired of telling Admiral Delabouche of the power of their tribe, and the uncanny secrets which they held.

"Some day," the Admiral told Bakali, "we'll go and find out these Monkey Men of yours."

But that was scarcely what Bakali wanted. "Why leave Mahomet Abdul's?" he asked. It was peaceful there, even though Mahomet Abdul did occasionally kick him in the ribs.

ADMIRAL DELABOUCHE gazed out of the window of his room at the travellers' hostel run by Mahomet Abdul, gazed out at the hot, dust-ridden street, shimmering in the noon-day sunshine. The street was deserted except for a long-legged chicken which, with its wings outstretched from its hot body, was searching amongst the debris outside the hostel door for any tit-bits, and Bakali, fat and comfortable, snoring on the doorstep. Bakali should be careful, thought Admiral Delabouche, glancing down at him, for one day his wives might come and catch him there.

Admiral Delabouche was restless; he suddenly felt an unaccountable distaste for Chembi, with its dusty streets and its houses like cardboard boxes in a row — a pettifogging civilisation thrust into the centre of a wild and interesting land, with not even the excuse of beauty for its existence there. He was filled with a quick rage that he could not rise up there and then and destroy it, rase the silly cardboard-box-like houses to the ground, and let the tall jungle orchids flower again in their place.

Admiral Delabouche had known the Congo in past and better days, days of great adventure, before the advent of tax-gatherers and missionaries and trading-store clerks. In those days he had been *Le Grand Delabouche,* King of the Congo River, and he and his *compagnie* of twenty blue-shirted, brown-breeched men, had swept up and down the Big River in their trading-canoes, respected and feared and admired by the black man.

But there was still adventure to be had in the land, thought Admiral Delabouche, looking away to the far blue mountains across the river, and beyond the dry brown plains of Akesi. Over behind those mountains was unexplored country where the Monkey Men lived; there, he felt sure, adventure lay. Old Admiral Delabouche felt that he would like to encounter adventure again, for he was becoming sedate and respectable, leading the hum-drum life that he did. Meeting the riverboat once a fortnight, the dominoes with Monsieur Lutz, his peddling expeditions to Akesi, these made up his life, he, *Le Grand Delabouche,* who in his day had slit a throat for a purse of gold, or the lure of a scarlet mouth.

Those Monkey Men now, behind the mountains, he would like to see them. He could take Bakali to shew him the way, and a bearer or two to carry food. Ruminating thus, Admiral Delabouche turned from the window, and taking down his gun from the rack over the door, began to clean it.

It was an ancient gun, and it had seen much service with him. Admiral Delabouche had a peculiar tenderness for this gun; he cleaned it as if it were some precious ornament of great value, thoroughly, and with the utmost care. As he worked upon it, he went through the episodes of his life : longshoremen, stoker, cowboy, trader, hunter, gambler, pirate, thief. Now he was old Admiral Delabouche, with a pedlar's licence, and stiff bones. Yes, he would go and have a look at the Monkey Men, and get rid of the stiffness in his bones. When he had finished the cleaning of his gun, he would descend and kick Bakali on the shins until he woke up, and together they would plan the route to the Blue Mountains and beyond.

The route, he found afterwards, when Bakali was uncomfortably awake and inclined to be peevish, was not definite. He would have to set his nose towards the mountain ridge and follow it. Bakali refused point blank to accompany him. He had known the Monkey Men in the days of his youth and he had no desire to renew the acquaintanceship. Besides, he was not an adventurer ; he was merely a fat old fisherman with a *penchant* for slumber, and a desire to lose his wives.

No, said Bakali firmly, he would not go with the white man. How could he catch his fish over on the mountains ?

As he never appeared to catch any, pointed out Admiral Delabouche, that was a point that did not matter.

But Bakali remained firm. "Well, you old black image," said the Admiral, "there are ways of circumvention," and he straightway went off to pay a visit to Bakali's wives in the village of Akesi, with the conse-

quence that they turned up next day at Mahomet Abdul's
and the howls of Bakali echoed up and down the street
outside the hostel.

Admiral Delabouche afforded Bakali no protection ;
he turned a deaf ear to the black man's cries for help,
and laughed quietly to himself when he saw Bakali rac-
ing down the street as fast as his fat legs would carry
him, with the younger of his two wives in hot pursuit.

Admiral Delabouche had never been at a loss to cope
with any situation ; he knew that after the advent of his
wives at the hostel Bakali would be disposed to consider
the proposition of acting as guide to the land of the
Monkey Men.

He was right, for the next day Bakali came to him,
downcast and ill at ease. Perhaps he would go with the
white man to the mountains after all, he said ; fish were
not plentiful in the river just then, and he had caught
nothing for three nights. But the white man must carry
a gun and plenty of food. There was no food to be had
on the mountains, and very little beyond, unless the
white man could shoot an elephant. Between the land
of the Monkey Men and the Blue Mountains was elephant
ground ; it behooved them to be careful there and watch
their step, for the elephants were dangerous when one
trespassed on their domain.

"You old faint-hearted son of a chicken, go and get
me four bearers," said Admiral Delabouche to Bakali,
"and tell them to be ready tomorrow at dawn."

Bakali went away with a great show of reluctance ;

he was not easy in his mind about this expedition of the mad white man's. True, all white men were mad and did the most unaccountable things, but this one was a little more so than the rest ; one never knew what he would be up to next. Still, as it was apparently a choice between accompanying a madman on a foolish enterprise or going back to his hut and being nagged at all day by his shrewish wives, Bakali decided that he had better go with the madman. Perhaps when he reached the ridges he would not want to go any further ; Bakali would help him in this by choosing bearers who could not walk very far.

ADMIRAL DELABOUCHE waited for the next day's dawn with a slight feeling of impatience. He had returned from the Tavern in the small hours of the morning somewhat more drunk than usual, and had slept off the effects of the whisky for a heavy hour or two. Now he was sober, wide awake, and anxious to be gone upon his travels. Monsieur Lutz had tried to persuade him against going the night before. "It will be strenuous walking across the mountains, and you are not as young as you once were, my dear Admiral," he had said in his slightly pedantic way.

Admiral Delabouche had resented this, and they had had their first real quarrel. As he stood by the window of his room, and watched a silver dawn being sifted on to the sky like so much luminous powder, he felt sorry that he had been so sharp with Monsieur Lutz. Un-

doubtedly he was getting old, as Monsieur Lutz had said ;
his beard was grey, it would soon be white, and he a
shaky old man in a Tavern corner spilling his whisky
from its glass.

His life had been like a flame ; it had burnt well, and
now it was burning out. He found himself thinking of
death and its finality. He had run the gauntlet — from
a polished floor reflecting the glow of yellow-flamed
candles, to the stokehold of a ship with sweat standing
out in great glass beads on the naked bodies of men. But
what had been consummated ? He pieced the pictures
of his life together and found they made an incongruous
whole ; there had been no harmony in his existence. He
had lived by his wits, given no quarter, and asked for
none. And yet it had been in some respects a grand
life, and he was not going to regret it now. He might
be old, but he was still unquenched ; he could yet go
out and adventure, and die with his boots on, if need be.

In this curiously sensitive and introspective mood
Bakali, with the four necessary bearers, found Admiral
Delabouche.

"Well, you old black rogue, lead on," said the Admiral,
losing his dreams of the past and returning to the actual,
the particular. "And if you don't lead me right, I'll put
a bullet in your chicken's heart !"

With the silver dawn turning faintly pink above the
cardboard-box-like houses of Chembi, Admiral Delabouche and his bearers set out for the Blue Mountains
and the land of the Monkey Men beyond.

THE bearers of Admiral Delabouche, true to type, discovered when they came to the rocky ridges of the Blue Mountains, that their legs would not carry them farther. Admiral Delabouche could bluster, threaten, and even prod them in the back with the butt of his rifle, but into the land of the Monkey Men they would not go.

"Well, you old black heathen," said Admiral Delabouche to Bakali, "I'm not to be done ; you and I will do the trip alone." This was scarcely what Bakali had planned, and his loud howls of protest sounded all across the ridge of the mountains. But willy-nilly the Admiral dragged the fat black man along with him.

"You see, O white man," pointed out Bakali when they came to the precipices that dropped down to a level plain on the other side of the mountains. "It is impossible to go on." Admiral Delabouche laughed. "If you have guided me wrongly, O Bakali," he said, "I'll turn you over to the Monkey Men without any compunction, when we reach their land." But Bakali assured him that the direction was right.

The two men slept on the mountain ridges that night, Bakali curled up between two great boulders to keep the icy wind from his naked body, and Admiral Delabouche getting what warmth he could from a fire that burned fitfully, the wood being damp, and a rug that he had taken from the packages of the bearers.

Upon the Little River, upon the settlement of Chembi, upon the grass-covered plains, the day broke warm and sultry with a hint of storms to come, but up on the mountain-tops it broke icily cold, with a wind to freeze the very marrow in one's bones. Admiral Delabouche, bestirring himself to go upon his journey, shivered and wrapped his blanket closer about his shoulders, as he fanned the dying fire into a blaze. He heated some coffee in a tin pannikin, and then woke Bakali by throwing the coffee tin at his head.

Bakali, when awake, with the thought of the precipices he had viewed the night before still in mind, shivered with more than cold. He cooked himself an unsavoury hash of mealie meal and beans, and then returned to his boulders to partake of it. Admiral Delabouche looked at the fat old fisherman making his meal, and then away to where the mountains dropped steeply down to a deep purple ravine. Bakali would never be able to climb down into the ravine, for he was too fat and soft, like a round, rubber ball; he would bounce down if he went anyway at all!

Bien, he would go on alone. It would be two days' travel at the most to the Monkey Men, for he could see the ridge of their jungle black upon the horizon. Admiral Delabouche set about dividing the food into two portions. "Now, you old son of a turnip," he said to

Bakali when he had finished. "Here is food for three days. I am going to the land of the Monkey Men alone ; you wait for me here."

Bakali was overjoyed. It was cold on the mountain-tops, certainly, but still the white man was leaving him his blanket and plenty of food, so that he would not be so badly off ; at least, he would be able to sleep in peace between his boulders for quite a long time.

Admiral Delabouche, taking his gun and a haversack of food, proceeded to descend the rugged slopes of the mountains. It was hard and exhausting work, and by the time the sun was high in the heavens, the Admiral was not very far upon his way. He was finding the descent more difficult than he expected. He slept through the noon hours in the limited shade of a stunted bush and then descended again.

It took him two days finally to reach the ravine, and then the jungle of the Monkey Men seemed farther away than ever. Between the ravine and the jungle stretched a wide, heavily-wooded valley. The air in this valley was heavy and oppressive ; the trees stood there tall and motionless, part of the heavy crushing stillness. It was like a valley enchanted. No wind could cool it, or waft away the vapour that hung low over it like a dense rain-cloud, for all around were the tall peaks of mountains, enclosing it like a castle wall. The vapour rising from the humid earth congregated in the tree-tops, and then, dissolving again, dropped from the foliage like rain. On the ground, rotting bananas, plantains, leaves and tubers mouldered into the earth, and the air was impregnated with the odour of fermenting fruit and rotting foliage.

Lichen and moss covered the tall tree trunks, and gnarled and venerable vines hung in rope-like formation from bough to bough. Everything was aged in the valley, aged and mouldering away to ruin, and the atmosphere was that of the tomb.

Beyond the dark forest rose the hoary heads of mountains, snow-capped and sparkling, as the bright sun shed its light upon their white raiment. High above the mist of the valley, they reared their proud heads, tier upon tier, until they passed out of sight, melting into the wide expanse of the blue sky. On the forest slopes of those mountains dwelt the Monkey Men which the Admiral had come to seek, but they were far away ; there were still many kilometres of the hot humid valley to traverse, and the atmosphere was beginning to tell upon the Admiral.

His progress was slower than before. He was beginning to feel his age — he was somewhere near seventy, he supposed. He had kept no exact count of the years between his childhood at the Cinq Francs Tavern, and his days on the Little River. Monsieur Lutz had been right, he was too old for such adventures. With iron obstinacy, however, he forced himself onwards through the pathless woods.

But he wanted to rest, to lay his weary old body down in the rotting foliage and sleep deeply, perhaps for ever.

There was some whisky in his flask, and he drank of it, and then, looking, saw that the sun was still high above the snow-capped mountain-tops. Drinking before sundown, the road to ruin in such a climate! *Ma foi,* if he were going down that road, it would have to be on better whisky than what he had just drunk. Madame Boulboul must have taken to watering the casks, for the liquor had no sting in it. He chuckled a little, recovering his good-humour. He had not paid his Tavern score for over a year; it was chalked on the wall just behind Madame's chair. When he paid it, he would deduct fifty centimes off the price of every whisky he had drunk, for the water that had been in it. Water, he would indicate to Madame Boul-boul, was to be had for nothing, especially in the rainy season, when the roof of the Tavern verandah leaked.

He went on with more vigour after that, chuckling to himself over the wordy duel he would have with Madame Boul-boul at some future date, and he was surprised at length to find himself unaccountably coming into broad daylight. The forest ended abruptly, and before him stretched a cleared and open space of ground. A strange spot, uncanny, hemmed in by tall trees and yet in itself devoid of any growth. Admiral Delabouche, leaving the woods and going forward, saw that he had entered upon an elephants' dying ground. All about were the bleached bones of elephants, and their tusks, yellow, and rotting with age.

"Dead bones," said Admiral Delabouche, bending over

to examine a tusk with the eye of an old hunter. Well, it was no use to him, too old.

Bakali had been right; this was elephant country and he would need to be cautious. He was taking his gun from his shoulder, when a sound, sudden, ominous, in the dead silence of the valley, caused Admiral Delabouche to glance about him quickly. On the far side of the dying-ground an elephant was rising upon his haunches, and trumpeting loudly with rage. An old and worn elephant, come there evidently to die; even in his rage at human intrusion of this sacred place, he was feeble and shaky, and his legs, as he rose upon them, were trembling under him.

Admiral Delabouche sighted his gun. Unless the elephant attacked, he would not shoot, feeling a strange sympathy for the great black beast, worn and weary with its age. A rogue elephant, he could tell, by the many scars upon his skin. "A rogue, come here to die alone," he muttered whimsically, as he waited quietly to see what the elephant would do.

Several times the great beast rose up upon his haunches, and then sank down again, trumpeting weakly with terror and rage. Then, as if making one last and great effort to revenge himself upon his life-long enemy, the elephant rose up firmly, and with one tremendous rush came upon the Admiral. He had only time to fire once, and he missed the vital spot, for his hands were unsteady upon his gun.

Maddened by the wound the bullet had inflicted, the

elephant came on apace. Admiral Delabouche raised his gun for a second shot, but he knew that it was too late. "A rogue," he muttered again, his whimsical humour not deserting him even at the ultimate moment, "come here to die alone." But this time he was not thinking of the charging elephant now almost upon him.

M'KATO did not see Humphrey Brown's arrival at Chembi, because his attention was taken up by a long cortege of bearers that was winding its way through the tall grass of the plains that stretched between the Little River and Akesi. Although M'Kato was forgetful of the passing of time, unheedful of the ominous sequence of days, he was not so of the scenes which time presented to him. He was aware of all the events which happened within range of his vision, aware of them quietly, inactively; they passed before him like one long, unbroken picture, and never disturbed the even tenor of his thoughts. He was there on duty, without curiosity, lost to all bodily emotions, looking without wonder at the turbulent, crazy life of the white man which had come to trouble for ever the magnificent solitude of river and jungle and plain.

The narrow little river like a thread dropped upon the land, the grass-covered plains, the dank marshlands, the Mission hill, Chembi, the jungle—this was his domain. It could be indicated with a sweep of the arm. Beyond its limits his sight did not go, and his thoughts were encompassed in its horizons. Outside this domain lay a world of regrets and burning memories, which he had chosen to lose. Once when he had been asked by some foolish traveller what lay beyond the hard line of jungle, he had answered briefly : "Illusion." The illusion of false hopes, perhaps, of fears and inextinguishable desires.

Now he had done with illusion, his actuality lay in the feverish, exotic life of the narrow river, on the bank of which he sat ; a life at which he gazed impartially, friends and enemies, black men and white alike. Herons winging overhead crying their song of reeds and rushes, the cloudy glory descending upon the distant mountain ridge at sunset, the call of animals in the far hillside caverns, neither these nor other disturbances in the elemental life of his domain ever drew his gaze to farther horizons.

A strange figure, against a landscape of barbarous colouring, which the crude sunshine illumined, and night fell about like a curtain. Black, withered, immobile as a painted form, clothed in some quality of patience, vast and impalpable, living through, on this insignificant little foothold of the earth, the queer odyssey of his revenge.

Into his domain, into his line of vision, into perhaps, this odyssey, now came a caravan of bearers, carrying on a hastily-improvised litter the body of old Admiral Delabouche. A party of big game hunters, in crossing the valley near the Blue Mountains, had come upon the body of the Admiral, crushed but not unsightly, and beside it, the rogue elephant, that had died as he had attacked. They carried the body of Admiral Delabouche with them up the mountain slopes, and there on the topmost ridge, found Bakali having his long sleep out. By signs he made them understand that the Admiral had come from the Little River beyond the plains, and so the hunters had deviated from their original route to bring the last of the Elizabethans home.

Slowly, at dusk, the cortege wound its way through the long grass of the plains, to the banks of the Little River ; it came to the ford, and stopped there to rest before crossing. M'Kato, watching the proceedings, allowed himself a moment of surmise as to whose body was being brought back to Chembi with so much pomp and ceremony. The big game hunters had constructed a litter from their hammocks, and upon this the bearers carried Admiral Delabouche, his body covered with the skins of two lions which the hunters had shot in the regions beyond the Blue Mountains.

With his attention taken up by the funeral cortege, M'Kato paid no heed to the river-boat arriving on its usual fortnightly trip, and at its usual hour of dusk. Thus he missed seeing Humphrey Brown cross the gang-plank to the shore. It was not till the next morning that he saw the Master of the Kafue, when the sudden bright light of sunrise (out of which murder was to dart forth in a lightning flash, as if from an accumulation of prayers that had risen to it) illuminated his figure on the opposite bank.

But not so Flore, the courtesan. While the *Prinz Friedrich* disgorged its passengers, she stood upon the river-bank, the last rays of the dying sun glinting in her flaxen hair, summing up the passengers as they came on shore.

Rich man, poor man, beggar man, thief! There was only one amongst them who had any resemblance to the first named, a man well on in his sixties, with a red, bloated face, and a corpulent body, Captain Humphrey Brown from the Kafue in Northern Rhodesia. Besides being faultlessly attired, he walked with that assurance and arrogance of bearing that comes from long and successful enterprise. Flore, in need of a new "friend" now that the Administrator's wife was on her way out from Belgium, smiled at him across a bunch of petunias from the Marist Mission garden (she had just come from a visit to Father Domenique), but it was Humphrey Brown's son who caught the smile, and the blood flowed warmly to his brain, making the pulses beat hard against his temple.

He heard someone close behind him say : "There's Flore," and thought that the name suited her, though he disliked the casual tone of the speaker.

His father turned to him and remarked : "A handsome woman for these parts." And suddenly Chicot Brown knew that he hated his father. There had been constraint between them ever since leaving the Kafue, now there was enmity. Humphrey Brown saw it in his son's eyes, and muttering : "You young fool," strode angrily away.

At the Hotel Blanc, where they took rooms for an

indefinite period, father and son had high words. They
had been three months upon their journey from the
Kafue, and had been constantly irritated by each other.
Now the irritation broke bounds and took the form of
angry words, though both forbore to mention the factor
that had brought them to this breaking-point—the large,
fair-haired, smiling woman on the river-bank.

Chicot Brown went back to the boat ; he had struck
up a friendship with the young *chef de bateau* on his
journey up the Little River, and now he sat upon the
hard bunk in the little cabin of the *chef,* and told him of
his infatuation.

"She's a remarkable woman," said the young philosopher, instantly turning the infatuation of the sentimental
young Englishman into a fairy story, a legend, but, with
his Gallic instinct for logic and common sense well-
founded in him despite his mad philosophy, seeing in it
no possible outcome but the most sordid. He could only
mutter again and again. "Well, what is going to become
of them ?" And then returning to his previous statement, he went on : "She kept that priest fellow at
Lourenço Marques for two years, and finally he died in
her arms, but quite happily. She told me all about it."

Chicot knew then Flore's calling. But it did not alter
his feeling for her ; he was quite definitely in love for
the first time in his life. He thought of her as he had
seen her on the river-bank, fair-haired and gracious, with
her white arms full of flowers, and he was touched once
again with his sudden mad desire.

He went to the door of the tiny cabin and looked out towards the river-bank. Through the waving branches of the mango trees which lined the bank, he could see the Hotel Blanc, and leaning from one of the first-floor windows was Flore, idly dropping the ashes from a cigarette onto the heads of some black children playing in the street below. He saw her mistily through the gathering dusk. Her name suited her indeed ; she was like a flower, a flower that would perfume his life. He felt a slow, accumulated rage against that priest fellow whom she had nursed for two years, and against her other — friends.

Scruples, fears — he pushed them all aside. Flore should come with him when he went down river. He would take her back to England with him. He said to the young *chef de bateau.* "Tell me all about her."

The young philosopher complied with as much of Flore's life as he was aware of. He managed to imbue the tale of her adventures with a kind of tangled glamour, for he was a born story-teller. The Administrator's mistress, a friend of Father Domenique's, the joy of the Boulboul Tavern, the genial companion of himself and other bohemians ! He repeated again when he had finished : "She's a remarkable woman."

The Englishman said : "You must help me in this," and left the doorway to come back into the cabin and sit upon the hard bunk. The youthful Monsieur Brown promised all the help that he could give. Night had fallen during this conversation, and a great silence had come upon the Little River, broken only by the water lapping against the sides of the moored river-boat.

The Englishman sat on the hard bunk, with his head bent forward and resting in his cupped hands. He seemed too distraught to speak again. The tall *chef de bateau* paced the cabin as much as its limited space would allow. His gaiety seemed to have deserted him for the moment, as if he were wrestling in his mind with some problem that was too much for him. Finally he stopped in his pacing to say suddenly, as if it was the only conclusion that he could come to for the moment : "Come, let us go to Madame Boul-boul's !"

BUT Madame Boul-boul's was dull that night, for the
death of old Admiral Delabouche had affected
everyone's spirits. Even the young philosopher felt that
this was no time to try to raise a carnival about him, and
sat quietly at one of the tables drinking his beer. Perhaps
if there had been laughter and gaiety at the Tavern, and
the young philosopher had given one of his lengthy discourses, Chicot Brown might have been roused out of his
absurd infatuation. As it was he sat morbidly engrossed
by it, watching Flore alone at her table, toying with her
glass of vermouth.

Flore had no feeling at all for this ridiculous young
Englishman with his mad chivalry, but the father——
She knew his kind, the men she had had to deal with
all her life, hard, brutal perhaps, but inclined to be generous with their money. The ridiculous young man, who
did not know what to do with his ideals, probably had
no money.

She sat waiting at her table for Humphrey Brown to
come to the Tavern, and when he did not come she went
home early, in a borrowed car. After her departure the
Tavern seemed duller than before. The parrot went to
sleep with its head twisted uncannily upon its back, the

thin cat sat ceaselessly washing its face, whilst Madame Boul-boul closed the lids over her boot-button eyes and took a rest from the counting of cash. Over in the far corner Monsieur Lutz sat in his usual place with the dominoes spread before him. He played the game out with himself, painstakingly putting himself in a partner's place and moving the dominoes with judicious care; sometimes he cheated a little, not matching the spots correctly, to help himself through the evening.

The lights of the Tavern were extinguished somewhat earlier than usual, and the automobiles crossed the plains in the darkness, like so many fire-flies on the march. Behind them on bicycles, came Chicot Brown and the young *chef de bateau,* travelling with distressing slowness, owing to the young Englishman's inability to master his machine. The plains for them were deserted. . . Not a soul, not a sound. Not even the cry of a curlew from the marsh-land. And above this complete solitude broke the dawn. It was a dawn of evil content. It did not break rosily, or in a pure silver light, bursting upon the sky in great brilliance, but came slowly in sombre greyness, and brought with it no fresh breeze to chase away the hot and humid atmosphere of night.

Chicot Brown drew his companion's attention to it. "The dawn has died young," he remarked.

But the young philosopher pointed out that the birth had been a false one. Word perfect always, he added the dramatic, the theatrical touch to his reply. "Light will break presently," he said.

The words sounded ominous, prophetic almost, as if light might be suddenly coming into the lives of those who had groped for so long in a seemingly destiny-ridden obscurity.

The cyclists continued their ride across the desolate plains to Chembi. At the door of a house in the town they stopped to return their borrowed machines, and then went on to the river-bank on foot. There no longer was a far horizon, a stretch of darkness in which sight was lost. The Little River ran on its way, and beyond it the Mission hill rose up, black and definite ; it seemed as if they had come once more into a world of decision, and were not wandering on misty flats where their souls might stretch out into space and reach unknown and lost ways of life.

During their ride across the plains they had tried to divert their thoughts from Chicot's unfortunate love by calling each other's attention to little things, such as the false dawn, the mist damping their faces like rain, the height of the grass through which they rode, but as they returned to the river-bank simultaneously their gaze turned to the Hotel Blanc, and the first-floor window there, that should have been ablaze like a beacon, but was dark, like a dead eye looking out at the world.

"Will you sleep ?" asked the young philosopher of his friend.

Chicot Brown answered that he would walk by the river until sunrise.

"Well, good night," said the young *chef de bateau,* "or

it should be good morning. As for me, I must go back to the boat. We leave at nine, and I have breakfast to prepare."

"There is no hope : it is just sheer madness," said the Englishman, nodding in the direction of the hotel. "But I shall take pleasure in watching her window. Goodbye."

The friends parted then, the *chef de bateau* going on board his boat, and the young Englishman along the river-bank. There was heavy distress in his heart, but he moved forward with a kind of restless energy, in an abstracted way, as if with the idea in mind that he must go somewhere, but it mattered not where. It was in moving thus along the bank that he came upon his father and Flore, the courtesan.

AT any moment during the dawn hour M'Kato might
have awakened from his sleep of the night and,
looking across the river, seen his long-awaited enemy
upon the opposite bank. But it was just at the coming
of morning that he saw him for the first time. A column
of golden light, shooting up from the horizon of the far
plains and spreading itself over the sky, announced that
the sun had risen and day begun. The brightness of the
sudden light, after the dreary dawn, disturbed M'Kato.
He opened his eyes and saw, across the river, on the
Chembi bank, three figures in white, gilded a little by
the early rays of the hot sun. A thin man, a stout man,
and a large and gracious woman. There was a quarrel
between them : for loud and angry voices came across the
waters. M'Kato reached for his assegai ; he had recognised instantly the stout man, with hand upraised, as the
Master of the Kafue.

He manœuvred the assegai into position between his
toes, and took careful aim, judging the distance, and
counting the effect of the light wind that was blowing
upon the river. The assegai sped swiftly across the Little
River for half its distance, then turned about lazily and
dropped into the river waters. It had not been sped with
sufficient force.

M'Kato rose from his squatting position and regarded the assegai, floating down stream towards the Boiling Pot, with something of the helpless air of a frightened god who had had, without warning, the business of dictating to destiny suddenly taken from his hands. Then a diversion on the opposite bank called his attention to his enemy. He heard the stout man threatening in a loud coarse voice, as he had so often heard him threaten at the Kafue, then saw the woman by his side sway and fall ; and immediately afterwards the body of Humphrey Brown went hurtling, crashing down into the Demon's Boiling Pot.

Bewildered, but still watching intently, M'Kato saw the long lean figure of the *chef de bateau* come out of the shadows of Chembi, pick up the limp body of the woman and disappear again swiftly in the direction whence he had come.

Standing alone and stiffly, like a sentinel on guard, remained the thin man, the son of Humphrey Brown, watching the swirling waters into which he had hurled his father. Humphrey Brown had made some coarse and sneering remark, and Chicot, lifting his revolver, had fired at him ; but the bullet had wounded Flore instead, for the Master of the Kafue had been quick to knock his son's hand aside ; Flore had uttered a cry of pain, and Chicot had seen the red blood flow from her breast. He had sprung then at his father's throat, and after that there had been an interval of tremendous noise, when he had felt the blood pounding in his ears and had

had a vision of the Crack of Doom. Now he found himself alone on the river-bank, amidst a marvellous quiet broken only by the confused murmur of waters.

WHEN M'Kato left the Little River for good he did not glance back, as he went, at the town of Chembi, at the Mission, the hospitals on the hill, at the long ribbon of a road winding across the plains to Madame Boul-boul's, and say, like a god who had indulged in creation : This is very good. For he had no interest in reviewing the means whereby his magic had come to fulfilment, and also his mind was filled with thoughts of another matter. He was feeling that intense disappointment which a child feels when some long-looked-for event does not turn out quite as expected. True, his enemy was dead (his magic, at least, had been strong enough to accomplish that) ; but he felt no pleasure when he saw Humphrey Brown's body issue forth from the rapids and float down stream, for he had missed, at the last moment, his personal revenge.

M'Kato was amazed that it should be so. The realisation was yet to come upon him of the time that had passed since first he had come to the Little River — the time, even, that had passed since that red-letter day, when after arduous moons of practice, he had first been able to speed the assegai across the river to the opposite bank. He had been a young man then however, now his muscles were weakened by the years laid upon him, and his bones creaked with their age. But he knew it not. The bitter futility of his life's work had not yet been brought home to him. That would come later, in his own hut, after long hours of pleasant sleep, and more fully still, on the plateau by the Kafue, where the remnants of what had once been the hut of Kundi, the witchman, sheltered a few broken idols and some bleached bones.

Now he was merely bewildered by a magic that had turned out somewhat badly and, in his confusion and bewilderment, he left behind him, hanging on the scrubby bush beside his accustomed place on the river bank, Father Domenique's rosary, with one uncounted bead — the last bead near the cross. He had thought to count it slowly and with relish for the killing of his enemy, but in his acute disappointment he had forgotten it. The bead remained uncounted, until Fra Angelico in the Certosa, just outside Florence, came to say his prayers by the rosary, and counted it to his great undoing.

The foolish stricken figure of the thin young man still stood upon the opposite bank when M'Kato turned to follow the river up stream. And the old black man gave a hoarse chuckle of delight when the thought came to him that the foolish young man might be called upon to pay, under the white man's law of a life for a life, for his, M'Kato's, magic. It was a good thought and he reviewed it with relish. The white man could make good laws as well as bad ones, as Tarvisio had once told him. Now it would not be necessary for him to swing from a tree on the Kafue — life for him would go on, and life was sweet. How he and Kundi would laugh together over this later on ; it would make up a little for the pain of his lost revenge.

He walked along the river-bank in lush grass that grew almost to his knees. The merry chirp of crickets rose out of the grass ; on the leaves of some palm-trees gay parakeets swung and chattered. In the jungle some-one was singing. A voice, young and distant, belonging probably to a woman going to the river for water.

> Open your eyes, O maiden,
> Come out from the hut of sleep.
> Oh why do you come, O lover,
> To break dreams so long and deep ?

There was a rhythmic lilt to the song. It spoke of joy, of love, of all things pertaining to the spring of the year. Suddenly M'Kato felt recalled to life. He was again in a world of seasons, of the mating season and the season of sterility, the planting and the harvest. A sweet urge arose in him that had been dead for so long.

In the river, two young women were bathing, navel-deep in the water. They were fine young women, with wide, deep loins. They smirked and giggled when they noticed M'Kato's gaze upon them. He beckoned, but they only laughed the more. An old man like that ! No, if they were to bear a child, it would be to some tall, upstanding young buck, with a straight back and good legs. They waved derisively to M'Kato as he turned away from the river and walked slowly in the direction of Akesi and his hut.

It was hot in M'Kato's hut, a kilometre or so from the
Little River, and there were many flies in it, buzzing and
humming under the roof, also Tela's scolding, nagging
voice ; but M'Kato slept there serenely all through the
long day and had very pleasant dreams.

In his dreams, he was once again herd-boy on the banks
of the Limpopo River, and while he watched his herds,
he whittled away at some reeds to make a pipe. He
could draw the sweetest music from the pipes that he
made, music with the song of the river in it, the whispers
of the trees, and the thoughts of the young green grass
pushing its way through the earth in the spring. Spring
was in the air, in the earth, and in his heart, and as the
day bent down to darkness, and the labourers came in
from the fields and walked along the river-bank to their
huts, M'Kato, eying them as they strung slowly by, chose
one of them for his wife. A comely, upstanding young
woman, who would bear him fine children. She would
till the ground and mind his hut, while he sat on the
river-bank with his herds and his pipes. With the shy,
white antelope of a moon stealing through the woods of
the sky, he made a song about it, and played it upon his
pipes, but he was awakened before the song was finished
by Tela's cross voice in his ear. Now that he had come
home, she demanded, was he going to sleep for ever ?

He reached up his arms to Tela, but she went mum-
bling away. He saw her, by the fading daylight coming
through the doorway of the hut, bending over her cook-

ing-pot, and he saw her as a soured, bent old woman, long past the age of child-bearing.

His dreams vanished. He was no longer a herd-boy or a whittler of reeds ; there was no longer spring in his heart but autumn. His foreshortened arms swung out into the line of his vision. He knew now why the women in the river had laughed at him ; why he had been too slow and uncertain with his assegai.

He was old—a weary, impotent old man whose arms ended sharply at the wrists.

At nightfall, he and Tela set out upon a long journey south. Tela carried on her head two bags of mealie meal, and led by a rope a goat that walked heavily, because she was with kid. M'Kato was going back to the plateau near the Kafue to pay Kundi what he owed him.